PAST SHADOWS

Recent Titles by Anthea Fraser from Severn House

ELEVEN THAT WENT UP TO HEAVEN
THE TWELVE APOSTLES

BREATH OF BRIMSTONE
MOTIVE FOR MURDER

PAST SHADOWS

Anthea Fraser

This first world edition published in Great Britain 2001 by
SEVERN HOUSE PUBLISHERS LTD of
9–15 High Street, Sutton, Surrey SM1 1DF.
This first world edition published in the USA 2001 by
SEVERN HOUSE PUBLISHERS INC of
595 Madison Avenue, New York, NY 10022.

British Library Cataloguing in Publication Data

Fraser, Anthea
  Past shadows
  1. Vacations
  2. Detective and mystery stories
  I. Title
  823.9'14 [F]

ISBN 0–7278–5726–6

Typeset by Palimpsest Book Production Limited,
Polmont, Stirlingshire, Scotland.
Printed and bound in Great Britain by
MPG Books Ltd, Bodmin, Cornwall.

THE CARLYLE FAMILY

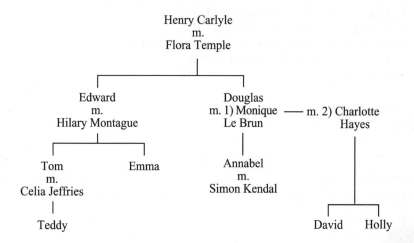

Henry Carlyle
m.
Flora Temple

Edward
m.
Hilary Montague

Douglas
m. 1) Monique —— m. 2) Charlotte
Le Brun Hayes

Tom   Emma
m.
Celia Jeffries

Annabel
m.
Simon Kendal

Teddy

David   Holly

One

One

A nnabel Kendal pushed open her front door, stepped over the morning's mail lying on the mat, and closed it with her foot before carrying her bags of groceries through to the kitchen. The house felt stuffy and hot with the day's stored sunshine, but the garden beyond the glass door beckoned her, and, dumping her carrier bags, she flung open door and windows, breathing in the scent of lilies of the valley.

As friends often remarked, the garden, with its terracotta pots, stone figures and tiny fountain, seemed to belong more in southern Europe than behind a Victorian terrace in Clifton, and coming home to it after a fraught day brought balm to her soul. Impossible, now, to recall the untended plot it had been when she and Simon bought the house.

On the kitchen wall behind her the answerphone beeped, demanding her attention, and she reluctantly turned back to deal with it.

'Darling,' said Simon's voice, with that forced heartiness that crept in more and more frequently, 'just letting you know I've asked some of the gang round this evening. Only half a dozen or so – shouldn't be a problem, should it? Something cold would be fine – we can eat outside. I'll bring some plonk. See you.'

'*Damn!*' she said forcefully, her voice loud in the empty room. Lately, he seemed to have acquired a compulsion to fill every spare moment with friends, outings or parties. After a day in a hot classroom, instilling French verbs into inattentive teenagers, it was the last thing she needed.

Instead of the relaxing evening she'd planned, she must now throw something hurriedly together, wash her hair, change—

Resignedly, she turned to review the contents of her larder. Just as well she'd bought those extra salad ingredients on her way home. There was cold chicken in the fridge, and she could boil some rice. As for dessert, fresh fruit would have to do. There was plenty of that.

She returned to the hall and picked up the mail, flicking through the buff-coloured envelopes until she came to a thick white one with a Cheltenham postmark. It had come, then. She'd been expecting it all week.

Dear Annabel and Simon,

she read, in her grandmother's elegantly flowing hand,

> As you will be aware, my birthday is once again approaching, and this year the celebrations will be held at Dunes Villa, between Exmouth and Budleigh Salterton, which, as usual, I have taken for a week from 27th May. A map is enclosed. I trust you will be able to join us.
>
> Yours affectionately, Flora Carlyle

Annabel could almost hear her grandmother's cultured voice as she read the words. Did she have to be so formal? Couldn't she just have signed herself 'Grandma', even if she wasn't, strictly speaking, Simon's? And as usual, she thought, giving full rein to her irritation, it would mean sacrificing her precious half-term week to spend it in the company of her relations, with whom she had little enough in common.

Leaving the letter on the hall table where Simon would see it, she went upstairs to change.

The evening seemed to be going well, though their guests

were more Simon's friends than hers. The 'half-dozen or so' had stretched to ten, including a couple Annabel had not met before, introduced to her casually as Martin and Mandy. Mandy was tall and languid, with improbably red hair and fingernails to match. She spoke loudly in a bored voice, and Annabel did not warm to her. Her long fingers were ringless, but as she continually addressed Martin as 'darling', it was clear she considered him her property.

Martin himself Annabel found even less appealing. Older than the rest of them – mid-forties, at a guess – he had overlong dark hair and deeply sunken eyes which, several times, she found regarding her with an oddly calculating look. To avoid it, she busied herself with her other guests. The food had been set out under the apple tree and they were engaged in serving themselves and, with laden plates, settling in groups either on the grass or round one of the white garden tables.

'The usual super spread, Annie,' Sue said appreciatively. 'And at the drop of a hat, no doubt. I don't know how you do it. I need at least a week's notice if *anyone's* coming to supper, let alone a horde like this!'

Catching Annabel's eye, Simon held up an empty wine bottle. She nodded and made her way back to the house, only realizing as she entered the kitchen that Martin had followed her.

'OK if I get a glass of water?' he asked rhetorically, going to the sink.

'Help yourself.' Annabel passed him a tumbler and bent to take the wine from the fridge. When she turned back, he was looking about him appraisingly at the cool white units, the slate-tiled floor and the side windows, through which the evening sunlight streamed.

'Attractive house,' he vouchsafed.

'Thank you. We like it.'

'Garden, too. With all these windows and glass doors, you can hardly tell where one ends and the other begins.'

'That was the idea.'

3

'Yours or Simon's?'

'We planned it together.'

He was leaning against the door frame, sipping his water and effectively blocking her exit. She started pointedly towards him, but he made no attempt to move. 'I hear you're related to the Carlyles?'

She stopped, looking at him in surprise. 'How did you know that?'

He shrugged. 'Simon must have mentioned it. I came across them once, in the course of my work.'

'Which is?'

'Journalism.' His eyes held hers over the rim of his glass. 'I was a cub reporter in Swansea when that woman was killed.'

Annabel tensed, and the coldness of the bottle spread from her hand to encompass her whole body.

'She must have been – what? – your aunt?' he continued, when she made no comment.

She moistened her lips. 'That's right, but I don't remember her – I was only a baby at the time.'

'All the same, I'd be most interested to talk to you about it, get the personal angle.'

'There isn't one. I told you, I was a baby.' She moved forward again, and this time he allowed her to pass.

'Odd that the killer was never caught,' he murmured as she stepped outside. Ignoring the comment, she walked steadily across the grass, her heart beating uncomfortably, and handed the wine to Simon.

For the rest of the evening she avoided Martin, though she was aware of his continuing scrutiny. When everyone had gone and she and Simon were clearing up, she remarked casually, 'I didn't think much of that new couple. Who are they, exactly?'

'Friends of Richard's – he asked if he could bring them. Seemed OK to me.'

'Did you tell Martin I'm related to the Carlyles?'

Simon glanced at her in surprise. 'Of course not. I

barely spoke to the guy, let alone delving into your family history.'

'He said you did.'

'You must have misheard him.' He went on polishing a glass, adding after a moment, 'Talking of your family, I see the Royal Command has arrived.'

'Yes.' She added without much hope, 'We could always make an excuse and opt out.'

He snorted derisively. 'You are joking? Though frankly I can't see why you get in such a state about it. It's a freebie, after all, with plenty of good food and wine thrown in. I book that week automatically now, as part of my annual holiday.'

'I thought that was so we could spend half-term together.'

'It is.'

She didn't pursue the point. She'd noticed before, though, that Simon seemed more at home with her family than she did herself. But then he hadn't all the hang-ups that bedevilled her. She looked across at him, tall, personable, good-looking: it was no wonder Flora approved of him more than herself. Annabel knew she'd not been forgiven for being Monique's daughter.

The familiar wave of sadness washed over her. Three years ago her mother had died in a road accident, and although the initial sharpness of grief had diminished, there were still times when a sense of loss overwhelmed her, particularly at this time of year.

She said aloud, 'It's Maman's anniversary tomorrow. You haven't forgotten we're going to George's?'

Simon turned, his guilty expression confirmation that he had. 'Hell, I wish you'd reminded me earlier; I've just fixed a game of squash with Phil.' He paused. 'Sorry, darling; I'll cancel it in the morning.'

'It doesn't matter, if you've arranged something. I can go by myself.'

He looked cautiously hopeful. 'But wouldn't George mind?'

'Not if I explain.'

'Well, as long as you're sure.' He kissed her cheek gratefully.

In fact, Annabel reflected, it would be easier all round. Though Simon got on well enough with her stepfather, he found the annual marking of Monique's death embarrassing. His absence would allow George and herself to reminisce more freely.

'Is he settling in OK?' Simon asked after a minute. Two months previously, George had sold the house in Bath and moved to Wiltshire to live with his married daughter.

'Oh, I think so. His part of the house is self-contained, so he still has his independence, but if he wants company, Cassie's on hand. It's an ideal arrangement.'

Dear George, she reflected fondly; he had been a father to her for over twenty years, and she loved him more than her real father – who, of course, would be at Budleigh with his second wife and family.

Which brought her thoughts full circle to the birthday celebration and, thanks to Martin's comments, to that same occasion all those years ago, during which her aunt had died. No, not *died*, she corrected herself impatiently. No more euphemisms: was *killed* – murdered – by person or persons unknown, as they said in Court.

Why was Martin still so interested in the case? He must have covered plenty of unsolved crimes over the years. And why had he wangled himself an invitation this evening? Had it really been as innocuous as Simon supposed? She gave a little shiver and, noticing, he put a casual arm round her. 'Feeling chilly? You go on up and I'll see to the doors and windows.'

She nodded and went out of the room, averting her eyes from the thick white envelope still lying on the hall table. Simon was right, of course, they'd have to go. Wearily, she started up the stairs.

Some forty miles away, Flora Carlyle sat propped up in bed,

a pillow at her back and a discarded book open on her knees. In her mid-seventies she was still a handsome woman; her hair had faded to a becoming pepper-and-salt, and though there were lines on her face, her skin was firm and the grey eyes had lost none of their directness.

Now, however, her thoughts were more ambivalent than usual. Her birthday was approaching, and though it would be good to have all her loved ones gathered under one roof, now that the invitations had been posted, she was, as always, conscious of unease. Perhaps, after all, Henry and Edward had been right, and she should have ended these birthday celebrations after Hilary's death. She recalled their horror the following year when she announced her intention to go ahead, unimpressed by her argument that the tragedy was no reason to abandon what had for years been family tradition.

Edward – understandably – had at first refused to attend, but she'd managed to talk him round – getting her own way as usual, as Henry had remarked with exasperation. But his white face was a constant reproach, reinforcing the subdued atmosphere that had hung over them all that year. There'd been a palpable air of relief when it was time to return home, even though she'd chosen a location as far as possible from the Welsh coast where the tragedy had occurred.

If only the killer could be caught and brought to trial! Perhaps then poor Hilary would cease to haunt them, as she undoubtedly still did. Flora's mind went back to that far-off summer, and the family as it had been then: she and Henry, Edward, Hilary and the twins; Douglas, Monique and baby Annabel. Life had seemed so settled, so safe, as though it would continue in similar vein for years to come. Now three of the group were dead, Monique fairly recently, though she'd ceased to be part of their lives long since.

Was it coincidence that she'd left Douglas the year after the murder? Flora had always felt the girl knew more about it than she admitted. Shocked and horrified though they'd all been, Monique's deathlike pallor had seemed, even at the time, excessive. It was not as though she and Hilary were particularly close. In fact, Monique, with what Flora regarded as typical French aloofness, had been close to no one, remaining, even after four years of marriage, a stranger in their midst. Thank God Douglas had been more successful in his second marriage; Charlotte had slipped easily into the family and in due course had presented him with a son and daughter, now twenty and seventeen respectively, who were both as pleasant and uncomplicated as their mother.

Whereas Annabel – Flora sighed. It grieved her that she couldn't feel the same fondness for the girl as for the rest of her grandchildren, though she hoped she managed to conceal it. Ruefully, she wondered if there was always something to worry about when one had a family. For worry she constantly did – not only about Annabel, but about Edward, who had never remarried, though a housekeeper, originally engaged to look after the twins, ran his home competently enough. And, of course, increasingly, she worried about Emma.

Flora's frown deepened. Only five at the time of the murder, Emma had been more affected than her extrovert brother and was still, at thirty-three, timid and lacking in confidence. Furthermore, during last year's holiday she had startled them with a sudden, obsessive interest in Hilary's death, endlessly quizzing them all on their memories of it. It had been most upsetting, and despite the counselling Edward had arranged on their return home, she seemed no better. An added reason, perhaps, for abandoning this year's celebration, which Flora had stubbornly ignored.

Her eyes moved restlessly round the room where she had slept since coming to Hazelwood as a bride. Family and continuity meant a great deal to her; both her sons had been born in this bed, her husband had died here, and in due course she hoped to do the same. Meanwhile, the room was full of memories. Light from the bedside lamp glinted on the silver frames of photographs clustered on the window table, though the faces they contained were in shadow. Shadows, too, softened the outline of the button-back chair where she had nursed her babies, while the pastel curtains, bleached in the dimness, hung like a silk waterfall down the far wall. And beyond this room, the rest of the house, solid and comfortable, also bolstered her amour propre: the drawing room with its grand piano and brocade upholstery, the dining room, solid in oak, the red Turkey carpet on the stairs – all as it had been, was now, and would be for years stretching into the future. Wouldn't it?

'All shall be well,' Flora said out loud. Then, with a shudder she couldn't explain, she switched off the light and settled herself to uneasy sleep.

The A4 seemed as busy as the motorway this Saturday morning, and Annabel was forced to brake yet again. She'd arranged to meet George at the cemetery in Bath, and was beginning to worry that she'd keep him waiting. The sky was overcast, which suited her mood, and the flowers on the back seat filled the air with their cloying sweetness. She would be glad when the next hour was over.

The traffic started to move again, gathering speed as though some unseen obstacle had been removed. Minutes later, she turned with relief into the road containing the cemetery.

George was standing patiently at the gate, a tall, thin figure holding the red roses he brought each year. For a brief, startling moment she saw him with a stranger's eyes, as an elderly, rather frail-looking man, and felt a shaft of fear that he too might be taken from her. Then, as she drew up and he stooped to open the door, he clicked into focus and she breathed a sigh of relief.

'Simon not with you?' he enquired, returning her kiss.

'He sends his apologies. Actually, he'd forgotten and arranged to play squash, and though he offered to cancel, I thought you wouldn't mind.' She lifted the flowers out of the car, locked it, and threaded her arm through George's. 'How are you?'

He made a little grimace. 'I'll be better when today's over.'

'Me too.'

They walked in silence up the curving drive to Monique's grave with its grey marble headstone, and stood for a moment looking down at it. There was the smell of freshly cut grass, and somewhere a bird was singing. Annabel read the inscription as she always did, though she knew it by heart.

Monique Woodbridge, beloved wife of George and mother
of Annabel. 1946–1997. Always in our thoughts.

Such a brief epitaph to describe a life, she thought, leaving so much unsaid: Monique's childhood in Rouen, her years in England as a foreign student, her marriage to Douglas Carlyle. There was no hint here of the woman herself, with her vibrant personality and sudden, rich laugh, her attractive accent and natural French chic. Remembering all those things, Annabel's eyes filled with tears. Yet perhaps the inscription contained all her mother would have wanted, the names of the two people most dear to her.

George broke into her thoughts. 'I feel I've deserted her, you know, moving to Marlborough and leaving her here.'

'She wouldn't want you to be alone,' Annabel assured him, 'and neither of us is far away.'

She unwrapped the flowers and they knelt together to push the stems into the sunken vase, making a splash of colour against the pale grey stone. Then Annabel stood up, brushing down her skirt, and went in search of a watering can.

'All right, darling?' George asked softly, as, having filled the container, she continued to stand looking down at the grave.

She gave him a shaky smile. 'I think so.'

'Ready to go?'

She nodded.

'Cassie and Nigel are coming in later, to do some shopping. One of them will drive my car back, so we can go home together instead of in convoy.'

'That's thoughtful of them.' Annabel knew her stepsister, too, would be bringing flowers. Fifteen when her father remarried, after initial resentment she had come to love his second wife as a mother.

The A4 was still congested as they continued along it towards Marlborough. Cassie and her schoolmaster husband lived on the western fringes of the town, and had recently built a ground-floor extension to their home to accommodate George.

'Have you settled in now?' Annabel enquired, turning into the driveway.

'More or less, though there are still some chests in the garage waiting to be gone through.'

She switched off the engine and surveyed the facade of the house in front of them. George's rooms had been added to the left-hand side, closing off access to the back garden. He had his own entrance, which mirrored the original front door, and the stonework of the walls merged perfectly into that of the main house.

'They've done it very well, haven't they?' Annabel commented. 'You can hardly see the join!'

It was beginning to rain as she waited for George to fit his key in the lock and push the door open. A smell of new carpet greeted her, and she sniffed appreciatively. The small hallway, lit only by the window alongside the front door, was papered in pale yellow, which gave the impression of sunshine even on this dull day. George opened the left-hand door and stood aside for her to go into the sitting room.

'Oh, you've turned it round!' she exclaimed.

'This is the summer arrangement. I want to look out on the garden during the long, light evenings, so I moved the dining area to the front. In the winter, it'll be cosier to sit up this end, near the fire.'

'It's lovely, George! You've done a lot to it since I was last here.'

'Well, I've not much else to occupy my time,' he replied, but she could see he was pleased. And indeed the room was most attractive, furnished with chairs, tables and lamps familiar from the house he'd shared with Monique, but which had somehow taken on different identities in their new surroundings.

She walked to the far end and stood looking through the patio doors at the large walled garden, colourful now with shrubs and flowers. George came up behind her with a glass of sherry.

'We're having salad,' he said. 'I hope that's all right. I see to my own breakfast and lunch, but Cassie insists on feeding me in the evening. I've an open invitation to join them, but usually opt for a tray in front of the television.'

Annabel nodded. She had shared Cassie's concern about George's frequently missed meals after Monique's death, but he'd resisted all suggestions that he move to Marlborough, despite the fact that the extension had been started within months of his widowhood. Perhaps the explanation lay in his comment at the cemetery, that he felt he was deserting his wife. However, a serious bout of flu before Christmas had been the turning point, and he'd finally given in.

'It's a perfect arrangement,' Annabel said warmly. 'And salad is definitely my favourite lunch.'

They sat at the small table by the window, using the familiar china that still brought a lump to her throat. The salad was good, accompanied by crisp new bread and a bottle of wine, with cheese and fruit to follow.

'The summons has come to Grandmother's birthday,' Annabel commented as they sat over coffee.

'Ah! Where is it to be this year?'

'On the Devon coast, near Budleigh Salterton.'

'And you don't want to go,' George suggested shrewdly.

'I *never* want to go!' She hesitated, eying him over

her coffee cup. 'George, why didn't Grandmother like Maman?'

He moved uncomfortably. 'We don't know that she didn't, love; it was only your mother's impression.'

Annabel brushed that aside. 'Was it because she was French, different from the rest of them? It seems very narrow-minded. But then,' she added reflectively, 'Grandmother *is* narrow-minded. All she cares about is the family, and even they have to toe the line. I suppose Maman wouldn't.'

'Probably not,' George agreed with a smile. 'Monique wasn't one for toeing lines. Seriously though, you get on all right with them, don't you?'

She grimaced. 'We haven't much in common, and I can never really relax with Daddy and Charlotte. I was thinking last night that Simon fits in better than I do. He conforms, while I feel as much of an outsider as Maman did. George –' her tone altered, became more sombre – 'what did she tell you about that Welsh holiday?'

Again he shifted on his chair. 'No more than you, I suspect. Speaking about it upset her, right to the end of her life.'

'But she must have said what happened? I never got the full story.'

He sighed. 'Well, as you know, you were all staying at this villa they'd taken on the Gower. On the afternoon in question, everyone had split up. I don't remember what the men were doing, but Monique had taken you for a walk in your pushchair, and Flora and Hilary were on the beach with the twins. At about four thirty, Hilary went back to the house to make a start on the twins' tea, leaving Flora to follow with the children in half an hour. In the meantime, Edward arrived home and found Hilary lying dead on the living-room floor. No sign of a weapon, but a heavy glass ornament was missing.'

He stopped speaking, and the little clock ticked into the silence.

'And that's all?' Annabel prompted, though she knew the answer.

'That's all. Despite intensive police work, the killer was never found and no motive established. The theory was that she'd disturbed a burglar, but if so, all he took was the ornament.'

'Was it valuable?'

'I shouldn't think so, in rented accommodation.'

'No fingerprints?'

'No suspicious ones.'

'Not even on the front door-knob?'

'Again, only those that could be accounted for.'

Annabel looked up. 'Which means what? That she must have let him in?'

George shrugged, adding after a minute, 'Edward was the prime suspect for a while, but only because the husband always is.'

He studied her anxiously. Though in many ways she resembled her mother, she had her father's colouring: pale gold hair that curved into her neck, and wide grey eyes which at the moment were pensive and inward-looking.

'Look, love,' he said gently, 'we've been over this before. Why bring it all up again?'

'Because,' she answered slowly, 'I met a journalist last night who'd been in Swansea at the time and had covered the story.'

George sat back in his chair, staring at her. 'Good God, after all these years?'

'Exactly; and what disturbed me was that he knew I was connected with it. He said Simon told him, but Simon denies it, and I believe him. He didn't know the man, a friend had brought him round.'

George frowned. 'You're saying this stranger arrives at your home, uninvited, and starts quizzing you about a murder that happened twenty-eight years ago?'

'Well, yes, though he wasn't a total gatecrasher – Richard had asked if he could bring him.'

'What's his name?'

'Martin something. That's all I was told.'

'And what did he say exactly?'

'That he'd heard I was connected to the Carlyles, and that he'd been in Swansea at the time of the murder.'

'That's all?'

'Except that he'd like to discuss it with me some time – and that it was odd the killer was never caught.'

'And what did you say?'

'Very little. I was – poleaxed.'

'Bloody cheek!' George said angrily.

'No doubt I overreacted, but it shook me, coming out of the blue like that, and when we'd just received this year's invitation. It was the fact that he knew who I was, and still remembered the case. It must have made an impression on him. Still –' she straightened her shoulders – 'I don't suppose we'll ever know the truth now.'

She pushed back her chair and began to help George clear the table, carrying the plates through to the small but fully equipped kitchen, which, like all the main rooms, overlooked the garden. They were silent for some minutes as George washed the dishes and Annabel dried them, both busy with their own thoughts. Then George commented, 'It's incredible, in the circumstances, that your grandmother should have continued with this week away. Monique said the atmosphere was very strained the first year. That was the last one she went to; she left Douglas soon after.'

He glanced sideways at her. 'But Flora continued to invite you. When I came on the scene, I used to take you myself and collect you at the end of the week. And to Cheltenham, for that matter, for half of every school holiday and the odd weekend between.'

Annabel smiled wryly. 'There's no escape, if you're a Carlyle. I was still Daddy's daughter, even after he'd remarried. And it wasn't really too bad. I quite enjoyed playing with my cousins, and when Pépé was alive, he always made a fuss of me. I was very fond of him. You remember him, don't you?'

'Yes, I liked old Henry. A gentleman of the old school. I always suspected that wife of his led him a dance, though to be fair, they seemed devoted to each other.' He emptied the washing-up bowl and rinsed away the suds. 'And talking of old times, I found some photograph albums when I was packing up to come here. I thought you might like to look through them.'

'I'd love to.'

They were still poring over old photographs and recalling the occasions they evoked when, at four o'clock, the doorbell rang.

'That'll be Cassie,' George said with a smile. 'She refuses to use her key – says it would be invading my privacy, if you please.'

'I'll let her in.'

Cassie Durham, with her round, unlined face and clear grey eyes, looked considerably younger than her forty years, an impression emphasized by the thick, curly hair which she confined in a tortoiseshell clasp at the back of her neck. 'How are you, Annie?' she asked, giving her stepsister an enthusiastic hug. 'I've not seen you for a while.'

'No, I'm sorry I've not been over, but life's somewhat hectic at the moment.'

'I've come to invite you both next door for tea. We brought back some luscious buns from Sally Lunn's.'

George was already on his feet. 'Say no more!'

Cassie kissed him affectionately. 'Your car's safely back in the garage, Pop.'

'Bless you.'

It was still drizzling as they went out of one door, along the front of the house and into the next. The Durhams' home always seemed welcoming, and Nigel, tall and bespectacled, was waiting to greet them. Annabel wished she could feel as relaxed with her father's family as she did with her stepfather's.

They settled down for tea in the large, comfortable sitting room with its deep armchairs, and in the general talk and exchange of news, Monique's name wasn't mentioned again. It was only as she was leaving that George said suddenly, 'Oh, I meant to tell you – I came across some papers of your mother's that you might like to have. There's a pile of exercise books and files, probably relics of her student days, but as they're written in French, I'm not much the wiser! Just hang on and I'll get them.'

He emerged from the house carrying three large cardboard cartons precariously balanced on top of each other, and Annabel opened the boot for him to put them inside.

'A task for a wet afternoon!' he said, smiling, as he fitted them in.

'Several, I should say! Now –' she closed the boot and kissed him – 'you must come to us soon. I've not seen enough of you lately.'

'It's that social whirl you live in!' he teased her, and as she drove away she reflected that he was right. The frenetic pace that Simon had been setting of late left them little free time. And at the thought of her husband, the little niggle of anxiety which she'd been trying to ignore moved inside her. Pushing it aside again, she settled down to the drive home.

Two

Simon's car was parked outside the house when she arrived home, but there was a space only two doors along and she slipped into it gratefully. One of the penalties of living in Clifton was the dearth of off-street parking, and none of the houses in their road had a garage.

It was still raining, and rather than struggle with the heavy cartons, she decided to leave them in the boot till morning. Turning up her collar, she made a dash for her own gate, looking forward, as she had the previous day, to a relaxing evening.

'Hello!' she called, letting herself in. 'I'm back!'

Simon looked up as she came into the sitting room. He'd switched on a lamp in the premature gloom, and was reading a magazine.

'Did you have a good game?' she asked, leaning over to kiss him.

'Yes, thanks. How did your day go?'

'As well as could be expected. We had tea with Cassie and Nigel.'

'Still raining?'

'Yes, it looks as though it's set in for the night.'

'That's a pity. We're meeting the gang at the Schooner at seven.'

She stared at him aghast. 'Oh, Simon, no!'

'What do you mean, no? I thought it would cheer you up.'

'All I want is to kick my shoes off and relax in front of the telly. I can't remember when we had a night in by ourselves.'

18

He gave an annoyed laugh. 'You sound like an old woman!'

'I'm beginning to feel like one. What's got into you suddenly, that we have to be doing something every free moment?'

'Oh, come on, you're exaggerating. We've nothing on tomorrow, have we?'

'Not so far, thank goodness; I've a pile of things to do – ironing and cleaning, as well as some schoolwork.'

'The ironing and cleaning are Mary's province, surely?'

'Mary comes one day a week, and there's only so much she can do.'

'Then have her more often.'

Knowing what he was leading up to, Annabel refrained from comment, but he continued anyway.

'And before you say we can't afford it, you know Mum and Dad would be happy to help out.'

'Simon, we don't *need* anyone more than once a week.'

'Fine, then you can come to the pub.'

'No; I'm sorry, but I really don't want to.'

He frowned, laying down the magazine. 'You're not serious?'

'It's been a difficult day and I'm tired. Anyway, they were all here yesterday. We don't need to see them every night, surely?'

'Annabel,' he said with heavy patience, 'it's Saturday!'

She merely shook her head and went in search of a glass of water, the act of pouring it reminding her of Martin and his intrusive questioning. Her temples began to throb. She stood sipping the water, staring unseeingly at the dripping greenery in the garden, the pools of water forming on the surface of the little iron table. Oh God, she thought, let it be all right.

It wasn't, in that half an hour later, Simon slammed out of the house without her. Perversely, though she'd told him she wanted to relax, she felt compelled to take out the ironing board and work her way through a dozen of his shirts, festooning them on hangers round the kitchen so that the room filled with the scent of crisp, damp cotton. Finally, at eight thirty, she made herself an omelette and took it through to eat in front of the television.

It was not, she thought miserably, the evening she had planned. The programmes were abysmal, and it was lonely sitting in the quiet room by herself. Her head, which had begun to ache earlier, grew steadily more painful. At nine thirty she switched off the set, put her supper things in the dishwasher, and went up to bed.

That night she had the dream again. It had come at irregular intervals for as long as she could remember, its very vagueness somehow adding to its menace. Nor could she explain why it upset her so much. 'It's just a presence,' she would say inadequately, in reply to anxious queries. 'Knowing someone else is in the room, and a terrible feeling of fear.'

As always, she awoke sobbing and screaming, struggling to escape from the bed. Simon, just back from the pub, came running, toothbrush in hand, to catch and hold on to her.

'All right – it's all right now,' he soothed, holding her rigid body against him and stroking her damp hair. 'I'm here – you're quite safe.'

She drew a deep, shuddering breath and sat back on her heels. 'Sorry!' she gasped.

He was looking at her anxiously. 'The dream?'

She nodded.

'What did you have for supper? Cheese?'

'It makes no difference what I eat. Every now and then, it just – comes.'

'Don't I know it? One of these days, you'll give me a heart attack, letting out that unearthly shriek.' He paused. 'Can I get you anything? A glass of water? Hot milk?'

'No, thanks. I'll be all right in a minute.'

He hesitated, still looking at her frowningly. Then, with a slight shrug, he returned to the bathroom. Annabel swung her legs to the floor, and, going to the full-length window, slid it back. Shivering slightly, she stepped through on to the terrace they had built on top of the kitchen extension. The rain must have stopped some time ago, because the paving under her bare feet was dry. She walked to the far end and stood leaning on the balustrade, staring down into the shadowed garden. The night air was chill on her overheated body but she welcomed it, raising her head to let the faint breeze lift her hair, aware of the scent of damp flowers rising from the garden below.

It was galling how this recurring dream could still reduce her – a normally balanced, self-confident adult – to a gibbering wreck. In the early days of their marriage, alarmed by her terror, Simon had suggested she seek help, but she'd refused. The dream came so infrequently, she insisted, it wasn't worth bothering about. Nonetheless, its after-effects lasted several days, leaving her tired and listless, and quite often once it had occurred, it repeated itself soon afterwards.

'Annabel!'

Simon's voice swung her round. He was at the open window, silhouetted against the lighted room behind him. 'What the hell are you doing?'

'Just coming,' she answered meekly, walking back towards him.

'I thought you were sleepwalking.' He took her arm and pulled her none too gently back into the room. 'You'll catch your death of cold, going out like that.'

She slid back under the duvet and after a moment he also climbed into bed and reached up to switch off the light. It was obvious he was still annoyed with her, but she needed his arms round her to dispel the last tendrils of the dream.

'You're right,' she acknowledged softly, 'I am cold. Will you hold me for a minute?'

Resignedly he turned on his side and pulled her towards him. His body was warm against her cool one, and she could smell beer on his breath.

'I'm sorry I didn't come with you,' she murmured,

stroking his neck and shoulder. 'I really was tired and headachy. Perhaps that's why I was susceptible to the dream.'

He pulled her a little closer. 'And I'm sorry I slammed out like that. I should have been more understanding, today of all days. Am I forgiven?'

'If I am.' And, feeling his arms tighten, she thankfully gave herself up to the comfort of his lovemaking.

The following morning, determined to shake off the clinging strands of nightmare, Annabel worked steadily, sweeping and dusting downstairs, finishing the ironing she'd abandoned the previous evening, and making a casserole for their evening meal. This afternoon, she resolved, she'd allow herself a couple of hours' gardening before settling down to prepare some classwork for the next day. But she had just changed into her gardening clothes when the doorbell rang, and she answered it to find herself face to face with Simon's parents.

Giles Kendal was taller and leaner than his son, with thinning sandy hair and faded blue eyes, but Sally was an attractive, youthful-looking sixty, her tanned face only faintly lined. It was from his mother that Simon inherited his dark good looks.

'Hello, darling.' Sally stepped forward and kissed the air on either side of Annabel's face. 'I hope we've not come at an inconvenient time?'

'Not at all, we're only gardening.' Annabel submitted to a scratchy kiss from her father-in-law. 'It's good to see you – come in.'

She led the way through the kitchen and out of the back door just as Simon emerged from the shed with the lawnmower.

'Hi there!' He came forward to greet his parents – with more enthusiasm, Annabel thought guiltily, than she had been able to muster. She supposed she was fond of them, but she did wish they didn't come round so often. Which was ungracious, since they'd welcomed her into the family with open arms, even if, as she suspected, it was not for herself but because she was Simon's choice. All his life he'd had only to ask to be given anything he wanted, a fact of which he took full advantage and which was an ongoing cause of friction in their marriage. Nor was their generosity limited to Simon; Annabel had learned early on that it didn't do to express a liking for anything, from a dress in the sales to a foreign holiday, since it would unfailingly be presented to her.

They all stood chatting for a few minutes, exchanging family news, then Sally said brightly, 'Now we don't want to interrupt, darlings; we know how precious your time is. Carry on with what you're doing, and we'll just sit here in the sunshine. It's always a pleasure to look at your garden – even more so, since we're not responsible for its upkeep!'

Annabel hesitated, feeling it would be impolite to disappear to the far end of the garden as she'd intended. Simon, however, with no inhibitions, promptly switched on the mower, raising his voice to say above it, 'OK, if you're sure you don't mind. We'll stop for a cuppa in an hour or so. I don't know that it's warm enough to sit outside, though – go indoors if you'd rather. The Sunday papers are there.'

Sally seated herself on one of the white chairs on the patio. 'It seems quite sheltered in this corner; we'll bring the papers out.'

Thus reassured, Annabel collected some tools from the shed and walked down the lawn, revelling in its green freshness. Minutes later she was on her knees, her hands in the warm, moist soil where plants and flowers crowded together in joyful abundance, their creams and pinks and blues harmonizing into a soft blur of colour.

She worked for some time, pulling out weeds, thinning and replanting, heeling in and patting down. The drone of the lawnmower, which had blotted out the sound of the fountain, also masked Sally's approaching footsteps, so that she jumped when her voice came from just behind her. 'Do carry on, darling. Giles has gone inside to watch the cricket, so I thought I'd come and chat.' She seated herself on the stone bench that faced down the garden and looked happily about her. 'I do adore these cherubs; wherever did you find them?'

'At a country house auction.' Annabel sat back on her heels and brushed her hair from her face with the back of her hand. 'I fell for them at once, though they were more than we'd meant to pay.' She hurried on, belatedly fearful that Sally might offer to reimburse them. 'Still, the ones at the garden centre are rather ordinary and we wanted something special for our special garden.'

'Quite right,' Sally approved. 'I think you've both done wonders with it.' She paused. 'Simon was saying you've received the birthday invitation.'

Annabel made a little moue. 'No escape, apparently!'

'Which reminds me, I met a charming young man at a dinner last week. His name's Martin Coutts and he's a journalist. You'll never believe it, but he was working in Swansea at the time your aunt was killed.'

She stopped, waiting for some reaction, and when none was forthcoming, added, 'He was fascinated to hear about you, and would love to meet you some time.'

'He already has,' Annabel said.

Sally looked surprised and a little deflated. 'Really? He didn't waste much time. Did he phone you?'

'No, he came on Friday with some friends.' She swallowed, trying to keep the accusation out of her voice. 'So it was you who told him about me.'

'Well, yes. That's all right, isn't it?'

Annabel looked down. 'Not really; it's not something I like to talk about.'

Sally was instantly contrite. 'Oh darling, I'm sorry! I thought you'd be interested to hear his views. It didn't occur to me it might distress you.'

'How did the subject come up, anyway?'

'The usual social chat. "What do you do for a living?" – that kind of thing. He said he was a crime reporter, and we discussed some of the well-known cases he'd covered. Then I asked how long a paper continued to run the story if no one was caught, and he mentioned the Swansea case. And I blurted out that it was my daughter-in-law's family who was involved. Oh, Annabel, I'm so dreadfully sorry! I wouldn't have upset you for the world.'

'I know you wouldn't,' Annabel assured her, relenting. 'To be honest, I don't know why it still worries me – perhaps because of my mother. She always refused to talk about it.'

'Did he try to question you?'

'Not really; I didn't give him the chance.'

'Well, if he gets in touch again, just say you don't want to discuss it. I'm sure he'll understand.'

Annabel's mouth lifted. 'A journalist?'

'Oh dear, I feel responsible now. I *am* responsible. Would you like me to contact him?'

Annabel shook her head. 'That would add too much weight. He might have got the message, anyway. I certainly wasn't very helpful.' She paused, adding in spite of herself, 'What did he actually say?'

Sally flushed and looked away down the garden. 'Nothing much.'

'Please?'

'Well, he – he said he'd always felt the family knew more than they were saying.' Sally looked down at her clasped hands. 'I wish to God I'd never brought this up,' she added in a low voice.

Annabel had never seen her mother-in-law so subdued. 'Look, it's all right,' she said awkwardly. 'Please don't blame yourself – it's my fault for being so touchy after all this time. Really, it doesn't matter.'

Sally bent forward impulsively and kissed her cheek. 'Bless you. I promise to guard my tongue in future.'

Annabel stood up, dusting down her jeans and aware

suddenly that the sound of the lawnmower had stopped. In the same moment Simon's voice called down the garden, 'The kettle's on!'

Both women started back towards the house, relieved that their tête-à-tête had been brought to a natural conclusion. In the kitchen Simon had set out mugs on a tray, together with a tin of shortbread. He winked at his mother.

'If Annabel had got here first we'd have had the best china, but I reckon this will do us.'

'Well, I'm here now,' Annabel retorted, 'and I happen to know your mother prefers her tea in a cup.'

'You two have cups, then,' Simon answered equably, taking them out of the cupboard, 'and Dad and I will slum it with mugs.' He poured boiling water into the pot and carried the tray through to the sitting room. Giles Kendal turned at their approach and switched off the remote control.

'That looks good.'

'Go on watching if you like,' Annabel invited, but he shook his head.

'It's not a very good match – I've seen enough.' He picked up the car magazine Simon had been looking at the previous evening. 'Thinking of getting a new car, Simon?'

Annabel said quickly, 'Not really, the Golf's fine, isn't it, darling?'

At the same time, Simon was saying, 'Well, I have been toying with the idea.'

Annabel flushed and turned to the tea tray. When she'd tidied and swept the room this morning she had put the magazine in the rack. Simon must have taken it out deliberately, so that his father would comment on it and give him an opening. There was no way they could afford a new car at the moment, and he was complacently waiting for Giles to offer to buy one for them.

While Annabel and Sally made conversation, the men discussed the merits of different cars, but as far as Annabel could tell, no definite conclusion was reached, and when the Kendals left soon afterwards she deduced from Simon's sulky face that his ploy had failed.

'I'm going to finish off the lawn,' he said, closing the door behind them. 'I didn't get the edges done.'

'Right. I have some schoolwork to do.'

She carried the tray through to the kitchen, loaded the crockery into the dishwasher and watched for a moment as Simon, shears in hand, started on the grass. They hadn't had a day to themselves after all, she reflected.

She returned to the sitting room, retrieved her briefcase from behind the sofa, and took from it a pile of French newspapers. The news items and articles provided good topics for her conversation classes. Seating herself at the little walnut desk that had been her mother's, she began to prepare lessons for the following day.

She worked steadily for an hour, and had almost finished when the phone rang in the hall. Pushing back her chair, she went to answer it.

'Annabel Kendal?' said a man's voice in her ear.

'Yes?'

'This is Martin Coutts. We met on Friday.'

Her hand tightened on the instrument, but she answered steadily, 'I remember.'

'I'm calling to thank you for your hospitality to unexpected guests.'

'It was a pleasure.' She waited, curious to see what he really wanted.

'Look, I'm afraid I rather got off on the wrong foot with you, didn't I?'

'In what way?'

'I think you know what I mean. I apologize; I handled it clumsily and you were right to be angry.'

'More surprised,' she said.

'Whatever. The point is, we didn't get the chance to talk, and I really would like to.'

'If it's about my aunt's death, you're wasting your time. You probably know more about it than I do.'

'Suppose you let me buy you lunch and we can discuss it?'

'I'm sorry, that's not possible. I teach at St Helena's and we all eat in Hall.'

'Afternoon tea, then, when you finish? I have some theories I'd like to test out on you.'

'I've told you—'

'Yes, but I'd still like to speak to you.'

There was a pause. Though she'd barely admitted it, even to herself, Martin Coutts had aroused her curiosity. He'd have been right in the middle of things at the time – reporters always were. He might have heard things she knew nothing about.

'Please, Annabel. Just a brief chat, and if you don't want to go any further, fair enough.'

'You won't contact me again if I ask you not to?'

'I promise. Just give me this one chance.'

'All right,' she said.

'Fine. What time do you finish?'

'I could meet you about five.'

'Five o'clock tomorrow, then, on the terrace of the Avon Gorge, weather permitting?'

'I'll be there,' she said, and put down the phone. What, exactly, had she committed herself to?

Simon was at the kitchen sink when she went through. 'Did I hear the phone?'

'Yes, it was Martin Coutts.'

'Who?'

'The man who gatecrashed with his girlfriend.'

Simon dried his hands. 'Does he want to speak to me?'

'No,' Annabel said slowly, folding her arms and leaning back against the counter, 'it was me he wanted to speak to. He's asked me to have tea with him tomorrow.'

Simon stared across at her. 'Am I missing something here?'

'Your mother put him on to me – she told me this

afternoon. Remember he asked about my family? He wants to talk about the murder.'

'But you don't remember anything!'

'So I told him. He still wants to.'

'Are you sure he doesn't just fancy you?'

She smiled. 'Quite sure. He has his hands full with Mandy. Anyway, we're meeting tomorrow at the Avon Gorge.'

'I'm surprised you agreed, when you get so worked up about it.'

'So am I, but it's the only way to get rid of him. He promised not to bother me again.'

Simon shrugged. 'Suit yourself. I'd have thought it was a bit late to be sniffing about now, though.'

'Of course it is. If the Swansea police couldn't come up with anything at the time, an ageing reporter isn't likely to now.'

Simon grinned. 'I'm not sure he'd like the "ageing".' He put an arm round her. 'Finished your work?'

'Just about.'

'Then I vote we have a peaceful evening with the Sunday papers.'

'That sounds wonderful,' she said.

The next day, Annabel found it increasingly hard to concentrate on teaching, wondering whether, by the evening, she would know more about the family tragedy than she did now.

Her preoccupation didn't pass unnoticed. 'Everything all right?' Stephie Lucas enquired in the staffroom at lunchtime.

'Yes, why?'

'You seem a bit abstracted. You walked right past me in the corridor after break.'

'Sorry. A lot on my mind.'

'Such as?

Annabel smiled. 'An appointment after school. I'm meeting A Man for tea.'

Stephie regarded her quizzically. 'I presume one doesn't jump to the obvious conclusion?'

'Correct. Strictly business.'

'His or yours?'

Annabel considered. 'Probably both.'

'Are you being deliberately infuriating?'

She laughed. 'Of course!' she said, and went out of the room. Stephie was a good friend, but not even those closest to Annabel knew her dark secret, and she intended, Martin Coutts willing, to keep it that way.

The Avon Gorge Hotel commanded an imposing position overlooking the Severn Estuary and the famous suspension bridge. As she emerged on to the terrace, Martin, seated at a table under a large umbrella, stood up to greet her. He was wearing a dark, open-necked shirt and jeans. His hair, she noted, was still shaggily unkempt and his deep-set eyes still calculating.

'Good of you to come,' he said, pulling out a chair for her.

'Did you think I wouldn't?'

'I wasn't too sure, to be honest. You might have changed your mind. Now that you *are* here, I can order tea.'

Annabel watched him walk into the bar to place his order. To her relief, she found that her qualms had disappeared, to be replaced by curiosity. Accordingly, when he returned, she forestalled him with a question of her own. 'Why did you say it was Simon who mentioned my family?'

'I said it *might* have been,' he corrected. 'It's known as protecting your sources.'

She raised an eyebrow, but made no comment.

'Now . . .' He offered her a cigarette, and, when she shook her head, lit one himself. 'I thought we might start by your telling me about the Carlyles.'

'Who you think might know more than they're saying about the murder?'

He threw her a quick glance, then, unexpectedly, smiled.

'An unguarded comment, which I hadn't expected to get back to you.'

'But why should you think that?'

'Because of the total lack of motive. Despite what they term "exhaustive enquiries", the police couldn't come up with any reason to kill her, and we all know there must have been one. Totally random killings are, thank God, few and far between. And if there are hidden motives, family members have to be the chief suspects.'

'Particularly the husband?'

'Possibly, but in this case, none of the men could produce an alibi.'

She hadn't known that.

'Whereas as far as could be checked,' Martin continued, 'the women's stories tallied.'

'The women?' Annabel echoed, taken aback. 'Surely they weren't suspected?'

'Why not? A woman's as capable as a man of hitting someone over the head. But it was verified that Hilary and her mother-in-law spent the afternoon on the beach with the children, while Monique took you for a walk along the cliffs, where she was seen by several witnesses.'

Which was what George had told her. Martin's shrewd eyes were on her face. 'How old were you at the time, Annabel?'

'Fifteen months.'

'Memories go that far back, you know. Even farther. Have you no recollection at all?'

'None.'

A waitress arrived with a tray and decanted it on to the table: sandwiches, scones with jam and clotted cream, a selection of cakes. He stubbed out his cigarette and, when Annabel had poured the tea, passed her the plate of sandwiches. Then he continued as though there'd been no interruption.

'My thought was that people frequently make unguarded remarks in front of young children. Though the words aren't

31

understood, they can be stored in the memory and dredged out years later, under the right stimulus.'

'Surely you'd do better with my cousins,' she commented. 'They were five when it happened.'

'Too old; discretion is shown in front of five-year-olds.' He sipped his tea. 'Odd how things work out, isn't it? I've not thought of the case in years – it was only the chance meeting with your mother-in-law that brought it back, and the opportunity to speak to someone who'd been on the spot was too good to miss.'

'I warned you I'd be no help.'

He leaned back in his chair. 'I'm not so sure about that. What is your earliest memory?'

She frowned. 'I've no idea.'

'Think back. A birthday party, perhaps? Or Christmas when you were very young? A particular present?'

After a minute she said slowly, 'I remember playing ball with my parents.'

'When would that have been?'

'I don't know, but they separated when I was two and a half.'

'So you could have been quite a bit younger. Were you aware of that memory before now? Playing ball?'

'No,' she admitted, 'it just came into my head.'

'See? All you need is the right trigger to bring things back.'

'And how,' she asked, keeping her voice light, 'do you propose to find it?'

'We'll come to that later. These family weeks away: Sally told me they still take place?'

'Yes; there's one at the end of the month.'

'Do you ever talk about the murder, or the victim, for that matter?'

'We never have, until last year.'

'And what happened last year?'

'My cousin Emma brought it up. In fact, she kept on about it the whole week. Everyone found it a bit embarrassing.'

'This is Hilary's daughter?'

'Yes. She's always been highly strung.'

'And what did she say?'

'Oh, she was asking everyone how they first learned her mother was dead – when they'd last seen her – what her last words to them had been. It was almost as though she resented the fact that Hilary was never mentioned, and wanted to force us to remember her.'

'How did her brother react to all this?'

'Tom? Oh, he's much more down to earth. He was as embarrassed as the rest of us, tried to make her stop.'

Martin pondered for a moment. 'Did your uncle remarry?'

'No.'

'Lady friends?'

'I never heard of any.'

Martin leaned forward and helped himself to a scone, piling it high with strawberry jam and cream. 'Do you remember your aunt at all?'

'No.'

'Not even faintly?'

Annabel shook her head. 'And my mother refused to discuss either her or her death.'

'What about your cousin's probing last year? Didn't anything come out of that?'

'It was all very vague and general.'

He was watching her with narrowed eyes. 'You don't like talking about it, do you, even now?'

'Not really.'

'Why? You don't remember your aunt, so you can't mourn her personally. Aren't you the least bit curious to know who killed her?

'Not,' she said with feeling, 'if it turns out to be one of the family.'

'But you must have wondered, over the years? The convenient tramp who materializes out of nowhere, does the dirty deed and then disappears again isn't really on, is he?'

She said aridly, 'What is it you want of me?'

'To come to Llandinas with me.'

She stared at him for a moment, then said vehemently, '*No!*'

He continued as though she hadn't spoken. 'I want to take you to the house you all stayed at – inside it, if possible. I want you to walk with me along the cliffs where your mother took you that afternoon. I believe that could provide the trigger we were speaking of, and you might remember what happened when Monique returned to the house. Which would at least give us somewhere to start.'

She pushed her plate away. 'And how,' she demanded, her voice shaking, 'do you imagine my family would react to my playing detective, if it resulted in one of them being charged with murder?'

He leaned forward, putting a hand on her wrist, but she shook him off and stood up. 'No. I'm sorry, but very definitely no. I can't stop you poking your nose in my affairs, but I'm damned if I'll help you.'

'Annabel – wait—'

'You promised that if I met you today you wouldn't contact me again. I shall hold you to that.'

She snatched her jacket from the back of the chair and, before he had time to rise, walked quickly into the hotel and through the door to the street. Cheeks burning, she let herself into the car and turned on the ignition.

'And that,' she said aloud as the engine started up, 'is the last I see of you, Martin Coutts.' Reversing swiftly out of her parking space, she turned in the direction of home.

Three

E dward Carlyle stared out of the window at the bustling thoroughfare of the Promenade. The chestnut trees were in full flower, their waxy candles glowing in the sunshine, the leaves still freshly green. It was, he thought, the time of year when Cheltenham looked its best. And when he felt the most down.

Today, he was especially low, and his shaving mirror had shown him a depressing image – eyelids heavy, forehead ridged with grooves, even his thick hair, now grey at the temples, finally beginning to recede. He looked, he thought, every day of his fifty-eight years.

He sighed, tapping his fingers distractedly on the desk. There was a pile of reports to read through before this afternoon's meeting, and all he could think about was his mother's forthcoming birthday. Had she any idea what hell she put him through, year after year? He and Pa had tried to reason with her after Hilary's death, but no matter how he'd raged and pleaded, she would not be swayed. Much as he loved her, he was only too aware of the streak of ruthlessness she could draw on to get her own way.

Even more unforgivable was the strain put on Emma – a strain which, after simmering beneath the surface all these years, was finally manifesting itself. Her mother's death had changed her from a happy, outgoing child like her brother into a timid little girl afraid of her own shadow. And, he thought sadly, the change had been permanent. In her thirties she still lacked self-confidence, wanting nothing better than to merge into the background and not be noticed.

At least, her father amended uneasily, that had been the case until last year. And, naturally, it was Ma's birthday that had been the catalyst. Out of the blue, Emma had broached the subject that had always been taboo – not only broached it, but refused to let it drop. Who had been the last to see her mother? What was the last thing she said to them? What was her favourite scent – food – book? On their return home, she had gone feverishly through old photograph albums, removing all the snaps of Hilary and making a collage of them for her bedroom wall. Even now, almost twelve months on, the obsession continued, and the coming week could only intensify it.

Edward's thoughts went back to that terrible, never-to-be-forgotten week in South Wales, when all their lives had changed and Hilary's had ended. Over the years he had dreamed unremittingly of his return to Llandinas that afternoon; he'd parked the car and stood for several minutes staring out at the glittering sea, blissfully unaware of what lay ahead. He sometimes thought they were the last completely happy minutes of his life.

Then he had turned and gone up the path to the villa. The front door wasn't locked, which meant somebody was in.

'Hello?' he'd called, and glanced into the sitting room . . .

Abruptly he put his head in his hands, remembering the nightmare of suspicion that had followed, the continuous police questioning, and, even worse, the corroding, all-pervading sense of guilt.

There was a tap on the door and his secretary came in. 'Some letters for you to sign, Mr Carlyle.'

'Thank you.'

'Are you all right, sir?' She was looking at him with a worried frown.

'Yes, I'm all right, Barbara. It's just that May isn't my best month.'

'I know,' she said softly. 'It doesn't get any easier, does it?'

He remembered belatedly that her husband had died of cancer two years before, and gave her a bleak smile. 'No, it doesn't.'

As she went out, he glanced at the framed photographs on his desk. One was of the twins taken soon after Hilary's death, so he could remember them as she'd last seen them. They were in school uniform, Tom staring confidently at the camera, tie askew, hair unruly, though Edward knew for a fact he'd been presentable when sent into the studio; and Emma, huddling close to her brother, eyes enormous, mouth slightly open as though her thumb had just been removed from it. As was probably the case.

And the photograph alongside it was of Hilary herself in shorts and T-shirt, sitting on a children's swing. With her long legs and fragile ankles, he'd teased her that she looked like the thoroughbred she was. Now he lifted the picture and studied it – the generous mouth, smiling eyes and thick mass of hair. The snap had been taken in Rex and Moira's garden, the year before her death. He remembered that Tom had fallen out of the apple tree that afternoon, fortunately escaping with nothing worse than a grazed knee. Thank God for Rex and Moira, Edward thought devoutly. He doubted he'd have survived those early years without them.

Which inevitably brought his thoughts to Suzanne, whom he'd met six months ago at their home and who now presented yet another problem. Of course there'd been women before – he wasn't a monk – though only half a dozen in nearly thirty years, so not a Don Juan, either. Sometimes the affairs had lasted a year or two, sometimes less than six months, but they'd always been discreet and Edward was confident that his family knew nothing of them.

With Suzanne, though, it was different; she'd complicated things by falling in love with him. He was fond of her, as he'd been of her predecessors – casual sex had never interested him – but that, really, was as far as it went. Despite his mother's nudging over the years he'd no desire to remarry, though admittedly Suzanne was a prime candidate.

Divorced a couple of years ago, she was tall, dark and slim, had excellent dress sense and was always perfectly groomed. She'd be a great asset in his business entertaining – and an exciting partner in bed, as she'd already proved. Furthermore, she'd no children of her own to complicate matters. He could do much worse than marry her – but he'd no intention of doing so, and the difficulty lay in making that plain without hurting her too much.

Women! he thought humorously; his life was ruled by them: his mother, his dead wife, his daughter, his mistress. Even his secretary, who would be in shortly for the letters he'd not yet even glanced at.

Pushing aside worries past, present and future, Edward finally settled down to work.

A few miles away, his brother Douglas had also been anticipating the holiday, and with little more enthusiasm.

'God knows why Mother insists on going on with this,' he had grumbled to his wife over breakfast. 'In the light of all that's happened, it's grotesque, to say the least. And if it makes me uncomfortable, how must it be for Ed?'

'He doesn't given any sign of minding,' Charlotte said mildly.

'It wouldn't do him much good if he did,' Douglas pointed out. 'She made that plain enough in the early days. I wonder if she realizes she's the only one who enjoys these get-togethers?'

'Oh, darling, surely that's not true?'

'Then who else does?' he challenged her. 'Certainly not Emma, as she proved last year. And I doubt if Annabel finds them very congenial.'

Charlotte was silent. She knew he was ill at ease in his elder daughter's company, though she did everything she could to smooth things between them.

'And you know we practically have to handcuff our two to get them there. I can't speak for Tom and Celia, but I doubt if they regard it as a bundle of laughs.'

Charlotte said peaceably, 'Never mind, this year we'll have baby Teddy to enliven the proceedings.'

'And keep us awake at night!'

She laughed. 'You're determined to look on the dark side, aren't you?'

He smiled without replying. He could hardly tell her that these annual excursions always brought Monique to mind. Sheer bad luck, of course, that, years later, she should have been killed in the same month, so was doubly in his thoughts.

They'd been so in love at the beginning, he reflected sadly, recalling her first visit to Hazelwood; how stiff Mother had been with her, and how he'd crept to her bed, very properly made up in the guest room, when the parents were asleep. He'd been too weak, too indecisive for her, that was the trouble, and had ended by getting on her nerves. Monique was a strong character and needed an equally strong partner, whom she could respect and depend on. Though he'd always wondered whether that birthday week the year after Hilary's murder had been the final straw. If so, he could hardly blame her.

Still, he'd been lucky enough to find Charlotte, who'd given him two more children, and there was no denying they were a happy family. A couple of years his senior, she had shown no impatience with his fluctuations, no resentment of his general underachievement, and it was her money that ensured they had a lifestyle comparable with the rest of the family.

But there was still Annabel, who had come to stay regularly after Monique's departure, who was punctiliously invited to family celebrations, and whose smile reminded him so poignantly of her mother. He would give a lot to be able to relax with her, get to know her better. Perhaps this year.

Charlotte watched the emotions playing over his face, and ached with love for him. Sometimes she wondered if he'd ever completely got over his first wife leaving him; certainly, when she had met him five years later, his self-esteem was still low. She had fallen in love with a suddenness and completeness that had taken her by surprise, and had set herself, gently and patiently, to make him love her in return, in which task she'd been unstintingly supported by Flora.

'Douglas has always needed someone to lean on,' she had confided to Charlotte. 'Monique lost patience with him – she was French, you know.' Charlotte smiled at the memory.

With Flora's help, though, she had broken through Douglas's self-protective shell to gain his confidence and, eventually, his love, and the arrival of the children had completed her happiness. Yes, Charlotte reflected, she had every reason to be grateful to Monique.

'So how did the tea go?'

'What?' Annabel spun round to see her friend's smiling face.

'Tea yesterday,' Stephie repeated patiently. 'How did it go?'

'Don't ask!'

Her smile faded. 'Is something wrong?'

'No – no, not really.'

'Look, Annie, this is me you're talking to. Something's upset you.'

'No, I—' Annabel broke off. She'd had a bad night, unable to stop going over her conversation with Martin. Even when she'd fallen asleep, it was to dream herself back on the terrace at the Avon Gorge, with his probing eyes across the table.

She'd tried, when she arrived home, to talk to Simon about it, but he wasn't really interested. 'I don't see the problem,' he said obtusely. 'If you want to find out more, do what he suggests. If you don't, just forget it. Seems quite simple to me.'

Stephie said gently, 'I could provide a willing ear, if that would help.'

Annabel looked at her consideringly. She was a couple

of years older than herself, divorced, but now living with someone. Her short hair and large brown eyes gave her a gamine appearance, but in fact she was highly intelligent and well versed in the ways of the world. They had been friends almost as long as Annabel had been at St Helena's, and she had proved herself someone to be trusted.

'It's a long story,' she said slowly.

'Fine. How about finding ourselves somewhere quiet after school, and you can tell me about it? If you want to,' she added.

For a moment longer Annabel hesitated, a lifetime's taboo fighting with her need to talk. Then she said slowly, 'Yes, I rather think I do.'

During the afternoon, the coming discussion loomed large in her mind, lurking beneath the surface of Molière and the use of the subjunctive. Stephie would, she realized, be the ideal confidante – someone who knew nothing of her family or their history, who would bring a fresh viewpoint to the familiar story. A pity they'd not had their talk before she met Martin.

By five o'clock the capricious May weather had changed, a wind had risen and clouds were scudding across the sky.

'The Downs?' Stephie suggested, when they met in the cloakroom.

'Ideal. The wind will blow away the cobwebs.'

Clifton Downs was only a brisk five minutes' walk from school, a large, open space of grass, scrubland and bushes where dogs raced, children played and the local youths set up games of football. Annabel's hair, longer than Stephie's, whipped stingingly across her face. For some minutes they walked in silence as she tried to think how to make an opening. Then Stephie ventured, 'A long story, you said. Does it begin, "Once upon a time . . ."?'

Annabel smiled. 'I suppose it does. It goes back to 1972, anyway.'

'Good Lord, it *is* long!'

Annabel clenched her hands and launched into it. 'My

family were all on holiday in Wales – grandparents, parents, uncle, aunt and cousins. We always go away for a week over my grandmother's birthday.'

Stephie nodded. 'And you resent missing out on half-term. You told me.'

'Yes. Well, one afternoon my mother took me for a walk – I was a baby, of course – and the men went their separate ways. Grandmother, Aunt Hilary and the twins were on the beach.'

'Yes?' Stephie prompted, when she didn't go on.

'Well, Hilary liked to do the twins' meals herself, even though we had someone in to cook for us, and she went back ahead of the others to make a start on it. And soon afterwards Uncle Edward – her husband – returned to the villa and found her dead on the carpet.'

Stephie stopped abruptly, turning to face her. '*What?*'

'She'd been hit over the head – with an ornament, they think; at least, one was missing. And that's it, really. They never found out who'd done it, or why.'

'Annie, that's *dreadful*!'

'Yes,' Annabel agreed flatly, and started walking again. After a minute, Stephie fell in beside her.

Eventually, she said, 'No unidentified fingerprints anywhere?'

'No; even those on the door-knob could be accounted for.'

'You won't remember anything about it, I suppose?'

'No.'

'Look, it *is* dreadful, as I said, but – well, it happened a long time ago. What's upset you now? And what has this man you met yesterday got to do with it?'

'Everything!' Annabel said, and told her about Martin Coutts.

'What a nerve,' Stephie exclaimed indignantly, 'sniffing you out like that!'

'That's why they're called newshounds,' Annabel said without expression.

Stephie glanced at her uncertainly, unsure if she was making a joke. 'It's my guess,' she said slowly, 'that you're torn between telling him to go to hell and going along with him, if only to try and tie up all the loose ends.'

'I don't see how I could, though.'

'Is it all right if I speak frankly?'

'Of course – that's why I told you.'

'Well – you say there were no unexplained prints on the door-knob.'

'That's right; which means either she let him in, or they met outside and went in together.'

'There is another possibility,' Stephie said.

Annabel glanced at her, pushing the hair out of her eyes. 'What?'

'That it was someone whose prints were *not* unexplained.'

Annabel came to a halt. 'Someone—?'

'Whose prints had every right to be there – one of the family.'

'Oh, God! I knew they'd been under suspicion, but the significance of the door-knob hadn't registered. No doubt it did with the police.'

'As I said, it's only a possibility. You might still be right, that she *did* let him in herself.' Stephie paused. 'You say the men were about their own pursuits. Where, exactly?'

'I don't know, only that none of them could produce an alibi.'

'Great! What does Simon think about your going back?'

Annabel shrugged. 'He says it's up to me. Go, if I'm interested, if not, forget it. Not much help, really. What would you do, in my position?'

Stephie pursed her lips, considering. 'I suspect that my curiosity would prevail.'

'Even though one of your relatives could be arrested?'

'If he killed her, he deserves to be,' Stephie said stoutly. 'He's already had twenty-eight years of freedom which he wasn't entitled to.'

'For what it's worth, I don't think it was premeditated.

43

He didn't go armed with a weapon, just seized the nearest thing to hand.'

'It doesn't make her any less dead. And at the moment he hit her, he meant to kill her. Why? There must have been a reason. What kind of person was she?'

'I don't know. There's no one I can ask.'

'Might she have had a secret lover?'

Annabel smiled. 'In our family it seems unlikely, but I suppose it's possible. You're saying my uncle might have found out?'

'Perhaps. Or perhaps he was the one with a liaison, and wanted his wife out of the way.'

Annabel shivered and pulled up the collar of her jacket. 'You do realize I'm just about to spend seven days in his company?'

'You've been in his company regularly over the last twenty-eight years. What's the difference?'

'Martin is, damn him, for bringing all this up again.'

'Then take the bull by the horns and go to Wales with him, before half-term. Something might emerge.'

'I can't, Stephie! What would everyone think?'

'You can't be the only one who still wonders. Your grandmother must, and your cousins – and presumably your uncle and father, too. Or at any rate, one of them.' She paused. 'You say someone did the cooking. Did they live in?'

'No; it's always part of the package – someone to cook and someone to clean, but they only come in as required.'

'Perhaps your aunt found them trying to nick something?'

'Even if she did, they'd hardly have murdered her. And they'd have been checked at the time.' She paused. 'I wonder what Martin's got up his sleeve.'

Stephie cocked an eyebrow at her. 'Do I detect a weakening?'

'Oh, hell, Stephie, I don't *know*! I can't go crawling back when I flounced out telling him not to contact me again.'

They were both silent, watching a young couple strolling towards them and throwing a stick for their dog. It was a spaniel, and as it ran its ears flew out behind it in the wind. It skidded to a halt not far from them, retrieved the stick, and dashed back to its owners. They exchanged a smile with the couple as they passed.

Then Stephie said, 'I'll go with you if you like.'

'Um?' Annabel's eyes were still on the dog, now jumping up at the stick the man held, begging him to throw it again.

'To South Wales. I'll go with you.'

Annabel stared at her. 'But – we wouldn't know where to start.'

'We can look up the old newspapers – they'll be in an archive somewhere. Then we'll know at least as much as Martin does. What was he proposing to do, anyway?'

'Take me to the villa where it happened – see if it stirred up any memories.'

'Do you know the address?'

Annabel shook her head.

'Well, the papers are sure to have given it. With a bit of luck it could still be rented out, and if it's between lets we might even get a look inside. At the very least we could see the outside, where it is in relation to the beach, and if there's anywhere someone could have been hiding, watching your aunt go into the house.'

Annabel said accusingly, 'You're beginning to enjoy this!'

Stephie smiled sheepishly. 'Call it exercising the brain.'

'Call it watching too much TV!'

'Well, I'm sure between us we're quite as capable of finding things out as Martin is. Always provided there's something to find. What's more,' she added cunningly, 'we would have the option of keeping quiet about it if you changed your mind, whereas he would obviously make a bid for the headlines, even if you didn't want him to.'

Annabel felt a stirring of excitement. It would never have

occurred to her to go to Wales had Martin not mentioned it, but she didn't see how anyone could object. Even if nothing came of it, she would at least see the house that had played such a traumatic part in the life of her family. 'When could we go?'

'Next weekend? Down Friday evening after school – with the Avon bridge it shouldn't take long – and back Sunday evening. It'll give us two clear days. And if we don't find out anything, then Martin probably wouldn't have, either.'

'You're on! But won't Charlie mind you being away all weekend?'

'He'll survive. We haven't anything planned. What about you?'

'There'll be something on – there always is – but it won't matter if I'm not there.' It hadn't on Saturday. 'The first thing to do,' she went on, her interest quickening, 'is to find out the name of a Swansea paper and ask if we can have access to their files for the week around 31st May '72. I'll do that as soon as I get back. I don't think we need to book in anywhere – there must be dozens of hotels and B&Bs.'

Stephie took her arm and squeezed it. 'I'm quite looking forward to it!' she said.

The *Swansea Gazette* did not offer any objections to her request, and she arranged to be at their offices at nine thirty on Saturday morning. She had just put the phone down when Simon arrived home.

'You'll be glad to know I've reached a decision,' she said lightly.

'About what?' He bent to kiss her.

'About whether or not to go to Wales. I'm going over for the weekend, to see what I can find out.'

'So Martin talked you round after all!'

'Actually, no, he didn't. I'm going with Stephie.'

Simon frowned. 'I don't get it.'

'Well, Martin put the idea in my head, but I didn't want to go with him, and I knew you wouldn't come. So we're going Friday evening, back on Sunday. You don't mind, do you?'

'I won't have to, will I?'

'I'll leave something in the freezer.'

'Don't bother; I'll be out both evenings, and go to Mum and Dad's for Sunday lunch.'

'If you see Martin while you're socializing, I'd rather you didn't say where I was.'

He gave a short laugh. 'Yes, I imagine he'd be pretty narked at your trying to steal his thunder.'

'I'm doing no such thing!' she said indignantly. 'It's my family who's concerned, after all.'

'Will you tell your grandmother?'

'I don't know. It depends on what happens.'

'Well, the best of British, but don't blame me if you land one of your relatives in jail.'

Friday evening was not the best of times to drive into Wales, especially when the forecast for the weekend was good. Traffic was slow, with frequent hold-ups. While they were waiting in a jam Stephie asked idly, 'Do you get on well with your family?'

Annabel shrugged. 'When I see them, which isn't often these days. We go up for the odd weekend, and of course there's the birthday week, but we're never there for Christmas, because we spend it rushing between my stepfather and Simon's parents.'

She felt in her bag for a tube of mints and passed one to Stephie. 'I knew them better when I was younger, and spent a fair bit of time at my grandmother's. I used to tag along with Tom and his friend Neil, even though they were quite a lot older. Looking back, I'm surprised they put up with me. They didn't with Emma.'

'Who is . . . ?'

'Tom's twin. She was always whining about being left out, but she couldn't climb or play cricket and she didn't like getting dirty, so the boys thought her a dead loss.'

'Describe them to me, so I can picture them.'

The traffic started to move and the car inched forward again. 'Well, Emma's still a bit wimpish. She's always been neurotic, and recently she's become obsessed with her mother's death, to everyone's embarrassment.'

'Asking about it, you mean?'

'Yes, and endlessly discussing it. I told Martin she was the one he should be speaking to.'

'Does she look like Tom?'

'In a faded kind of way. They have the same features, but her hair is lighter than his and she's paler. She doesn't wear much make-up, which I'm sure would help, and she goes around in these long flowered skirts and ethnic tops. Tom, on the other hand, is quite a go-getter. He's married to Celia, who adores him, and they have a six-month-old baby. He's tall like his father, with thick browny-gold hair and hazel eyes – not bad looking, really, though for me he was always overshadowed by Neil. I had a crush on him for years!'

'Tell me about Neil, then.'

'He's the doctor's son. His parents are friends of the family, so we saw quite a lot of them.'

'Is he still around?'

'Not in Cheltenham. He's an artist, and doing very nicely, thank you. He's had several exhibitions in London.'

'Married?'

'No, but he's been living for years with a girl he met at art school. Marina, her name is. From what I hear, it's a very stormy relationship. Perhaps that's what's needed to produce great art – I wouldn't know. Sounds rather stressful, though.'

Stephie was silent for a minute or two, then said, 'What's your uncle like? The widower?'

'To look at, an older version of Tom. I'm fond of Uncle Edward; he's quiet and considerate and has always been very kind to me.'

Stephie frowned. 'Meaning some of them weren't?'

'No one was *un*kind, but my grandmother's not particularly fond of me, though she tries to hide it.'

'Oh, Annie, come on!'

'It's the truth, believe me. She didn't like my mother, either, even before she left Daddy.'

'And what about your father? Are your feelings for him equally ambivalent?'

Annabel manoeuvred her way past a row of lorries, seemingly travelling in convoy. 'He's all right, but we're not close – and I can't help wondering why my mother left him. She must have had her reasons. Anyway, he married again, and I think of him as David and Holly's father, rather than mine.'

'What a complicated family! Mine seems quite tame by comparison.'

'They're happy enough. Charlotte's a year or two older than Daddy; she mothers him, and he laps it up. He certainly wouldn't have got that with Maman.'

'The Peter Pan syndrome,' Stephie observed. 'Some women go for it, but not me, I'm afraid.'

Annabel looked surprised. 'I hadn't thought of him like that, but you could be right.'

She frowned, seeming to consider her father in a new light, and Stephie felt a little uncomfortable. But they were at last coming into Swansea, and their attention switched from the Carlyles to the more urgent question of finding accommodation.

Fortunately the problem was soon solved, and they installed themselves in a small hotel near the centre of town. The twin-bedded room was basic but adequate, and much the same could be said of the meal served in its restaurant.

'When in Rome, do as the Romans do,' remarked Stephie, ordering leek and potato soup, and Welsh lamb as her main course. Annabel's appetite, though, had disappeared, and she opted for melon, followed by salmon salad. Even so, she was unable to finish it.

'Nerves?' Stephie asked sympathetically.

Annabel nodded. 'I'm beginning to wish I hadn't come.'

'If you hadn't, you'd never have stopped wondering about it, whether or not you might have found out something.'

'I'm not sure I want to. When you think about it, we've all managed to survive for twenty-eight years without—'

'All except Hilary,' Stephie put in.

Annabel sighed. 'You're right, of course. Well, let's see what tomorrow will bring.'

At nine thirty the next morning, they presented themselves at the office of the *Swansea Gazette*. A pleasant-faced woman, who introduced herself as the librarian, conducted them through the press cuttings and photographic library to an adjacent room furnished with three desks, each bearing a machine she referred to as a 'reader'.

'It's the week of 31st May '72 you're interested in, isn't it?' she said in her lilting Welsh voice. 'I've put the film in for you.' She pulled over an extra chair for Stephie. 'It was a Wednesday that year, but you can go either forward or backwards. Do you know how to work it? You press the button here to move from page to page. Let me know if there's anything else you need.'

She went out of the room, closing the door behind her, and they seated themselves in front of the machine. 'Well, here goes,' Annabel said.

As they'd expected, the murder was front-page news. The first reporting of it appeared on the thirty-first itself – Flora's birthday.

WOMAN MURDERED IN HOLIDAY VILLA screamed the headlines.

Mrs Hilary Carlyle, 28, of Cheltenham, was found dead yesterday in the lounge of the family's holiday villa, Bay View, at Llandinas. She had been dealt a severe blow to the head, but no weapon was found at the scene. The dead woman's husband, Mr Edward Carlyle, who found the body, was being comforted by relatives last night. Police are anxious to interview

50

anyone who might have seen someone approaching the house between four thirty, when the victim left the beach, and ten minutes past five, when her husband found her. The number to phone is . . .

Over the next few days, various additional pieces of information were vouchsafed. The inquest had been adjourned after establishing cause of death. The victim was the daughter of Sir Francis and Lady Montague, of Chelsea. A man was 'helping police with their enquiries' – Edward, Annabel surmised. A day or two later he was released without charge. One or two shocked neighbours were interviewed. By the end of the week, the story had been relegated to the inside pages.

Annabel went on hopefully turning the handle, but the case seemed to have fizzled out, mirroring the lack of progress made by the police. She sat back, turning to look at Stephie.

'Hardly worth coming!' she commented.

'We've got the name of the villa,' Stephie reminded her. 'That was one of our objectives. We can ask about estate agents as we go out.'

They pushed back their chairs, thanking the librarian on their way back through the library. At the desk, they were given the names of half a dozen local estate agents, which Annabel jotted down in her diary. Then, slightly deflated, they made their way back to the hotel.

'Let's have some coffee, then go up to our room and start ringing round. If Bay View is still rented out, someone must handle it. Today's Saturday – changeover day – which might help.'

They struck lucky with the fourth name on the list, a firm called Jones, Meredith. 'Yes, it's on our books,' they were told, 'but I'm afraid it's fully booked till the end of August.'

'We don't want to rent it, just have a quick look round. Would that be possible?'

'I'm sorry, viewing is restricted to prospective tenants.

51

We have several other properties we could show you—'

'Right, thank you, we'll come in. How do we find you?'

Annabel took down the directions and looked up. 'We won't get anywhere trying to explain over the phone. Anyway, the girls on the desks couldn't give us permission. Let's go round and see the manager.'

Mr Elwyn Davis – his name was on the door – was a bald, bustling little man, who looked at them doubtfully over the top of his spectacles. 'I believe my staff explained, ladies, that there are no vacancies at Bay View until the end of August. However—'

Annabel leaned forward. 'We don't want to rent it, Mr Davis. It's very important to us that we should see it – in fact, that's why we came to Wales this weekend.'

'Then I'm sorry you had a wasted journey. I—'

'You see,' Stephie cut in, 'I'm writing a book about the murder that took place there in 1972.'

Annabel held her breath, watching the man's face change. 'A book, is it?'

'Yes, and I'm sure you'll appreciate how important it is to get your facts straight.' She paused. 'Is anyone in possession at the moment?'

He hesitated, but he was clearly impressed. 'Well now, this week's tenants had to vacate by ten a.m. –' he glanced at his watch – 'so the house could be prepared for the new arrivals.'

'Who are due – when?'

'They're collecting the keys at two o'clock.'

'That should give us time, then.' Annabel smiled at him expectantly.

'It's most irregular,' he began, reverting to his slightly pompous manner.

'We'll send you an autographed copy!' Stephie promised shamelessly.

'Well, I suppose it'll do no harm. As long as you're quick, mind, and don't hold up the cleaners. The turnover time is tight enough as it is.' He pulled a pad towards him. 'I'll need your names and addresses, for the record. You say you're staying in Swansea?'

'Just for two nights.' Stephie gave him her best smile. 'We really are terribly grateful to you.'

'Well, we must do what we can to help research, mustn't we?' He picked up the phone on his desk and spoke into it. 'Gwilym, are you free to take two ladies out to Llandinas? They want a look round Bay View between lets.' He looked up. 'You're ready to go now?' Annabel nodded eagerly. 'Five minutes at the front desk,' said Mr Davis into the phone.

Gwilym was about twenty, a small, dark young man with black hair that fell over his brow. He had parked on a yellow line, and was eager to bundle them inside as quickly as possible before a prowling traffic warden appeared on the scene. Their insistence on seeing the villa seemed to have aroused curiosity in the outer office, and Annabel noticed the quick, interested glances he darted at them in the rear-view mirror.

'Sorry if we're disrupting your morning,' she said.

He flashed her a smile. 'Glad to get out of the office, to tell the truth. Working Saturdays isn't my idea of fun.' He hesitated, clearly wondering how to get round to the subject which interested him. 'Looking for somewhere to stay, is it?'

'No, we know Bay View's not available. We just want a look at it.'

'Why would that be then, if you don't mind me asking?'

Stephie repeated her falsehood. 'I'm writing a book about the murder that took place there.'

His face lit up. 'A writer, are you? Are you famous?'

Stephie laughed. 'I'm afraid not. Perhaps I will be after this book.'

'My nan told me about it – the murder, that is. She was living out on the Gower then. Afraid she'd be murdered in her bed, she said. They never caught him, did they?'

'No,' Stephie agreed.

'Looking for more evidence, are you?'

Too close to the truth; she quickly denied it. 'Hardly, after all this time. But it helps to see the place you're writing about, so you can visualize it properly and get the facts right.'

They were leaving Swansea and its suburbs behind, and Annabel looked out of the window as fields began to replace the straggling houses. The sky was wide and blue and every now and then there were glimpses of the sea. Alongside the road, sheep grazed the short grass and in the distance a group of wild ponies stood under the trees.

They must have driven along here all those years ago, she thought, unaware of the horrors that awaited them. Was Martin right, that being at the villa would bring things back to her? Did she want to remember them? Despite the sunshine she felt cold, with a sick, heavy feeling in her stomach.

'Nearly there!' Gwilym said cheerfully, and her nails dug into her palms.

A signpost appeared on the left, reading *Llandinas, 2 miles*. He turned off the main road and they wound their way between high hedges until, rounding a bend, they found themselves in the village, a cluster of white-painted houses, a church, and a general-purpose shop. The pavement outside the shop was cluttered with postcard stands and buckets crammed with spades, paper flags and flailing windmills, and a group of holidaymakers eating ice creams stared at them as they went past.

They drove on, past half a dozen bungalows with deck chairs in the gardens and a guesthouse with a notice reading 'Vacancies'. Ahead of them they could see several cars parked facing the sea, which was now visible some way below them. As the car followed the road round to the left, three widely spaced villas came into sight, separated from each other by screens of trees. Annabel leant forward to read the names as they passed: Cliff Top, Sunnyside, and, finally, as Gwilym drew to a halt, Bay View.

In front of the house was a garden enclosed by a white fence. There was a garage alongside and a car stood in the drive – presumably belonging to the cleaners. Beyond the far fence a small copse extended for several yards, then the land opened out to scrubland and the road came to an end. The house itself was, like its neighbours, painted white, the woodwork picked out in dark blue. It was single-fronted, and its windows stared blankly out at them, as though daring them to uncover its secrets.

Annabel and Stephie sat motionless, gazing up at it, and Gwilym, surprised they made no move to leave the car, turned to look at them. After a moment he cleared his throat. 'Well, ladies, if you'd like to see inside – ?'

They nodded and climbed out, and a stiff breeze ruffled their hair. On the sea side of the road was a stretch of scrubby grass and a steep path leading down to the beach. Above it, gulls soared and swooped, uttering their raucous cries. Stephie took Annabel's arm and gave it an encouraging squeeze. Still in silence, they followed Gwilym up the path to the front door. He opened it with his key, calling, 'It's only me – Gwil. I've a couple of ladies here wanting to see round. We won't get in your way.' Then he stood aside for them to enter.

Ahead lay a fairly narrow hall tiled in brown and white, with a staircase facing them on the right. There was a door on the left and one at the end of the passage, opening on to what was obviously a kitchen. Annabel's heart had set up a heavy, uneven thumping and her legs felt like lead. Stephie pulled her over the threshold and she stumbled slightly, the dark hall blinding her after the brightness outside.

'This is the lounge,' Gwilym announced, opening the door on the left with a flourish. 'Where it happened, like.'

With her heart fluttering at the base of her throat, Annabel allowed herself to be led inside. She had a blurred impression of a long room with windows at both ends, of a fireplace with a fitted gas fire, of the outlines of chairs and table. Then the darkness that had been hovering ever since they left Swansea enveloped her and, with a little moan, she slid to the floor.

She came round moments later to find herself lying on a sofa and Stephie bending anxiously over her, while Gwilym hovered in the background with a glass of water. She struggled wildly to sit up, straining to see past them, still in the grip of terror.

'Annie – Annie, it's all right. I'm here – you're all right.' Stephie took the glass from Gwilym and held it for her. She drank thirstily. Gradually the fear began to recede and her breathing slowed. She lay back and put a hand to her head.

'Is she OK?' whispered Gwilym's awestruck voice.

Then Stephie's: 'Yes, she's fine now. Just give her another minute.'

'What happened?'

Stephie improvised wildly. 'Well, you see, she's psychic. She – gets vibrations from the past.'

'Did she see who did it, then? The murder?'

'I – don't know.' And God help her, Stephie thought, that's the truth. Annabel had gone the most ghastly colour, and she still looked like death. Stephie shivered at the cliché, noticing with relief that she was now swinging her legs to the floor.

'OK, love?'

'Yes. Sorry about that. I don't know what came over me.'

'For one thing, you've hardly eaten anything for the last twenty-four hours. Are you up to seeing the rest of the house, or shall we just go?'

'No, I'm OK. We might as well look round while we're here.'

Out into the hall again and along to the kitchen – small but reasonably well set up. And in any case, Stephie reflected, they'd had outside help. Through the window she could see an enclosed garden, mainly lawn, with a few shrubs. There was a washing line and some rather tired-looking garden furniture.

On the first floor they came across the cleaners, two large and cheerful women armed with vacuum cleaner and brushes.

'You go ahead, love,' they invited, 'we've finished up here anyway.' And they clattered away down the stairs.

There were four double bedrooms, the largest of which had been adapted to incorporate an en suite shower. Annabel doubted it had been there twenty-eight years ago. Other than the main bathroom, that was all. The house was simply what it purported to be – a moderately sized holiday home, close to the beach. It was not its fault that it had been catapulted into notoriety.

They returned downstairs, Gwilym called goodbye to the cleaners and opened the front door. Carefully avoiding glancing towards the lounge, Annabel went thankfully through it, drawing a deep breath of the fresh, salt air.

It took a moment for her to realize that another car was now parked in front of Gwilym's, and leaning nonchalantly against it, watching them, was Martin Coutts.

Four

Annabel clutched Stephie's arm as Martin straightened and walked to the gate to meet them.

'I thought I'd find you here,' he said.

Annabel moistened her lips. 'Stephie, this is Martin Coutts. My friend, Stephanie Lucas.'

They nodded warily at each other. Perplexed, Gwilym looked from one to the other.

'And this,' Annabel went on with an effort, 'is Gwilym – I'm afraid I don't know your last name – who kindly showed us over the house.'

'They're writing a book about the murder, see,' Gwilym explained, anxious to clear his position.

Martin raised an eyebrow and turned back to Annabel. 'Any repercussions?'

'Fainted clean away, she did!' Gwilym told him. '*Vibrations*.' His Welsh voice spoke the word with relish.

'Indeed?'

Still puzzled by the atmosphere, Gwilym glanced at his watch. 'We should be going, ladies, if you're ready.'

Martin said smoothly, 'Don't worry, I'll run them back.'

'No!' Annabel said involuntarily.

'It's the least you owe me, Annabel.'

Gwilym hesitated. 'We always return clients to the office, sir. To complete the service, see.'

Annabel said, 'Martin, I don't feel well, and I'm not up to being harangued all the way to Swansea. I want to lie back and close my eyes for a while. I admit I owe you an explanation, and you can have it, but at the hotel, when I've had time to recover.'

'Where are you staying?' His voice was clipped.

She told him, and turned to Gwilym, who opened the rear door for her.

Martin said shortly, 'I'll see you there, then. For lunch.'

Unable to fight him any further, Annabel merely nodded and got into the car.

'How the hell did he know you were here?' Stephie demanded in a low voice as they drove away.

'He'd have seen Simon at the pub last night.' Either Simon had given her away, or Martin had simply jumped to the right conclusion.

'I don't blame you for not wanting to come with him.'

Annabel leaned her head back against the cushions, closing her eyes, and, taking the hint, Stephie said no more.

The drive back was completed almost in silence. God knows, Stephie thought, what story would go round the estate agents' office. As they approached Swansea, Gwilym said diffidently, 'If you like I could drop you at your hotel. It's not really out of my way, and it would save you walking, like.'

'That's very kind of you. Thank you.'

'Do you think it helped, then,' he asked as they got out at the hotel, 'seeing the house for yourself?'

'I'm sure it did,' Stephie replied warmly. 'We're very grateful to you, and to Mr Davis for arranging it.'

'And your friend.' His eyes followed Annabel, who was moving slowly towards the hotel steps. 'Will she be all right, do you think?'

'As right as rain,' Stephie assured him.

They went up in the lift to their room on the second floor. Stephie unlocked it, and Annabel went in and flopped on her bed.

'You need to eat,' Stephie said, frowning in concern.

'I don't know if I'll be able to, with Martin glaring at me.'

Stephie retrieved a packet of biscuits from the tea-making tray. 'Have these now. At least there'll be something in your stomach.'

Annabel sat up and dutifully ate them.

'How do you feel?'

'All right. Just a bit weak.'

'What caused it, do you know? You looked absolutely ghastly.'

Annabel smiled wanly. 'Thanks. I don't know what it was; I'd been feeling progressively worse all the way there. I really didn't want to go into that house.'

'You should have said.'

'But it was so illogical. We'd come specially to see it. I can't really explain – I was frightened of something, but Lord knows what. It was – the same feeling I have in my dream.'

'What dream?'

'Oh, just a vague kind of nightmare I've had all my life, where I'm sitting or lying in a room somewhere, and watching the door.'

'And what happens?'

'Nothing, really. I'm just aware of being terrified, and of someone in the room with me, and then I wake up.'

They were interrupted by the strident ringing of the bedside phone. Stephie lifted it, and reception announced, 'Mr Coutts is waiting for you in the dining room, madam.'

'Thank you. Tell him we'll be down in five minutes.'

Annabel stood up, running her fingers through her hair. 'I'll have a wash and brush-up. That'll make me feel better.'

In the bathroom she sluiced her face with cold water and paused to study herself in the mirror. She'd regained some of her colour though she was still pale, and as always when tired or unwell, her eyes, usually light grey, had deepened to slate. She sighed, applied fresh make-up and brushed her hair. It was the best she could do, and, with no further excuse for delay, she went downstairs with Stephie.

Martin rose from a corner table as they were shown in. There was a glass in front of him, and, seeing Annabel glance at it as she sat down, he said, 'Can I get you an aperitif?'

'No, thank you.'

The waiter spread napkins on their knees and presented each of them with a menu. To her surprise, Annabel found that she was ravenous. When they had given their orders, she looked across at Martin, to find the dark, assessing eyes on her face.

'How did you know I was here?' she challenged him.

'Simon solo last night, and very evasive when asked where you were.'

Idiot! Annabel thought. Why couldn't he just have said I had a headache? 'But at the house?' she persisted.

'It was my idea you hijacked, remember, and coming to the house was the crux of it.' He paused, sipping his drink. 'Incidentally, what was all that about writing a book?'

'That was my idea,' Stephie admitted. 'They weren't keen on letting us look round, but that did the trick.'

'Brilliant!' he said ironically. 'So, Annabel, why the unilateral declaration of independence?'

She'd prepared for that. 'Because if I do find out anything, I want the option of not publicizing it.'

'You're beginning to accept it was one of the family?'

'Not necessarily, but you sowed the seeds of doubt.'

'Oh, come on! You've lived with it all your life.'

She shook her head. 'I never thought about it – I'd trained myself not to.'

Their first course arrived, and the waiter poured wine. When he had moved away, Martin resumed his interrogation. 'So, with the doubt duly planted, you decided to pull a fast one, and hope I wouldn't find out. Did it pay off?'

'At least I've seen where it happened,' she said steadily.

'And fainted dead away into the bargain?'

She flushed. 'It was the strain, that's all.'

'The *vibrations*?' His voice mimicked Gwilym's.

'I passed it off by saying she was psychic,' Stephie explained.

Martin looked at her with mock admiration. 'Another stroke of genius!' He turned back to Annabel. 'And were you aware of any stirrings of memory?'

She moistened her lips. 'It's impossible to say.'

'You mean the faint obliterated them?'

'Perhaps,' she answered evasively, and began to eat her mushrooms.

'Or,' he continued remorselessly, 'was it the memories themselves that made you faint?'

'Hey, ease up there!' Stephie protested, seeing Annabel flinch. 'Can't you see she's still feeling delicate? Grill me, if you must.'

Martin stared at her for a minute before saying levelly, 'Very well. Tell me what else you've been up to.'

'Well, we started off at the newspaper office.'

'Scene of my youthful endeavours.'

'Which is where we learned the address of the villa, but not much else.' She paused. 'Annie said you worked on the story; did you interview any of the Carlyles?'

'Alas, no; I only saw them from a distance, getting in and out of cars. The husband was under suspicion for a while, but only for lack of anyone else. There wasn't any evidence against him, and they had to let him go. It was mainly on lack of motive that the case foundered.'

He poured more wine into their glasses. 'What added to the publicity was that the victim came from one of the big county families, the Montagues. Box at Covent Garden, Royal Enclosure at Ascot, and all that. That's why the nationals picked it up. There was even an obituary in *The Times*.'

Stephie glanced enquiringly at Annabel, who shook her head. 'I only know what we read at the *Gazette*.'

The waiter approached with their main course, and they were silent while it was served. Then Martin continued. 'Hilary Carlyle was still in her twenties when she died, but she'd already made quite a name for herself – helped, of course, by her family background. With her father an MP and her mother active in local affairs, she grew up believing you should be involved in your local community. Consequently she was already on several boards and committees, and according to hearsay, making her presence felt.' Martin smiled crookedly. 'By which I mean – and again, this is only hearsay – she was inclined to be self-opinionated.'

'Which might have made her some enemies?'

'The police went into that pretty exhaustively. Of course there were people who didn't like her – thought she set herself up and was too officious. But it was generally acknowledged that she did a lot of good work, for charities and so on – and as I said, nothing remotely resembling a motive ever emerged.'

'And still hasn't,' commented Stephie. 'All in all, we don't seem to have got much further.'

'I wouldn't say that; I think Annabel's passing out was significant. If she'd also walked along the cliffs, as I originally suggested, there's no saying what might have come back to her.'

'Can we please change the subject?' Annabel asked rockily. 'I've had as much of this as I can take.'

Martin looked sceptical, but Stephie promptly embarked on a lengthy story about an eccentric relative, and the subject of the murder wasn't raised again.

When they had finished their coffee, Martin signalled to the waiter for the bill. 'I must be getting back to Bristol,' he commented. 'I was supposed to be cutting the hedge this morning.'

As they walked together out of the dining room, Annabel said a little stiffly, 'Thank you for lunch.'

'Don't mention it; it was the only way to get you to talk to me!' And with that, he strode across the foyer and out through the swing doors.

'Now what?' Stephie asked.

The answer came, unexpectedly, from the receptionist,

who leant forward holding out an envelope. 'Ms Lucas? A letter has been handed in for you.'

'For me? It can't be – no one knows I'm here.' She took the envelope and glanced down at the name before tearing it open. Then she gave a low whistle. 'Listen to this, Annie: *Dear Ms Lucas, I hope you don't mind me contacting you, but I heard from a friend who works at Jones, Meredith that you're writing a book about the murder at Bay View. I have some information that might be of interest, if you'd like to ring me on the above number. Yours sincerely, Janet Evans.'*

'How does she know your name?' Annabel asked, frowning.

'We gave it to Mr Davis, remember. And Gwilym knows we're staying here. Do you want me to phone her, or have you had enough for one day?'

'"Information",' Annabel said reflectively. 'It sounds important, but if so, why doesn't she go to the police?'

'Perhaps she has.'

'Let's ring her, then.'

The phone at the other end was picked up immediately. It seemed Janet Evans had been waiting for their call.

'This is Stephanie Lucas, phoning in reply to your note.'

'Yes, Ms Lucas. Would you like me to come round to see you?'

'Well, I – don't want to put you to any trouble. We could meet somewhere else, if you'd rather.'

'No, no, I'm not far from the hotel – I can be there in quarter of an hour. You won't be able to miss me – I have red hair!'

'Right – in the lounge, then? At –' Stephie consulted her watch – 'three thirty?'

'I'll be there.'

In fact, she was a few minutes early. Having positioned themselves so they could watch the door, they saw her at once, a tall, red-haired woman in a bottle-green suit. As she paused in the doorway, Stephie raised her hand and she smiled and made her way over to them.

Stephie introduced herself and Annabel, and Janet Evans sat down and immediately began ferreting in her bag. 'You don't mind if I smoke?'

Her fingers, long and blunt-nailed, shook slightly as she lit a cigarette, inhaled deeply, and sat back in her chair.

'That's better! I hope you won't feel I'm butting in, but this is by way of easing my conscience. They say confession's good for the soul.'

'Confession of what, Mrs Evans?'

'Janet, please.' She sat back in her chair and regarded them both. 'Well, you see,' she said, 'I think I saw the murderer.'

For a minute no one spoke, and the sounds of the lounge – a light laugh from across the room, the clinking of tea-cups – were of another world. Annabel's hands had clenched convulsively on her lap.

'Go on,' Stephie said into their stillness.

'I was on the cliff-top that afternoon, with my boyfriend. Seventeen I was, just left school and thought I knew it all. He was in his twenties, with a wife and baby. My parents had found out I was seeing him, and the next day I was being packed off to my aunt in Llandudno, to attend secretarial college. I'd been ordered not to leave the house, but I managed to slip out, phoned him from the box on the corner, and arranged to meet in the usual place. He was a postman, so afternoons were a good time for him.' She drew deeply on her cigarette and exhaled, sending smoke circles spiralling towards the ceiling.

Annabel was consumed with impatience. What did she care about the intricacies of Janet Evans's love life? Who had she seen, and when?

Some hint of her tension must have reached the woman, because she smiled apologetically. 'Bear with me – I do need to explain the background, as you'll see. The "usual place" I mentioned was in the trees beyond the villas at Llandinas.

They formed a thick screen and no one ever went into them. What was more, it was only minutes from home – useful when our time together was limited. We'd found a little clearing in the middle, and could lie there watching people walking along the cliff path, knowing we were invisible. It added to the excitement.

'That afternoon, as you can imagine, I was in a terrible state at having to go away and leave Ivor. Anyway, eventually we said our goodbyes and promised to write – all the usual – and we were just about to go when he caught my arm and pulled me back into the trees. Someone was coming up the path from the beach – a young woman in a straw hat. Obviously we didn't want to be seen, so we waited. She was wearing a short towelling robe over her swimsuit, and her arms and legs were tanned. I remember Ivor giving a low whistle, and I nudged him in the ribs.

'Well, she crossed over the road making for the villa nearest to us, and reached the gate at the same time as a man coming from the opposite direction. He seemed to be in quite a state, and began gesticulating with his hands as though trying to explain something.'

'What did he look like?' Annabel demanded, unable to keep quiet any longer. Janet Evans looked surprised; she'd expected Stephie, as the author, to show the most interest.

'Tall, brownish hair, wearing jeans and a sports shirt. Anyway, the woman started shaking her head, and he got even more upset. He caught hold of her arm, but she shook him off, walked quickly up the path and let herself into the house. But before she could close the door, he pushed his way inside.'

So he didn't touch the knob, Annabel thought. The legitimacy or otherwise of the prints on it didn't matter after all.

'And?' Stephie prompted, when Janet didn't go on.

'Well, that's it, really. It didn't seem important, and what with going away the next day, and leaving Ivor and all, I was too wrapped up in my own misery to wonder about it. Aunt Et did say something about a murder at Llandinas, but

I assumed it would have been at the pub – they were always having trouble there – and didn't pay much attention.'

'What about Ivor?' Stephie asked.

Janet smiled ruefully. 'Never heard from him again, but he could hardly come forward and say he'd been there, now could he?'

Annabel swallowed painfully. 'And when did you realize? That what you'd seen might be important?'

'Bless you, not till about five years ago. I became friendly with someone who works at Jones, Meredith, and she just happened to say one day that they had "the murder villa" on their books. I asked what she meant, and then, when I worked out the timing, the significance struck me. I was shattered, I don't mind telling you.'

'Did you go to the police?'

Janet stared at her. 'After more than twenty years? Not much point, was there?'

'But the case is still open,' Annabel said.

'They're never still looking for him?'

'Officially, yes.'

The woman moved uncomfortably. 'You think I should report it, then?'

'Yes, I do. They might be able to trace Ivor, too.'

'He couldn't tell them any more than I can.'

'I suppose you didn't hear anything they said?' Annabel asked desperately.

'No, we were too far away.'

'And there's nothing else you can tell us about the man?'

She shook her head. 'I can tell you what time it was, though – just gone twenty to five. I checked my watch when we got up to go.' She smiled ruefully. 'You must wonder at me being so certain, after all this time, but my da was due home at five, see, and I had to be back in my room by then – he was sure to check. Anyway, I've relived that last afternoon with Ivor so often over the years, every detail of it is etched on my mind.'

Twenty to five. It fitted, allowing Hilary just under ten minutes to climb the steep path from the beach. It had been a hot day and she wouldn't have been hurrying.

'You didn't see him come out?'

'No, we didn't hang about. They'd held us up as it was, and like I said, I was anxious to get home.' She hesitated, looking at Annabel. 'You went over there, didn't you? This morning?'

'Yes.'

'And were taken ill?'

'It wasn't anything.'

'I've heard that violent deeds are somehow stamped on the atmosphere, and sensitive people can tune in to them.'

Stephie said quickly, 'I'm so sorry – we haven't offered you tea. Would you like some?'

For a moment longer Janet's eyes lingered on Annabel's closed face. Then she picked up her handbag. 'No, ta, I must be going. I hope it's helped, what I've told you – though I'd rather you didn't mention Ivor and me!'

'Not by name,' Stephie smiled, 'you can count on that.'

'And you really think I should go to the police?'

'Yes. I don't know if it will help at this stage, but you mentioned having a conscience. That might help to clear it.'

They all stood up and shook hands. 'Thanks so much for contacting us. It was an unexpected bonus.'

They watched her walk out of the room, then sat down again.

'Well!' Stephie said. 'What do you make of that?'

'At least we know how he got into the house without touching the knob.'

'And that she knew him.'

Annabel nodded soberly.

'But that's about it, isn't it? It could, technically, still be either your grandfather – he mightn't have been grey then, your uncle, or your father.'

'Or none of them.'

'True.' Stephie hesitated. 'Will you tell Martin?'

'I might, if I see him.'

There was a brief silence. 'Shall I order some tea?'

Annabel shook her head. 'I'm still full of lunch. Let's go for a walk on the beach. Langland Bay isn't far – I saw it signposted this morning.'

'Good idea,' said Stephie, brightening. 'I could do with a good blow!'

It was good to feel the sand under their bare feet and the wind in their hair. At the edge of the water children were playing with plastic buckets, their little bodies reddened by the sun.

'I hope they sleep tonight,' Stephie commented.

They walked in silence for a while, swinging their shoes in their hands. Then Stephie said, 'Do you want to walk along the cliffs at Llandinas?'

Annabel shuddered. 'No, thanks. If I passed out there, I could go over the edge!'

'I was just wondering—'

'What?'

'Whether your mother might have seen the man, when she was coming back from the cliffs. What time did she get back, do you know?'

Annabel stopped, staring out to sea. 'I don't know; as I said, she would never talk about it.'

Stephie said gently, 'Have you ever wondered why that was?'

Annabel turned to her with a frown.

'Why she should have been so upset that she would never refer to it again? Was she very close to Hilary?'

Annabel's mouth was dry. 'I don't think so.'

'I mean, it's natural to be shocked at the time – everyone would have been. But to refuse to discuss it for the rest of her life? It seems a bit extreme.'

'All right,' Annabel said slowly, 'we'll go back. Tomorrow morning. We've exhausted all other possibilities.'

'I'm not trying to twist your arm.'

Annabel smiled. 'Much! You're right, though; we might as well finish off what we started, and tomorrow's free.'

They walked for an hour or more, sometimes talking, sometimes silent. The families on the beach began to pack up and drift back to hotels and guest houses for tea. The wind grew stronger, the sun disappeared behind a cloud. By unspoken assent, they turned and made their way back to the car.

That night, Annabel had the dream again. As always, she was lying in a room, but this time the presence was more defined, separating itself into two shadowy figures that shifted and merged in the doorway. Fear escalated, and as she cried out in panic, her mother's face, white and strained, bent over her.

She woke, trembling and sweating, to find Stephie shaking her arm. 'Annie! For God's sake, what is it?'

For long minutes she lay gasping as the nightmare slowly faded. Then she pushed her damp hair off her face. 'Sorry – did I wake you?'

'And half the hotel, I shouldn't wonder! I've been expecting the manager to come thundering on the door, asking who's being murdered!' She bit her lip. 'Sorry, that was a stupid thing to say. Were you having that nightmare?'

Annabel nodded. 'It often comes when I'm tense, strung up about something.' She paused. 'There was a slight difference this time, though. Obviously the day's events have been weighing on my mind.'

'How was it different?'

'For one thing, my mother was bending over me.'

'She's never appeared before?'

'No; it must have been because we were talking about her. And I could make out shadowy figures, too.'

Stephie sat down on the edge of the bed. 'And you were still sitting or lying – below normal height, at any rate?'

'Yes – looking up.'

'Have you—?' Stephie broke off. 'It doesn't matter. You know, I've been thinking: there's no proof it was the murderer Janet Evans saw. All right, the man went into the house at twenty to five, but that was still half an hour before your uncle found her dead. He could easily have left – Janet wouldn't have seen him – and someone else could have come.'

'Are you trying to discount the only positive thing we've learned?'

'Just being realistic, that's all. OK, it's a long shot, I grant you.

'We have them arguing – he apparently asking for something and she refusing. It's a start, at least, in this motiveless crime.'

'Yes, you're right. OK, we'll keep him as prime suspect.'

Annabel lay back. 'What time is it?'

'Half-past three.'

She groaned. 'Let's try to get back to sleep.'

They didn't wake again till after eight, and were among the last to go down to breakfast. The day was warm and cloudy, but at least the lack of sun made for more pleasant driving. They checked out, put their cases in the boot, and set off once again for Llandinas. The same sheep cropped the grass, the same ponies stood under the trees.

As they rounded the bend and the villas came into sight, Annabel said, 'Drive past and stop just after the copse. I'd like to see how much of the house is visible from there, though admittedly the trees will be denser now.'

In the garden of Bay View, two children were riding up and down on tricycles. 'I bet Jones, Meredith don't advertise the history of the place,' Stephie commented. They parked just beyond the trees and got out, locking the car.

'It's thicker than I thought,' Annabel said, surveying the copse dubiously. 'Still, in the interests of research—' and she set off among the trees.

'They were on their way out, remember,' Stephie said from behind her. 'We don't have to go right in.'

They stopped and turned. 'About here, then? The road and the path are just visible.' She glanced to her right. 'And look, you can see Bay View – it's only about twenty-five yards away. They'd have had quite a good view of the meeting.'

'I wish they'd stayed a bit longer,' Stephie said. 'They might have seen him leave. I wonder if Janet will go to the police.'

They made their way out of the trees and turned in the direction of the cliff path. Annabel had imagined it to be higher, looking down on the villas, but in fact it was on the same level, winding round the bay to the next village. It was clear that no one on the path could have seen the villas from any distance.

'Bang goes that theory,' Stephie said cheerfully. She looked sideways at Annabel. 'Any vibes here?'

'Not a flicker.'

'Well, it was worth a try. What do we do now?'

Annabel stopped and looked about her. 'I think I've had enough of Llandinas, lovely though it is. I suggest we make a start for home, and stop somewhere nice for lunch. That way we should beat the traffic. You know what Sunday evenings are like.'

They put the plan into effect, leaving the motorway to drop down to Cardiff, where they had a pleasant and leisurely lunch.

Over coffee, Annabel said suddenly, 'You think my dream's connected to the murder, don't you?'

Stephie looked startled. 'Well – the possibility had crossed my mind.'

'Why?'

'Because recurring dreams often have their roots in a trauma of some kind.'

'There's more to it than that, though, isn't there?'

Stephie toyed with the mint on her saucer. 'This sensation

72

that you're lying down, looking up at something. It struck me that you might have been – at toddler height.'

Annabel drew in a sharp breath. 'It's just not possible,' she said. 'If I'd been there, so would my mother. In which case he'd either not have killed Hilary, or killed all of us.'

'Um.' Stephie didn't sound convinced.

'And the fact that I saw Maman this time doesn't mean a thing. She must often have bent over to comfort me.'

'Of course, but we come back to why the room should affect you so badly that you passed out cold. Martin thought it was significant.'

Annabel leaned forward emphatically. 'Hilary was alone in the house, Stephie. Last summer, when Emma was asking all her questions, she wanted to know if the front door was ever left unlocked, and Grandmother said the arrangement was that each couple had a key. The first back left the door on the latch for the others. *If* someone had been there, Hilary wouldn't have had to use her key.'

Stephie said quietly, 'We don't know that she did. Janet just said she "let herself in".'

They looked at each other. Then Stephie reached into her handbag, extracted her mobile and, after a moment's searching, the note Janet had left for her. 'Lucky I kept this,' she observed, dialling the number.

'Janet – it's Stephanie Lucas. Sorry to bother you again, but could you put us straight on one point?'

'If I can. What is it?'

'How did Hilary – the woman you saw – let herself into the house?'

There was a pause, and Annabel leaned closer to hear her reply.

'Well,' Janet said uncertainly, 'she had a key, didn't she?'

'Had she? Did you see her use it? This could be important.' Crucial, even.

'Yes – yes, I'm sure she had. I remember now; as she hurried up the path she took it out of her pocket. And –

it's coming back to me – she had to fiddle a bit to get it in the lock – that's what gave him the chance to catch up with her.'

'You're certain?'

'As certain as I can be.'

Which would have to do. 'Thanks. Sorry to have bothered you.

'OK, you're right,' Stephie said, crumpling the slip of paper and dropping it into the ashtray. 'There was no one else in the house.'

Annabel closed her eyes briefly. Then she bent and picked up her own handbag. 'Well, if you've finished, we might as well be going.'

As they walked to the car, Stephie said hesitantly, 'Sorry if I've been overzealous in expounding my theories.'

Annabel tucked her hand through her arm. 'Don't be silly; unless we put ideas forward, we're not going to get anywhere. I'm grateful that you're taking such an interest in my problems. Thanks for coming with me, Stephie – I do appreciate it.'

'You know me – can't resist a puzzle. Though we've not done too well on this one.'

'At least we found Janet. Or rather, she found us. If she does go to the police, it might open up a new line for them. Someone might remember seeing the man in the village, or something.' Though in a holiday area, where people were constantly coming and going, who would have noticed him?

With a sigh, Annabel unlocked the car, and minutes later they rejoined the motorway and headed for home.

Five

S imon was surprised to hear that Martin had turned up in Wales.

'God knows how he sussed that out – I never told him,' he assured her, all innocence.

They were on the patio having a drink while Annabel related the events of the weekend. Knowing Martin was sure to mention her blackout, she glossed over it as lightly as possible, and though Simon looked at her sharply, all he said was, 'I warned you not to get het up about it. Why you want to dig it all up again is beyond me.'

'We did at least unearth a new witness.' She told him about Janet Evans.

'Fat lot of good that'll do, after all this time. Even if they find the guy, how could she possibly identify him? He'll have changed beyond all recognition – and from what you say, she didn't get a close look at him any-way.'

Which was depressingly true. In the brief silence, the splashing of the little fountain formed an accompaniment to the song of a thrush in one of the trees. She'd meant to buy irises to plant round the fountain, but the trip to Wales had put them out of her mind. Perhaps Simon was right, and it had been a wild-goose chase. She'd have done better spending her time here, in the garden.

She roused herself. 'Anyway, how about you? Did you have a good weekend?'

'All right, thanks.'

'How are your parents?'

He looked down at his drink. 'Actually, I didn't see them. Something else came up.'

'Oh, what?'

'The group decided to drive up to the Cotswolds to try out a new pub, so I went along.'

Annabel studied his face, conscious that he was holding something back. After spending both Friday and Saturday evening with his friends, surely the prospect of an excellent lunch with his parents was preferable to a snack in an unknown pub?

She asked merely, 'Was it any good?'

He was staring down the garden, eyes narrowed against the evening sunshine. 'OK. Nothing special.' He paused. 'By the way, I shall be out on Wednesday evening, so don't bother about dinner. Business thing.'

She waited for more details, but none were forthcoming. Was this business engagement a change of subject, or did it link in his mind with the trip to the Cotswolds? She knew that if she asked any more questions he'd accuse her of nagging, so, with a mental shrug, she let the subject drop and went inside to see about supper.

Simon was surprised and relieved that Annabel hadn't questioned him more closely about his Wednesday engagement. Even to himself, he had sounded evasive. He'd had a story ready if she persisted, but he was a great believer, in such circumstances, in saying as little as possible. That way, you were less likely to tie yourself in knots.

Not, he assured himself, that he was doing anything underhand. Meeting a work colleague could, loosely, be referred to as 'a business thing'. The fact that the affairs of Stratford and Keene would be the last thing on their minds was neither here nor there.

It was sheer chance that Lucy and her sister had come into the Schooner last night. At work, their paths seldom crossed, and to the best of his knowledge he'd never seen her outside the office. In fact, it took him a moment to recognize her; in jeans and ribbed top, and with her hair carelessly caught up in a ponytail, she seemed very different from the efficient, severe-looking young woman in charge of the accounts department. He'd paused at their table on his way back from the bar.

'I didn't know this was one of your haunts,' he commented.

'It isn't,' she replied. 'We've been for a walk on the downs and worked up a thirst. This is my sister, by the way. Simon Kendal from work, Debs.'

He nodded at the other girl, and Phil, who was passing with two foaming tankards, paused to say, 'Who are your friends, Si?'

'Lucy Cox, from the office – and Debs. Meet Phil Baines.'

'Come and join us!' Phil said expansively, and moved over to the table they had commandeered.

Lucy looked at Simon uncertainly, and, though taken aback by Phil's invitation, he'd felt bound to repeat it. 'Yes, do, if you'd like to.'

And that was really all there was to it, he reflected, listening to Annabel moving about in the kitchen behind him. Or would have been, if he hadn't been in one of his moods. But he'd been annoyed all week about the old man not stumping up for a new car, a lapse that had never occurred before and which he wasn't at all sure how to deal with. Added to that, when he got to the pub on Friday the comments about Annabel's absence did nothing to help, particularly as she'd asked him not to say where she'd gone. What had started as mild teasing – 'Gone off and left you, has she? Can't say I'm surprised!' – had, over the course of two evenings' drinking, become wearisome.

So when the Tetbury trip was mooted – in which Lucy and Debs were automatically included – he decided to go along for the hell of it. It would show them all he wasn't fretting about Annabel's absence, and at the same time punish his parents who, he knew, would be disappointed when he cancelled his planned visit. Perhaps next time the old man wouldn't be so tight-fisted.

But no sooner had he committed himself than it turned out that Debs was going back to Bridgewater the next day, leaving Lucy and himself as 'singles'. 'Come up with us, both of you,' Phil had invited. Which was how the two of them had ended up together in the back of Phil's car, while he and Polly argued amicably in the front.

Simon took another drink, savouring the liquid in his mouth before swallowing. OK, so he was attracted to her. Perhaps, more annoyed than he admitted by Annabel's desertion, he had even flirted a little. But Lucy was no giggling eighteen-year-old who would get the wrong idea; she was, as he'd learned during the outward journey, a single mother with a young son, who knew exactly what she wanted out of life. What's more, she seemed to have organized that life pretty successfully. When she split with her partner she'd returned to live with her parents, who had proved to be doting grandparents, only too happy to baby-sit so that she didn't miss out on a social life.

Furthermore, though she enjoyed her job at Stratford's, she would stay only as long as it suited her. Having taken a couple of exams to increase her qualifications, she was eager for promotion, and if it weren't offered would not hesitate to move on.

'But that's enough about me!' she'd said, turning to smile at him. 'Tell me about you. You're married, aren't you?'

'Yes, but my wife's gone to Wales for the weekend.'

She raised her eyebrows. 'Do you often take separate holidays?'

'It's not really a holiday; she's doing some research on her family, and knew it wouldn't interest me.'

'She comes from Wales, then?'

'No, it's not historical research, just – something she wanted to check up on.'

To his relief, she didn't pursue the subject.

As a temporary pairing, they had sat together over lunch,

continuing their conversation both then and on the return journey, and by the time Phil pulled up outside her parents' house, what Simon had embarked on as a means of scoring off Annabel had developed into genuine interest. Getting out of the car to say goodbye, he said on impulse, 'Are you by any chance free for dinner on Wednesday?'

She'd stopped and turned to look at him. 'Do you think that's a good idea?'

'I think it's an excellent one.'

'The last thing I want is any gossip to jeopardize my job.'

'I'm discretion itself.'

While he waited for her reply, he was surprised at how much he wanted to see her again. There was an air of independence about her that intrigued and at the same time challenged him.

'All right,' she said at last. 'If you're sure you know what you're doing. We must leave the office separately, though; I'll meet you at Luigi's Brasserie at six.'

'Fair enough. See you then.'

He had reached home only half an hour before Annabel, and during that time had fluctuated between excitement at the thought of an evening with Lucy, and a panicky desire to phone and cancel the arrangement. Now, having cleared it with Annabel, he was committed. It was only dinner, he told himself – a one-off, no big deal.

'Supper's ready,' Annabel called, and, glad to be diverted from his thoughts, Simon went inside to join her.

Annabel had half-expected Martin to phone, and when he did not, wondered if his reawakened interest in the Carlyles had faded, or if he was pursuing some secret agenda of his own. She spent a lot of time thinking about the weekend: the tall house on the cliffs that had witnessed the tragedy, her reaction to it, and the unexpected appearances of first Martin, then Janet Evans. Had the brief visit been worthwhile? Were they any closer to the truth? She very much doubted it.

On the Wednesday evening she decided, since Simon was out, to go through the cartons of her mother's papers that George had given her, and as soon as she'd eaten she retrieved them from under the stairs and carried them into the sitting room.

Though George had given them an obligatory wipe there was a dusty smell about them, and when she lifted the flaps of cardboard old spiders' webs stuck to her fingers. With a grimace, she went for a duster.

The first pile of papers, loosely clipped together, seemed to confirm George's theory, for they were a varied selection of exam papers, exercises and essays. The sight of her mother's bold, confident handwriting brought a lump to Annabel's throat, reminding her of the daily letters she'd received during her enforced stays at Hazelwood.

She ran her eyes rapidly over several pages that seemed of little interest, and, reaching for the wastepaper basket, dropped them inside. No point in keeping these; letters or photographs would be a different matter.

Two further piles, lifted out and riffled through, proved to be more of the same, but as she bent over the box for another bundle, she found herself looking at a single page which seemed to be torn off a pad. The writing – in French, like the rest of the contents – started in mid sentence:

> which is now almost at an end. His examinations will take place soon, and I think they fear I might distract him from studying. Later in the summer he will return to live here in Cheltenham, which I do not like to think about.
>
> Madame then asked me what I did. I told her that after studying French and English Literature at the Sorbonne I had come to London to do a course in teacher training, which I had just completed.

Annabel sat staring at the sheet in her hand. It looked

like part of a diary of some sort, and must surely have been written soon after her parents had met. With growing excitement, she delved back into the box.

The next few papers, all loose, were a mixed bag: a few more pages from the pad, an empty envelope addressed to Mlle Monique le Brun and postmarked June 1968, and what looked like an old shopping list. Dropping it and the envelope in the bin and laying the pages aside, she impatiently searched for more. And came at last to what appeared to be the beginning of the extract, since it was headed by a date. Immediately beneath it lay a wad of half a dozen or so pages, still stuck together with the original binding of the pad. A quick glance confirmed her first impression: what she was looking at was her mother's account of her first visit to Hazelwood.

It took a few frustrating minutes to sort the pages into order, then, sitting back on her heels, she read them quickly through.

Cheltenham, 13th July 1968

Today I met Douglas's family for the first time, but I regret they are not as I expected. Douglas is so friendly and relaxed I thought his parents would be the same, but that is not the case. In fact, I do not think that Madame his mother likes me. Perhaps she guesses at our liaison and does not approve. *Tant pis*, for I mean it to continue.

Typical of Maman, Annabel thought with a smile. It seemed that she and Grandmother had clashed from their first meeting.

The home of the family is in Cheltenham, which is an elegant town with wide, tree-lined streets and many Georgian buildings. They live in a large house called Hazelwood in Regency Drive, a street of other large houses, separated from each other by spacious gardens.

They did not come out to greet us but awaited us in the drawing room, where Madame accepted the flowers I had brought with apparent pleasure. Nonetheless, I had the impression I am not welcome.

Madame is tall and straight-backed. She has large, well-shaped hands, a prominent nose and short hair of a nondescript brown. Her voice is deep but she is softly spoken, and although her clothes are not *à la mode*, they are of good quality and typical of an English lady.

Monsieur seems more *sympathique*. He is tall and broad-shouldered, with fair hair like Douglas, though mixed with grey. He walks with a limp, and calls me 'm'dear'.

The drawing room is a large room at the front of the house. There is a piano, with silver-framed photographs standing on top of it. As yet, I have not liked to go and examine them. The furniture is old-fashioned but comfortable. Douglas sat next to me on the sofa and took my hand, which I could see did not please his mother. We were served very dry sherry in tiny glasses and they asked Douglas about his course, which is now almost at an end. His examinations will take place soon, and I think they fear I might distract him from studying. Later in the summer he will return to live here in Cheltenham, which I do not like to think about.

Madame then asked me what I did. I told her that after studying French and English Literature at the Sorbonne I had come to London to do a course in teacher training, which I had just completed.

'So now you will return to France?' she asked – hopefully, I thought.

Before I could answer, Douglas said with a laugh, 'Of course not, Mother! The whole point of taking her teaching diploma here was so that she could teach in England.'

Madame kept her eyes on me. 'But you have family over there, surely?'

'My parents are dead,' I told her. 'My only relative is an aunt in Rouen.'

'And is she happy for you to stay here?'

'I think she expects it.'

'You should apply to the Ladies' College!' Monsieur said with a chuckle.

Madame glared at him and, seeing my bewilderment, explained, 'It is a world-famous girls' school here in Cheltenham. My husband was not being serious.'

'But why not?' Douglas asked eagerly. 'It would be great to have her here!'

'Douglas, really!' I could see his mother was annoyed. 'You don't, surely, imagine that – Monique – could just walk into a post at the Ladies' College?'

'Why not?' he repeated stubbornly. 'She has the necessary qualifications.'

At this point, to my relief, the maid tapped on the door to announce lunch was ready, thereby putting to an end what threatened to become a heated conversation.

As we crossed the hall, I heard Madame say in a low voice, 'I do wish you would not make facetious comments, Henry. That was quite embarrassing.'

Obviously they do not think me good enough for their precious school.

The dining room has heavy, highly polished furniture and oil paintings on the walls. We were served soup, then cold chicken and salad, followed by apple charlotte. During the meal, talk was of the rest of the family, of Edward, Douglas's brother, and his wife Hilary, who have year-old twins.

'They have invited you both to dinner this evening,' Madame said. I was glad, hoping the brother and his wife would be less stiff and formal than the parents.

After lunch I was shown round the garden. It is large and beautiful, with immaculately cut lawns, colourful herbaceous borders and graceful old trees. There is a small wooden *pavillon* that they called a summer-house, which Monsieur told me could swivel round to face the sun. Afterwards, Douglas and I walked into the town centre and looked at the fountains and the shops and had 'afternoon tea' at the Queen's Hotel, which is a very imposing building.

At seven-thirty, we drove to the house of Edward and Hilary on the other side of town. I liked Edward at once, particularly as he greeted me in schoolboy French, which I thought charming. He is two years older than Douglas and his features are similar, though his hair is darker, taking after his mother rather than his father. In character he seems quieter and more reserved.

His wife is tall and thin and has a mane of curling red-brown hair. Her voice is high-pitched and she speaks in what Douglas tells me is an upper-class accent. To my embarrassment, I had difficulty at first in understanding her. We were taken upstairs to have a look at the babies asleep in their cots. They are *mignons*.

We had just returned to the hall when the doorbell rang and another couple were shown in, and introduced to me as Rex Cameron – a doctor – and his wife Moira, close friends of the family. The doctor has a pleasant manner and his wife went out of her way to be friendly to me. She told me they have a little boy called Neil, who has just had his second birthday.

All in all, it was a most enjoyable evening. The meal was delicious, with quite a strong French influence, but whether this was for my benefit, or because Hilary always cooks in that manner, I do not know. I was quite sorry when it was time to leave and return to Hazelwood.

Sunday

I had just closed my journal last night when there was a soft tap at the door and Douglas came into my room. I was quite alarmed.

'Your parents will hear us!' I whispered, but he shook his head and climbed into bed beside me.

'We will be like mice,' he said. 'I could not leave you all alone, your first night in a strange house, now could I? Anyway, I have been wanting to make love to you all evening!'

So a day of mixed emotions ended in his arms, and all was well.

Annabel laid her hand tenderly on the pad, tears in her eyes. Though she felt uncomfortable at reading such intimate details, it was fascinating to have this glimpse of her parents' romance; and, after all, nothing she did now could hurt Monique.

For as long as she could remember, she had thought of her parents as being on separate sides, suspicious and hostile towards each other. That they must once have loved each other she had never until now consciously considered, and the full impact of their divorce struck her for the first time. How tragic, when they had been so much in love, so full of confidence in themselves and each other, that it should have ended as it did.

She flipped the page over, sorry to see it was the last of the attached sheets.

When I woke this morning, with sun streaming on to my pillow, he was gone. The maid brought me a cup of tea at eight o'clock and informed me that breakfast would be at nine.

I discovered, however, that this was served not in the dining room but the 'breakfast' room. Is this its sole purpose, I wonder? I must ask Douglas later. Monsieur and Madame were talking about going to church, and it was clear they would have liked Douglas to go with them. It seems my being catholic is another obstacle. I tried to explain I am not a strict observer and would be happy to accompany them, though I could not take mass. Madame said, 'I think not, dear. And we call it communion.' Regrettably, I have to say I do not like Douglas's mother, but I must not let him see this. They are a close family and he is very fond of his parents.

While they were at church, we sat in the garden and talked. Always we have so much to say to each other. On their return we drank sherry again, in the garden this time, and then we ate a large lunch with roast beef and pâte à crêpes, which they called Yorkshire pudding. I thought 'pudding' meant *dessert*, but when I said so, they only laughed.

After lunch, it was time to leave. Madame shook my hand and said, 'It was pleasant to meet you, dear.' She did not say, 'I hope we meet again,' and I did not dare. So we came back to London, but in a few weeks Douglas will be returning there permanently, and I must be with him. *I must!*

To Annabel's frustration the excerpt ended there, but surely there must be more of it; it was unlikely that Monique would have recorded only that one episode. She glanced impatiently at the papers strewn about her. She had intended going through everything systematically, but now an overwhelming desire to find more of the diary took precedence. Scooping the discarded papers back into the first carton, she turned her attention to the next one. Once she'd accumulated as much of it as she could find, she could assemble it in some sort of order and read it chronologically.

The task took her over an hour, by which time she'd retrieved a considerable number of pages and sorted them roughly into piles, in an attempt to keep those that seemed related to each other together. At first glance, the 'journal' seemed to be not a continuous diary but random accounts written at irregular intervals. Though the initial pages of each excerpt were dated, subsequent ones were not, and had often become separated from what went before. Even the dated sheets didn't always give the year, but they seemed to cover a fair period, since more than once she caught sight of her own name. Some sections were still stuck together like the original ones, others were single sheets seemingly unrelated to any other.

Annabel stood up and stretched. Her back ached from bending over them, but at least she was satisfied she'd extracted all that there was of the journal. She replaced the cartons under the stairs, fastened the different piles of sheets together with paperclips, and slipped them into the drawer of her desk. As soon as she had the chance, she promised herself, she'd start putting them in order.

The clock struck ten and she yawned. Simon had not said what time he'd be back, but he wouldn't expect her to wait up. Pleased with her evening's achievement, Annabel went to bed. It was only as she was falling asleep that a sudden thought jerked her awake. *Suppose her mother had written about that holiday in Wales?*

She was halfway out of bed before reason reasserted itself. Even if such an account existed, the separate pages would need to be first located, then patiently fitted together like a jigsaw before she'd be able to make sense of it. And, with the amount of spare time she had available, that could take weeks or even months. Nothing would be gained by a feverish search now; she would have to possess herself in patience.

Lying down again, she determinedly closed her eyes.

They met at Luigi's as Lucy had suggested, but, after a quick drink, drove out to a country pub, to lessen the chance of being seen together. The constrained atmosphere between them, so different from the ease of the weekend, might, Simon thought, be at least partly due to the formality of their work clothes; in her tailored suit and blouse, her chestnut hair confined in a chignon, Lucy was once again Head of Accounts, and he could find no trace of the girl with the ponytail. Seated across the table from her, he noticed for the first time a network of fine lines round her eyes. She was not as young as he'd thought – mid-thirties, at a guess. What the *hell* was he doing here? he thought in sudden panic. He should be at home with Annabel.

'Tell me about your son,' he said, more to break the silence than out of any interest in the child.

She smiled, rummaged in her handbag and extracted a snapshot, which she passed across. 'He's two now, and a regular handful. Keeps my parents on their toes!'

Simon studied the picture of a little boy in a paddling pool, murmured something conventional, and handed it back.

'Does he see his father?' he asked, and saw her lips compress.

'No,' she answered shortly.

'When did the two of you split up?'

'Before Sam was born. Rick didn't want "responsibilities". His loss.' She paused. 'Have you any children?'

'Not so far.'

The waiter came with the menu. Anticipating the enjoyable and lengthy discussion of it in which he and Annabel indulged, Simon was taken aback when, after a quick glance, Lucy immediately gave her order, forcing him to an equally rapid decision, which he almost immediately regretted. The wine list was disposed of equally summarily; in answer to his enquiry if she'd prefer red or white, she specified the precise vintage of her choice, leaving him merely to nod concurrence to the waiter.

During the meal they kept the conversational ball in play, but talk was light and inconsequential, of a totally different calibre from their weekend discussions. The evening was a mistake, Simon thought, furious with himself; he should have left well alone. It was playing with fire to meet anyone from the office, not to mention the ribald comments of the group should they get wind of it – which they doubtless would. And though the lads were loyal to a man, the girls would doubtless have Annabel's interests at heart.

As had he, damn it. All right, they had their differences, and her criticism of his extravagance infuriated him, especially when she refused to accept money from the parents. He'd also been aware, these last few months, of a feeling of restlessness – not boredom, exactly – which was why he'd embarked on the frenetic social round that he knew she didn't enjoy. They'd work through it, though; basically they were sound enough, and by seeing Lucy this evening he was putting everything at risk.

'A penny for them,' she said.

He smiled, making a dismissive gesture. 'Not worth it.'

The evening petered to an end. She had a brandy with her coffee, which, in view of the drive home, he declined, and they emerged into the starlit night, no easier with each other than they'd been at the start of the evening. During the drive to Bristol they made a few sporadic remarks but soon, to his relief, she leaned her head back and closed her eyes, absolving him from further conversation. Thank God the evening was nearly over. It had been a narrow escape, but he'd learned his lesson.

'This is the road, isn't it?' he asked twenty minutes later, breaking the long silence, and she sat up and looked out of the window.

'Yes, just past the third lamppost.'

He drew up, and was about to thank her formally for her company when, to his astonishment, she caught his face between her hands and kissed him hard on the mouth. Then she sat back, smiling at his stunned expression.

'Well?' she challenged him. 'That was why you asked me out, wasn't it?'

'No, I – no, of course not. I thought—'

'Don't tell me – it was my beautiful nature!'

He laughed shakily.

'Relax, Simon,' she said, a slight edge creeping into her voice. 'You're quite safe – I shan't attack you again.'

The implication that he'd been her pawn infuriated and at the same time excited him, and on impulse he pulled her towards him and began to kiss her in earnest.

It was several minutes before she drew back. With her hair, which he had freed from its chignon, loose about her face and the top buttons of her blouse undone, she presented him with a third version of herself, neither the carefree girl nor the efficient business woman but a passionate, dangerous stranger.

'So!' she said, amusement in her voice. 'Where do we go from here?'

He didn't reply, still struggling to control the deep, tearing breaths that shook him.

After a moment, she continued, 'Look, I might as well be honest. I've missed having a man around since Rick went, and I reckoned that if you fancied me, then why not? If your conscience doesn't bother you, why should mine? My only loyalty is to Sam, and this isn't going to affect him, one way or the other.'

Still he made no comment, and again she went on: 'But I have one stipulation, and that is that no one – *no one* – is to know about this. My job is far more important to me than a spot of nooky, with you or anyone else.'

Resentful, furious, and still ravaged by desire, Simon at last found his voice. 'Which puts me firmly in my place,' he said stiffly. 'But don't worry, I have no intention of troubling you again. Your job prospects are quite safe.'

There was a brief pause. Then she said, 'Very well. No skin off my nose. Thanks for the dinner.'

There was a rush of cool air as she opened the car door, and then she was gone. Simon lowered his forehead to the steering-wheel and sat motionless for long minutes. Bitch! he thought furiously. Cow! Whore! Having the bloody nerve to lay down her conditions when he hadn't even asked her to sleep with him! God, though, he wanted to! Her scent still lingered in the car and he frenziedly wound down all the windows to dispel it.

With the breeze cool on his hot face, he turned to look at the house into which she had disappeared. The hall light went out as he watched, and a minute later a front bedroom light came on. Turning the key in the ignition, he drove quickly away.

Six

Annabel told Simon about her discovery of the journal over breakfast the next morning, but he was obviously only half-listening. It was the same, she thought resentfully, with her visit to Wales; nothing she did or said seemed to interest him at the moment. What was the *matter* with him?

To show him she was still interested in *his* affairs, she passed the ball into his court. 'How did the business meeting go last night?'

'Oh – all right.' He lifted his cup and quickly drained it.

'Who was it with?'

'An associate. No one you know.' He pushed back his chair. 'I must be going – I've a meeting at ten, and there are some papers to sort through first.'

He kissed the top of her head as he passed – she couldn't remember when this gesture had supplanted a proper kiss – and a minute later the front door banged behind him.

Reflectively, Annabel poured herself another cup of coffee. She could, of course, tell Stephie about the journal, but just for the moment, for no reason she could pinpoint, she wanted to keep it in the family. And if Simon wasn't interested, she thought defiantly, George certainly would be. Furthermore, she'd promised to arrange a visit. She'd check with Simon that the coming weekend was free. Decision reached, she stood up and started to clear the table.

*   *   *

'George? We were wondering if you were free to come over this weekend?'

George Woodbridge bit his lip. It was the first time he could remember when he hadn't unreservedly welcomed an invitation from Annabel.

'I'm not entirely sure—' he began feebly, but she cut in.

'Do come! I'm sorry it's such short notice; I tried to phone you last night, but there was no reply.'

'I went to the bowls club,' he said.

'Come tomorrow, if you like, and stay the night. I've something I want to show you.'

'What is it?' he asked warily.

'You'll have to wait and see! And it must be this weekend, because after that we're off to Devon for a week.' She paused, and when he didn't speak, asked, 'Have you something else fixed?'

'Nothing definite,' he admitted. Nothing at all, in fact.

'Well, then?'

He gave in, fabricating a reason for his hesitation. 'Sorry, darling; I thought for a moment I had something on, but that's the following weekend. Yes, of course I'd love to come. Just for the day, though, whichever one suits you.'

'Sunday? It'll get me out of going to the in-laws!' She laughed, to show she wasn't serious.

'Sunday, then.'

'Perfect! About twelve? Then we can have our talk after lunch.'

'How's Simon?' he asked quickly, as she seemed about to ring off.

'Fine, why?'

'No reason. I haven't seen him for a while, that's all.'

'Well, you can soon put that right,' she said. 'Look forward to seeing you.'

'Me too.'

He put the phone down and stood staring out of the window. On the bird table some starlings were squawking and squabbling over the food Cassie had put out, knocking the best part of it on to the grass, where an opportunist blackbird was busily engaged in eating it.

Is it possible Nigel had been mistaken? George wondered for the hundredth time. He'd admitted the room was dimly lit, and that they were over at the far side. But he'd been adamant that it was Simon he'd seen on Wednesday evening – Simon having dinner with some woman. A pure fluke, of course, that Nigel should have been there himself; one of the school governors had invited him over. Almost, George wished he hadn't been, that if Simon were indeed meeting someone else, he didn't have to know about it. Nigel and Cassie had, it seemed, deliberated for some time before telling him.

'We didn't want to worry you, darling,' Cassie'd said, with that anxious crease between her eyebrows. 'But finally we thought it best you should know.'

As his daughter came to mind, George reached for the house phone, and immediately her cheerful voice answered him.

'I've just heard from Annabel,' he said. 'They've invited me over to Sunday lunch.'

'Ah!'

'She says she has something to show me. God knows what.'

'It'll give you a chance to see how they are with each other.'

'But I don't *want* to!' he said miserably. 'I hate the thought of sitting there accepting their hospitality and watching their every move.'

'Oh dear,' Cassie murmured. 'Perhaps we shouldn't have told you after all.'

'Too late now. Run through it again, would you – exactly what Nigel saw?'

'Just Simon and this woman sitting over a meal. They didn't seem particularly close, or anything. Perhaps it was just a business colleague, and Annie knows all about it.'

'Perhaps.' But he didn't believe that, and he knew she didn't.

'You won't mention it, will you?' she said after a minute. 'To either of them?'

'Certainly not to Annabel.'

'Nor Simon, Pops. If it *is* serious, we don't want to stampede him into going off the rails.'

'If he does anything to hurt her—' George began fiercely.

'Yes, I know; but time enough to worry if that happens.'

George sighed. 'You're right, my love; all we can do is keep a watching brief.'

Though how he'd be able to be civil to Simon, knowing what he did, George had no idea.

Suzanne Harcourt came into the bedroom, surprised not to find Edward there. Following what had become established routine, they had returned to her house after an early dinner and she'd preceded him upstairs. Usually, by the time she'd had her shower, he was waiting for her. Tonight they'd lingered over coffee, it was already ten o'clock; and Edward was punctilious about leaving no later than eleven thirty. Their affair seemed dominated by continuous clock-watching.

She hated the subterfuge, did not understand why he wouldn't acknowledge her openly, as his 'partner' – her lip twisted on the euphemism – if nothing more. Both of them were free; they were hurting no one. This constant keeping out of sight, being discreet, made her feel like a kitchen maid skulking under the back stairs.

Still, since that was the price for being with Edward, she'd accepted it. She hadn't intended to fall in love with him, nor with anyone else for that matter, and had initially been relieved that he felt the same. It was not his fault she'd broken the rules.

She looked round the softly lit room with its beautiful furniture, its watercolours and rich furnishings. Miles had been generous over the divorce settlement and she led a very comfortable life. Why could she not be satisfied with that?

Still no sign of Edward. Pulling on a silk dressing gown, Suzanne went down the broad staircase and into the drawing room. Edward was sitting where she had left him, the heavy glass in his hand still showing the same level of whisky. He turned as she came in and half rose, but she waved him down.

'Sorry, love, are you ready?'

She seated herself next to him on the sofa and he put an arm round her silk shoulders, drawing her closer.

'What's the matter?' she asked softly.

He sighed. 'It's this bloody holiday hanging over me. I wish to hell I didn't have to go.'

'But you do, I suppose?'

'Too right. I have to drive down on Friday with Ma and Emma, to get the place ready, allot bedrooms, and so on.'

Suzanne was silent. Soon after she'd met Edward, she had overheard a conversation in the ladies' room between two members of the bridge club. Edward's name had come up – she didn't remember how – and one woman said, 'You know, of course, that he was suspected of murdering his wife? Might well have done it, too; no one else was ever charged.'

She remembered how her stomach had lurched, and the sick feeling that had stayed with her all day. At the first opportunity she had questioned Moira, at whose house she'd met Edward, and Moira told her the story as far as she knew it.

'He didn't do it, Suzanne,' she had finished. 'I've known Edward for over thirty years, and I'm quite sure of that.'

'Then who did?' Suzanne had asked tautly.

Moira shrugged. 'We'll probably never know.'

Edward himself had never gone into details, but now, surprising her, he suddenly said, 'You'll have heard the story, no doubt?'

She looked up quickly, and he gave a rueful smile. 'Yes,

I thought you would. Well, it was on one of these infernal holidays that it happened, and every year – for me, anyway – the whole thing is resurrected.'

'Doesn't your mother realize that?'

'God knows. It didn't stop her the first year, and it hasn't since.'

'I think that's – barbarous.'

He said hesitantly, 'It's Emma I'm really worried about. I know you think I'm overprotective, with her being in her thirties and so on, but she's never really got over her mother's death. It's . . . blighted her life, and this last year things seem to have got worse.'

'Darling, I'm so sorry.'

'I'm not a wife-killer, Suzanne.'

'Edward – don't!'

'I shouldn't blame you if you wondered; I'm sure even the family does, sometimes.'

'I'm quite sure they don't, and nor do I.'

'Thanks for the vote of confidence.' He gently traced her chin with one finger. 'Don't get too fond of me, Suzy.'

'Too late for that!' she answered lightly.

'I mean it; I don't want to hurt you, but I shall never marry again. If you'd rather we ended it, I should quite—'

'No!' she said swiftly, catching hold of his hand. 'I'm quite happy as things are. Except that it's nearly ten thirty, and we're still sitting demurely down here!'

He laughed, breaking his mood, as she had intended. 'Then by all means let us stop being demure and go upstairs.'

When, just over an hour later, he left her, she lay thinking over what he had said. Why was he so adamant about not remarrying? Because of the way his first wife had died? Or because he was afraid it might happen again?

By the time George arrived at midday on Sunday, Annabel was impatient to share the news of her discovery. After Simon's lack of interest she hadn't mentioned it to him again, nor had she broached the subject with Stephie. The previous day, having hurried through her housework, she had spent another couple of hours sorting through her mother's papers and had managed to slot a few more into some semblance of order. She wasn't sure yet what date they were, but it was obviously after her parents' marriage. Edward's name had cropped up once or twice, and the Camerons'.

'So,' George began, comfortably seated with a glass in his hand, 'what's this mysterious thing you have to show me?'

'Wait till after lunch,' Annabel said. 'I can't settle now, I have to keep dashing in and out of the kitchen.'

Simon glanced from one of them to the other, shaking his head as if to dissociate himself from the whole affair. But it was all right for him, Annabel thought rebelliously as she basted the meat; both his parents were alive and well, and there were no question marks in his background.

During the meal, it occurred to her that George was being a little stiff with Simon. Had he minded, after all, that he hadn't accompanied her on Maman's anniversary? He'd said not at the time. Simon, however, obviously unaware of any constraint, was at his most entertaining, telling a stream of anecdotes and stories, and Annabel suspected he had started drinking some time before George's arrival. But that was simply Simon being Simon, and couldn't be the cause of George's reserve.

He redeemed himself, when the meal was over, by offering to clear away and stack the dishwasher, leaving them free to their discussion, and, gratefully accepting, they went through into the sitting room.

'So, what's all the mystery, my love?' George enquired, seating himself where she indicated.

'It's not a mystery, just something very interesting. You know those cartons of Maman's papers that you gave me?'

George was suddenly still. 'Yes?'

98

'Well, they weren't all exam papers and student things. She kept a journal, George. Did you know that?'

He was staring at her, and to her concern she saw he'd gone pale.

She knelt quickly beside him. 'George? Are you all right?'

'Yes – yes, of course.'

'*Did* you know about the journal?'

'She mentioned it, yes; she said jokingly that she'd been very indiscreet in her youth, and before she was too old and decrepit she would ceremoniously burn it.' His voice cracked.

Annabel said softly, 'But she died before she had the chance.'

'Perhaps we should do it for her.'

Annabel gazed at him aghast. 'Oh, George, don't ask me, please! It's so wonderful to read about her being young, and meeting the family for the first time and everything! And I shan't show it to anyone except you, I promise.'

'We're probably the ones she didn't want to see it.'

Annabel sat back on her heels. 'Does she refer to the Welsh holiday?'

'I don't know.' His face was grey.

'She didn't mention it in connection with the journal?'

'Annabel, she never mentioned it – you know that.'

She looked down at the sheets of paper in her hand. After a minute she said hesitantly, 'You remember that recurring nightmare I used to have?' Better to speak of it in the past.

He nodded.

'Did Maman ever discuss it with you?'

'How do you mean, discuss?'

'Did she tell you what it consisted of?'

He frowned. 'I never asked her. One time when you were particularly distressed, I did suggest taking you to a child psychiatrist. I thought he might be able to get to the bottom of it, but she wouldn't hear of it. Said she wasn't having

99

anyone messing with her child's mind, and that you'd grow out of it in time.'

Had her mother been afraid of what a psychiatrist might find?

'What *did* you dream?' George asked with sudden unease.

Stephie's theory came into her mind, and without conscious thought she accepted it. 'I was in a room somewhere – at a low level. About toddler height.'

She saw him tense, his hands clench.

'There were two other people there, though I couldn't see them properly, and a – a pervading sense of fear. I used to wake screaming and crying, trying to get away.'

George moistened his lips. 'It sounds like a typical nightmare.'

'Yes. But the last time I dreamt it, Maman was bending over me.'

He didn't speak, and she went on, 'There's something else I should tell you. Remember I mentioned that journalist who'd been in Swansea at the time?'

'Yes?'

'Well, I – met him for tea at the Avon Gorge.'

He frowned. 'Why on earth?'

'I suppose to see if he knew any more than I did. He didn't – or only very little – but he wanted me to go back to Llandinas with him, to the house, and see if I remembered anything.'

George gave a startled exclamation. 'I hope you did nothing of the sort!'

'Not with him, no. But I – I went with a friend, and we were able to go inside. George, it was terrifying – I passed out.'

He stumbled to his feet and lurched over to the window, gazing out at the garden.

Annabel also rose. 'Is it remotely possible that I was there? When it happened, I mean?'

'How could you have been?' he demanded harshly, without turning. 'You were with your mother.'

Annabel said, so softly she wasn't sure he'd hear, 'Could we *both* have been there?'

He didn't answer, and she thought perhaps he hadn't. But after a moment he put both hands up to his face. They stood without moving, and the clock ticked into the silence. Eventually, Annabel broke it, her voice sounding strange to her own ears.

'Stephie – the friend who went with me – wondered why she refused to talk about it to the end of her life, when she hadn't, by all accounts, been particularly fond of Hilary.'

'Yes,' he said in a strangled voice, 'I asked myself that.'

Annabel moved towards him and put a hand on his arm. 'I didn't mean to upset you,' she said softly, 'and I hate to do this, but I've got to ask you: do you *swear* to me that she never told you anything about the murder?'

He turned then to face her, putting both hands on her shoulders. 'I swear it, darling. I know no more than I've told you, but I've always had this dreadful fear that she knew more than she admitted.' He smiled bleakly. 'And I never thought I'd say that to a living soul.'

Annabel moved closer, putting her arms round him, and they stood holding each other.

Finally she said, 'I have to find out. You realize that, don't you? Having come this far, I just have to know.'

'My darling girl, if the police haven't found the answer in twenty-eight years, how will you?'

'Actually, I found a new witness in only two days.'

He frowned down at her. 'Who? How?'

Again she recounted the meeting with Janet Evans. 'So you see, there *are* new facts waiting to be uncovered.'

'You could be putting yourself in danger, you know.'

'I'll be careful.'

'Annabel – have you thought what you'd do if you found your mother *was* involved?'

She shook her head dumbly, staring at him.

'I think you should work out all the options before you

go any further. And darling – don't put too much emphasis on that nightmare. You know what they are – a mixture of buried fears, imagination, stories one's heard. Don't fall into the trap of regarding it as a genuine memory. And don't forget there were several people who swore to seeing you both on the cliff path that afternoon. She had an alibi.'

Annabel nodded. 'I know.'

Simon's cheerful voice said from the doorway, 'Have you finished your discussion? Is it safe to come in?'

'Just about,' Annabel replied, putting the papers back in the desk drawer. George hadn't so much as glanced at them, but in any case they were in French and she'd have had to translate.

'Then how about a game of croquet? I've set it up.'

'Good idea!' George said heartily. It was clear he'd had enough soul-searching for one afternoon, and, following the men out into the garden, Annabel resolved to keep any further discoveries to herself.

That evening, Sally Kendal phoned. 'Darling, we haven't seen you for weeks and you're about to disappear to wildest Devon! Could you spare us an evening to come over for dinner?'

After a quick consultation with Simon, Thursday was agreed on.

'Lovely!' Sally enthused. 'About seven thirty? Such a shame Simon had to cancel last weekend. Oh, and Giles says ask him to bring that magazine of the car he's interested in.'

So once again his strategy had worked, Annabel thought resignedly; if he didn't get his way immediately, a short sulk always brought his parents round.

'Your father says to take that car magazine,' she told him on her way out of the back door, and saw the glint of satisfaction in his eyes. How could she hope to instil some sense of responsibility in him, when his parents constantly if unwittingly undermined her?

*   *   *

The Kendals lived in one of the country hamlets east of the A38, about half an hour's drive from Bristol. Simon was in the driving seat, on the unspoken assumption that, leaving him free to drink, Annabel would do the return journey. As usual, he went much too fast, and after leaving the main road, barely lessened his speed as they zoomed down narrow, twisting lanes with high hedges on either side, which gave no chance of seeing any oncoming traffic. She tried not to think what would happen if they met a tractor coming the other way, but any request to slow down only made him accelerate.

His parents' house – or cottage, as they referred to it – was set at the end of a broad drive between lush lawns, and Simon drew up with a flourish at the front door, scattering gravel. Sally and Giles came out to meet them, she slim and tanned in a navy silk dress splashed with large white daisies, he in open-necked shirt and cravat.

'Darlings! How lovely! As it's such a splendid evening, we thought we'd have drinks on the terrace.'

They walked together round the side of the house, pausing to admire the vividly coloured plants that filled the beds and the terracotta birdbath, new since their last visit. A table, laid with wineglasses and an ice bucket, was set up under an umbrella, with cushioned chairs arranged round it. As they seated themselves, Simon laid the car magazine on the table.

Giles glanced at it, said merely, 'Ah, yes,' and opened the bottle of wine.

'So – what have you been doing, both of you?' Sally asked, settling back in her chair. She turned to Annabel. 'I hear you had a girls' weekend away?'

Of course she knew; that's why Simon had arranged to have lunch with them. Until, for no clear reason, he'd changed his mind.

'That's right,' Annabel said neutrally.

'To Swansea, wasn't it?' Sally pursued, raising her eyebrows enquiringly.

'Yes.'

'On the trail of the family skeleton,' Simon put in breezily, taking the glass his father passed him.

'Really? That's why you went? I thought you didn't like reminding of it?'

'I don't,' Annabel said shortly, 'but it's been rather forcibly brought to my attention lately.'

'Oh dear – that journalist? Mea culpa!'

'He tried to talk her into going to Wales with him,' Simon said. 'She wouldn't, but she went with someone else instead. Then he turned up anyway.'

'And – was the trip worthwhile?'

'It's hard to say.' Annabel looked at Simon, willing him not to mention her faint, and whether or not he understood, he said no more. His parents were still waiting expectantly, so she reluctantly added, 'We did find someone who was up there that afternoon.'

'Really? How incredible!' Sally leant forward, eager for further details, which Annabel dutifully supplied.

'Just shows, doesn't it?' Giles commented, raising his glass in a silent toast, which they all reciprocated. 'Police been on the job for years, but if you lift up the right stone, you can still come up with something.'

'Did you tell them?' Sally asked. 'The police, I mean?'

'We asked Janet to.'

'Do you think she will?'

Annabel shrugged. 'I really don't know.'

'Shouldn't you check, to make sure?'

'It wouldn't be much use anyway, after all these years,' Simon said deflatingly. 'How could she possibly recognize him?'

'They might have photographs taken at the time,' Sally said, then flushed and looked down, sipping at her wine.

Of my family, she means, Annabel thought. *Would* Janet be able to identify one of them, from an old photo?

'Anyway,' she went on quickly, 'there's no proof that the man Janet saw was the murderer; someone else might have been already there, or arrived later.'

Simon, bored with the conversation, picked up the magazine and handed it to his father. 'You wanted to see this, Dad?'

'Yes, I thought we might have another look at it. Page seventeen, wasn't it?'

Annabel stopped listening. Sally had excused herself and gone into the house. A smell of roasting beef drifted out to them, and Annabel was reminded of Monique's first visit to Hazelwood, and the dubiously regarded Yorkshire pudding. And that in turn brought back her own memories of meals eaten in that same dining room, with the furniture and oil paintings seemingly unchanged since her mother had first seen them.

As far as she knew, the entire family still assembled once a month for Sunday lunch. In the early days she was the youngest, and down the years her grandmother's voice still rang in her ears: *Sit up straight, Annabel . . . Put your knife and fork together when you've finished . . . Don't talk with your mouth full.*

Tired of her memories and uninterested in the continuing discussion of cars, she stood up and wandered down to the pond, where she stood watching the darting golden fish and the tiny new frogs basking in the shallows. This time next week they would all be in Devon, in yet another of the villas they occupied in May each year. She thought of the house on the cliffs at Llandinas, and the long, narrow room that had frightened her so much. Was it the one featured in her dream, or had it been subconsciously superimposed on her memory?

She gave a little shiver and turned to face the house, its mellow brick and thatched roof warm in the sunshine. From this distance she felt detached, an onlooker, as though it were a picture she was looking at. The two men were still sitting under the umbrella, Simon's dark head and Giles's ginger one bent close together over the wretched magazine. Then, as she watched, Sally appeared in the open French windows behind them.

'Dinner's ready!' she called, breaking the spell, and Annabel walked back across the grass to join them.

To her relief, there was no more talk of her family or the past, or even of the forthcoming holiday, and in the car going home, Simon remarked with satisfaction, 'Dad's going to stump up for the Peugeot after all.'

'We don't need it,' she said flatly, threading her way through the narrow lanes.

'What's need got to do with it? Anyway, we'll get a good part-exchange on this one.'

'I *like* this one,' she insisted stubbornly.

'Oh, for Heaven's sake, Annabel!' he burst out. 'Why do you always have to put the dampener on everything?'

A wave of heat washed over her. 'I don't; I just feel we shouldn't have to rely on your parents' generosity every time you want something new.'

'Why not? They can afford it.'

There was no point in arguing with him. Feeling completely isolated, she drove the rest of the way home.

School closed at lunchtime on the Friday for half term, and Annabel walked to the car park with Stephie.

'You're off tomorrow, then?' Stephie asked.

'Yes. Lamb to the slaughter.'

'I hope it won't come to that!'

Annabel's skin rippled, remembering George's warning. 'So do I.'

Stephie turned and surveyed her through narrowed eyes. 'You're not really nervous, are you? I mean, you've been going to these things all your life.'

'Yes, but I've never before given so much thought to what happened in Wales. It seems so fresh in my mind. And what worries me is that Emma could easily provide the flashpoint.'

Briefly, she was tempted to mention her mother's diary, but she resisted. Perhaps when she came back. In any case, there wasn't time to go into it all now.

'If I were you,' Stephie said, 'I'd put all the question marks out of your mind and treat it simply as a holiday. We're all in need of one.'

'Good advice. I'll do my best to follow it! Enjoy yourself, and I'll see you a week on Monday.'

With a wave of her hand, Stephie wandered on to her own car. Annabel drove slowly out of the gates and turned towards home. It wasn't only the past that was worrying her, she thought miserably; there was still this barrier between herself and Simon. And what was more, she knew he'd expect her to go with him to the Schooner this evening, and Martin, who seemed to have effortlessly insinuated himself into the group, would doubtless be there.

Annabel's apprehension was justified; Martin and Mandy were the first people she caught sight of when they walked into the pub. She'd not seen Mandy since that first evening when they'd come to the house. Now, she was sitting on a bar stool, one hand resting casually on Martin's shoulder. Her startlingly red hair was piled on her head and she was wearing a cream silk shirt, emerald-green trousers and gold sandals. Colourful was the word that came to mind, Annabel thought drily, feeling positively drab in her sleeveless black dress.

'Well,' Mandy drawled as they approached, 'if it isn't our psychic friend!'

Annabel looked quickly at Martin, and saw the gleam of malice in his eyes. No doubt he had regaled his girlfriend with full details of his time in Swansea. She nodded to them both, then, taking the glass Simon handed her, turned thankfully to Sue and Richard.

Later in the evening, Martin waylaid her as she was returning from the washroom.

'I hear from my contacts that you came up trumps in

Swansea,' he said. 'Another little secret you were keeping from me?'

She regarded him warily. 'What do you mean?'

'Don't play dumb, Annabel. The missing witness, no less. She told the police she'd been advised to see them by "a lady who's writing a book about it". Why didn't you tell me?'

'You weren't there, and I didn't know how to contact you.'

'Not very convincing. You could have found me if you'd tried.'

'Perhaps.'

'And tomorrow, I hear, you're off again for another family jolly.'

'That's right.'

'Well,' he said, moving on past her, 'let's hope that history doesn't repeat itself.'

Seven

Emma sat in silence, resigned to the fact that the noise of their movement as they sped down the motorway made conversation between the front and back of the car difficult. Daddy and Gran talked quietly from time to time, but she couldn't catch what they said and eventually she stopped trying.

It always seemed to be good weather for these birthday weeks; the sun shone from a cloudless sky, and less fortunate drivers had wound down their windows to create a breeze. As they flashed past, she could see their red, sticky faces, their brown arms resting on the sill. Inside the Rover, the three of them sat in air-conditioned comfort.

She smoothed down her flowered skirt, despite her efforts already creased. What would Mummy have worn to travel to Wales? However hot it had been – and cars weren't air conditioned then – Emma knew she'd have been cool and unflustered. She closed her eyes, trying to remember her mother's clothes as portrayed in the snaps she'd purloined from the family album. On holiday, of course, they'd been mainly swimsuits, shirts and tops, but even in these she managed to look elegant.

Emma sighed. Every time she badgered family or friends to describe her mother, she hoped someone would add, 'You look rather like her,' but they never did. Hardly surprising, since she and Tom favoured the Carlyles. But even there she missed out, for although feature by feature the two of them were very similar, the overall impression couldn't have been more different. In a nutshell, Tom was good-looking and she was plain.

She moved restlessly, gazing unseeingly out of the window. After last year's traumatic holiday she'd persuaded Tom, against his will, to take her to Wales. They had stood across the road from Bay View, their backs to the sea, staring up at the house. Then, at her insistence, they had gone down to the beach, to roughly where they'd been that last afternoon. She'd expected to find the spot straight away, since it was where they always sat and she remembered the formation of the sandhills behind. But over the years the sandhills had shifted and they'd had to make a guess, using the cliffs at the far end for guidance.

They'd sat for some time, hugging their knees and looking out to sea, oblivious of bathers and running dogs and crying children. Then, having extracted a promise from Tom to wait five minutes before following her, she had started back alone on a private pilgrimage, walking slowly up the steeply sloping path to the road above. There'd been a smell of hot grass, the sun on her back, the wide blue arc of the sky and the wheeling, screaming gulls – all of which Hilary would also have experienced.

After she had left them on that long-ago afternoon, Emma had glanced up and seen her halfway up the path looking down at them, the turquoise of her towelling robe bright against the brown and green of the cliffside. She'd waved, and Hilary had waved back. That distant splash of colour had been her last ever sight of her mother.

So, pursuing her re-enactment, Emma, too, had paused at that point and turned to look down on the beach she'd just left, making out the diminished figure of her brother, solitary amid the family groups. Then she'd continued climbing, tears pouring unchecked down her face, the backs of her knees aching at the steepness of the path and her breath laboured. What had her mother been thinking about on that final climb? The things she and Gran had been discussing? About driving into Swansea to buy some shorts for Tom, and perhaps going on to the Disney film they'd seen advertised? Or about what she was going to cook them for tea? At least she could have had no inkling that only a few minutes more of life remained to her. There was a bleak comfort in that.

But what had happened next, Emma agonized, after Hilary passed out of her sight? Had she met someone up on the road? Waiting at the house? Or had she gone in alone? The attack must have come at once, since no food had been taken out of fridge or freezer and she was still in her swimsuit and robe. Why had she gone into the sitting room – to speak to someone?

'All right, darling?'

Her father's voice broke into her musings, jolting her back to the present. He glanced briefly over his shoulder to smile at her. Poor Daddy, he dreaded these annual excursions as much as she did.

'We'll be stopping for lunch soon,' he said rallyingly. 'I don't know about you, but I could do with stretching my legs.'

The rest of the party wouldn't be down till tomorrow. Anticipating their arrival, Emma thought first, as always, of her brother. Now that he was married and a father she no longer had exclusive rights over him, but Celia was very kind. Realizing Emma might feel jealous, she always made her welcome, and had asked her to be Teddy's godmother. It would be good to see the baby again; he'd probably changed in the last few weeks.

The thought of her little godson cheered her, as did the imminent prospect of lunch; she realized she was hungry. And after lunch, it would be only a short drive to Dunes Villa, where the holiday would begin. This year, she was determined not to be neurotic and weepy, spoiling things for the rest of them; but this did not mean her resolve had weakened. She had not forgotten her mother, even if the rest of them had, and she was determined, somehow, to solve the mystery of her death.

*　　*　　*

Dunes Villa was, Annabel thought, an improvement on Bay View, being considerably larger. Its sitting room had enough seating to accommodate them all, as had the separate dining room, though an extra table had had to be brought in. Upstairs, its two single bedrooms had been allotted to Grandmother and Uncle Edward, the double ones to her father and Charlotte, and Tom, Celia and the baby.

After a brief inspection, she and Simon walked over to their own room in the annexe, a single-storey building at right angles to the house, which they would be sharing with Emma, Holly and David. It was the custom, on arrival, to settle into their rooms and unpack, the first formal coming together being for drinks at seven. Traditions, traditions, thought Annabel mockingly.

She stood in the centre of the room and took stock. The sea wasn't visible from the window, which looked across an expanse of grass to the swimming pool, one of the main attractions in view of the stony beaches along this part of the coast. Beyond it, some croquet hoops had been stuck in the grass. It might be fun to have a game.

The room itself was furnished with a double bed, dressing table, wardrobe and two easy chairs. Much like a middle-of-the-road hotel bedroom, really, with the requisite bathroom en suite, containing somewhat cramped facilities.

'So – here we are again,' Simon said behind her.

'Yes.'

'I hope to God we're not going to be treated to any histrionics from Emma. I don't fancy being stuck out here with her, I can tell you; the only ones who can deal with her moods are Tom and Edward, both of whom are over in the house.'

'I'm sure she'll be all right,' Annabel said. At the moment, she felt quite an affinity with Emma.

'So what do you want to do for the next hour or so? Take a walk along the front?'

Annabel shook her head. 'Not this evening; I'm happy just

to relax and have a long soak in the bath.' Time enough to explore their surroundings the next day, when they would be in a crowd. For the moment, she didn't want to be reminded of that other sea front at Llandinas.

'Well, I think I'll go out for a breath of air. I'll be back in time to get changed.'

Left to herself, Annabel finished her unpacking, finally lifting from the bottom of the suitcase a large envelope containing her mother's rescued papers. With luck, some of her unaccustomed free time this week could be spent getting them in order.

She had just spread them out on the bed when there was a tap on the door, and she heard her name called.

'Yes?' She quickly fumbled the papers together, but had not time to cover them before the door opened and Emma's face appeared round it.

'I thought I heard Simon go out. I've just made some tea, and wondered if you'd like a cup?' Her eyes fell on the papers on the bed and she came into the room. 'What have you got there? Not schoolwork, surely?'

Oh, *damn*! Emma was the very last person she wanted to know about the diary.

'No, it's – nothing important.'

'That's French, isn't it?' She was peering curiously at the upside-down papers.

Annabel nodded and, offering no explanation, slipped them into the envelope and put it back in the case. She didn't want to leave it in a drawer, which Simon might inadvertently open.

'I'd love a cup, thanks,' she said brightly, cutting off any other comment, and, steering Emma gently out of the room, followed her into her own much smaller one. It was odd, she reflected as Emma poured the tea, that although her cousin was four years older than she was, Annabel always thought of her as younger. There was an essential immaturity about her, a lack of confidence which was at the same time touching and irritating. Yet she had a responsible job at the local library, where she was highly thought of; perhaps it was only in her family life that she felt insecure. It could be that they'd all tried too hard to protect her.

Emma handed her the thick white cup and saucer with her peculiarly sweet smile. If only she'd try to make something of herself, Annabel thought despairingly. She was wearing one of her many long, flowered skirts, this one in blues and purples, and a white peasant-style blouse embroidered with flowers, with a red ribbon slotted through the neckline and tied in a bow. She looked, Annabel thought, like a refugee from the Tyrol.

'I'm looking forward to seeing little Teddy,' she remarked, breaking a rather awkward silence. 'I haven't seen him since the christening.'

Neil Cameron was one of his godfathers, she remembered, but he'd been on a painting trip in South America and David had stood proxy for him.

'You'll notice a big difference. He's sitting up now.'

They talked about the baby, and school, and Emma's job, and finally Annabel stood up. 'Well, I promised myself a leisurely bath, so if I'm to be ready for drinks, I'd better go and have it.'

Emma also rose. 'Nice to have a chat, anyway.'

'Yes. Thanks for the tea.'

'Annabel—'

She turned, her hand on the door-knob.

'I'm – sorry if I rather messed things up last year. Pestering you all about Mummy, I mean. It won't happen again.'

'It can't be easy for you,' Annabel said gently, 'but if you're saying you've come to terms with it, that's fine.'

'No, that's not what I meant. Just that I shan't bother anyone else with my problems.'

Annabel hesitated. 'The police won't have given up, you know. If any new evidence comes to light—'

'Let's not pretend they're looking for any. All right,

the case is still open, but it's hardly at the forefront of anyone's mind.'

'Just don't let it prey on yours,' Annabel advised, and with a quick smile, let herself out of the room.

Should she confess about her visit to Wales, she wondered as she ran her bath. She'd need to think about it, see how composed Emma appeared during the next few days. She was having enough trouble trying to rationalize her own feelings at the moment, without upsetting anyone else's.

Charlotte stood at the window of her room, watching Emma's foreshortened figure walk across the garden.

'I'm sorry for that girl,' she commented.

Douglas came and joined her, slipping an arm round her waist. 'I know Ed's concerned about her.'

'What was Hilary like?' Charlotte asked curiously. 'Not physically – I've seen her photos – I mean her character. Can you imagine anyone wanting to kill her?'

Douglas gave a brief laugh. 'To shut her up, perhaps.' He sobered quickly. 'Sorry, that was below the belt.'

'How do you mean, though?'

'Well, she had a high, upper-class voice that could go right through you. Her family were loaded, you know. Rather like yours!' he added, giving her a squeeze.

'Come on, Douglas, I'm serious.'

'It was her bossiness that got me, and her conviction that she was always right. She'd never concede that anyone else might have a point.'

'Do I gather you didn't like her?'

Douglas shrugged. 'Not particularly, if I'm brutally honest. To give her her due, though, she was involved in all kinds of good causes, worked her socks off for charity, and all that. As a result, perhaps, she had very high standards, and woe betide anyone who fell below them.'

'Emma seems to have idolized her.'

'Rose-coloured glasses, if you ask me. Oh, she was a reasonable enough mother, but she was out a great deal, and in my opinion imposed very much on Moira's good nature. Before they started school she used to dump the twins on her day after day.'

'Why didn't she have a nanny?' Charlotte asked. 'You say money was no problem.'

'Because she *said* she wanted to look after her own children. She just didn't put it into practice.'

'How did Edward react to all this busyness?'

'Gave her a free rein – what else could he do?'

'He didn't worry about the children?'

'He never said so, but then he wouldn't. Edward has always played things close to his chest.'

Charlotte was silent for a moment, her eyes on Emma's now-distant figure. 'Were they happily married, would you say?'

Douglas moved uncomfortably. 'I told you, Edward is a very private person. He doesn't discuss things that matter to him.'

And still waters run deep, reflected Charlotte. 'But what was your impression?'

'There was occasional friction, as there is in any marriage.' He paused. 'But we're on dangerous ground here, my love, in the light of what happened.'

'Yes, of course. I wasn't suggesting—'

He stopped her words with a kiss. 'Time to get ready for dinner,' he said.

The dining room was buzzing with conversation, and Flora looked about her contentedly. The renting agency had overcome the seating problem admirably; there were seven of them round the large table, and the remaining four on a smaller one alongside, close enough to join in the general conversation. They would, of course, change places each evening.

She had chosen menus for the whole week from the choice offered by the caterers, and was delighted with this first meal. The food was excellent, and the staff serving it unobtrusive and efficient, which augured well for the rest of the week.

It was so wonderful to have the whole family together, she thought happily. This custom of going away for her birthday had started early in her marriage and continued even while the boys were at school, since the date fell conveniently within half-term week. Later still, when they married, it was a way of ensuring that they spent a reasonable amount of time together; although – with the exception of Annabel – their homes were within a ten-mile radius, they all lived busy lives, and frequently the only time they saw each other was at the monthly Sunday lunches she had also maintained.

Flora viewed this annual week away as a means of reinforcing ties which, in the normal hurly-burly of life, might possibly weaken. It was because of this that, against all opposition, she had insisted on continuing the custom after Hilary's murder. She hoped that Edward had now forgiven her.

She looked down the length of the table to where he was engaged in conversation with Holly. The child had blossomed in the last year, Flora thought fondly. She was doing well at school, and hoped to follow David to university next year. What a comfort Douglas's second marriage was.

Her eyes moved to her second son, seated next to Annabel, and she noted their somewhat stilted conversation with a frown. She still felt guilty about the girl, though she'd made every attempt, when she was younger, to keep her in touch with her father, claiming regular visiting rights which, given the chance, Monique might have let slip and Douglas been too idle to insist on. Yet for all that there seemed to be a gulf between father and daughter which it was probably too late, now, to rectify.

'This salmon is perfect,' remarked Celia on her right, bringing Flora back to her duties as hostess. 'Do you think they could be persuaded to give me the recipe?'

'If anyone could get it out of them, you could!' Flora

replied with a smile. Most people smiled at Celia; she was such a happy little soul, bubbling over with good spirits, and her adoration of Tom was a joy to see. Flora was also aware how kind she was to her sister-in-law, ensuring that Emma felt welcome at their home. And Emma could be possessive of Tom, as her grandmother had frequently observed.

'All quiet upstairs,' Flora added, seeing Celia's eyes stray to the baby alarm on the sideboard.

'Yes, thank goodness. I fed him as soon as we arrived, and he went down without a murmur.' And Celia, not doubting the older woman's interest in her great-grandchild, launched into an account of her son's latest achievements.

Annabel, listening to her father's account of a holiday in France, was aware of a shift in perception. This tall, rather gangling man, with whom she'd never felt at ease, had once been the impetuous young lover who won her mother's heart. Until now, she had all her life taken Monique's 'side', had instinctively assumed that her father must be lacking in some quality for her mother to have left him. She should have been adult enough to realize there were two sides to every situation. Though Monique had never actively run him down to her, the words 'your father' had always been spoken in a slightly derogatory tone, and odd phrases, overheard from her conversation with friends, had been unquestioningly accepted: *too lazy to make anything of himself . . . no backbone . . . living off his second wife's money – her father had to find him a place in his business.*

Uncomfortably, Annabel wondered for the first time if her mother had in some way resented Douglas's second, and obviously happy, marriage. This story he was telling her now, about the fool he'd made of himself in France, seemed suddenly, painfully, endearing. She said impulsively, 'I wish I'd been there – I could have saved you the embarrassment.'

He turned to her in surprise. Then he said quietly, 'I wish so, too. I don't see nearly enough of you, Annabel.'

'No.' She swallowed past the sudden lump in her throat. 'Perhaps you and Charlotte could come for a weekend sometime?'

Oh God, what was she doing? Would she regret this?

'We'd love to,' he said warmly. 'Thank you.'

To Annabel's relief, they were interrupted at this point by a burst of laughter from Holly, and conversation became general again.

But further angst awaited her. In the sitting room over coffee, Emma, who had had more wine than she was used to, made a general announcement that for the next week she intended to do nothing more strenuous than lie in the garden or pool.

Tom laughed good-naturedly. 'I give you two days at most before you'll be bored out of your mind.'

'Far from it!' she declared. 'I shall revel in doing absolutely nothing. Unlike Annabel, who's actually brought some work with her.'

Annabel felt her face flame. 'I haven't – really!' she protested, willing Emma not to go on. In vain.

'But I saw it – a whole sheaf of it, written in French.'

There was a bewildered silence, then Simon said theatrically, 'Oh, God, Annie, you haven't brought it with you, have you?'

They were all looking at her, and she said hastily, 'It's only some papers I'm trying to sort out.'

'What sort of papers?' Flora asked, her voice cool. The word 'French' had obviously alerted her.

As Annabel hesitated, Simon answered blithely, 'They're her mother's, aren't they, darling? A diary of some sort – from the year dot, apparently.'

Douglas said slowly, 'Yes, I'd forgotten that; she did keep what she called a journal.'

'It's all mixed up,' Annabel said desperately. 'A lot of loose papers. I'm just – trying to make sense of it, that's all.'

'When was this diary written?' Flora asked.

'I – don't know; as I say, it's not in any kind of order.'

'But during her marriage to Douglas, I assume?'

Douglas spoke sharply, surprising them all. 'Mother, please! She's told us she doesn't know; can't you see you're embarrassing her?'

'I'm sorry, I'm sure,' Flora said stiffly. 'I was interested, that's all.'

There was a brief silence, then Emma sprang to her feet and ran out of the room. Tom, with an apologetic glance, went after her.

'Back to square one,' Simon muttered under his breath.

'Well,' Charlotte said after a moment, 'are there any plans for tomorrow?'

After a somewhat rocky start, conversation gradually resumed. Neither Emma nor Tom rejoined them. Annabel, hands locked tightly together, longed to escape as well. She was burningly conscious of her grandmother's disapproval and the curiosity of the rest of them, impotently furious both with Emma, whose gaffe had led to this disclosure, and with Simon, who had compounded it.

At last, after what seemed a very long time, the party broke up and they made their various ways to bed.

As soon as they reached their room, Annabel rounded furiously on Simon. 'What the *hell* were you thinking of?' she demanded. 'Why in the name of Heaven did you have to mention Maman, let alone her diary? Didn't you realize what the outcome would be?'

He had taken a step back at her onslaught, and was now regarding her with an air of injured innocence. She saw that he, too, had had a lot to drink, and that therefore any remonstrances would be useless.

'It wasn't my fault!' he protested predictably. 'It was you who let Emma see the papers. If you didn't want people to know about them, you should have been more careful.'

Which she couldn't deny. 'But you didn't have to say what they were! I was the one Grandmother was speaking to – why didn't you let me answer?'

'You were taking all day about it.'

'You *know* that any mention of Maman is like a red rag to a bull, and it was embarrassing for Daddy and Charlotte, too.'

'I don't see why,' Simon argued stubbornly, taking off his tie. 'Just because people get divorced, you can't pretend they never existed. Now calm down, Annie, there's a good girl, and get ready for bed. It'll all have blown over by the morning.'

It seemed he was right; Flora always breakfasted in her room, but to Annabel's relief there was no hint of awkwardness among the rest of them, and Teddy in his baby bouncer provided a welcome distraction, greeting each newcomer with an engagingly toothless grin.

When Annabel came out of the dining room, Emma was waiting for her.

'I'm going to get the Sunday papers for Dad,' she said. 'Would you like to come with me?'

'I thought you weren't leaving the garden?' Annabel reminded her.

'I've changed my mind.'

In truth, Emma was the last person she wanted to spend time with this morning, but she could think of no reasonable excuse. 'All right,' she agreed resignedly. 'I'll just tell Simon where I'm going.'

As they set off along the uneven cliff road, Emma came straight to the point. 'You've probably guessed that I want to apologize for last night. I'd no right to blurt out what I did – it was none of my business. But I never dreamt it was anything to do with your mother. I hope you believe that.'

'Simon was right, I shouldn't have brought them with me. It was asking for trouble.'

'I hope I haven't soured things between you and Gran. I know she's always a bit sticky with you.'

Annabel glanced at her, surprised by her perception. 'I can never get close to her,' she admitted, 'I don't know why. I wish I could call her Gran or Grandma as the rest of you do, but I just can't. There's some sort of barrier between us.'

They walked for a few minutes in silence. Then Emma said wryly, 'Isn't it strange that neither of us can talk about our mothers? I know I forced the issue last year, but only because they always skirt round the subject. You know, I can remember the day Mummy died quite clearly; when she left us to go and make our tea, she stopped halfway up the path and looked down at us. I waved to her, and she waved back. We didn't know it, but it was goodbye.'

'What happened when you got back to the house?' Annabel asked in a low voice.

Emma gave a little shudder. 'That's much more confused. Daddy came out and hugged us, and there were people milling around and we had to go to a hotel for the night. I kept asking for Mummy, but they said she wasn't there. And you wouldn't stop crying. I remember that. Each time Aunt Monique tried to put you down, you screamed for all you were worth. I remember Gran saying, "It's odd how babies sense things," but I didn't know what she meant.'

Crying. Her mother bending over her . . .

Annabel said hastily, 'You asked everyone else what they remembered about your mother, but what do *you* remember?'

'Bad things as well as good,' Emma replied surprisingly. 'Gran once said that it's easy, when someone you love very much dies, to sort of canonize them – forget the things that irritated you or made you unhappy when they were alive. I think she was talking about Grandpa. And she said the result is that they become less real, not truly themselves any more. I didn't want that to happen to Mummy. I wanted to remember her exactly how she was – yelling at us sometimes, often not being there when she'd promised, at school sports and concerts and things. But whatever time she came home at night, she always came up to kiss us goodnight, even if we were asleep. We always knew that she loved us.'

Bad things as well as good. Had she, Annabel wondered,

been guilty of canonization? Certainly it was the good things she remembered about her own mother – her warmth, her sense of humour, the happy times they'd shared. But Monique had also been strong-willed, and quite ruthless in going after what she wanted. As, of course, was Flora. Perhaps that was why they'd clashed.

It hadn't occurred to her that she'd been filtering her memories, but as she looked more deeply into them, others, less welcome, began to surface: the frequent rows between George and Monique in the early days, when, having been woken by raised voices, she would tiptoe out of bed and sit on the stairs, trembling at the anger in her mother's voice; the rare occasions when, in a flash of temper, Monique had lashed out at her, only to scoop her up immediately afterwards, with kisses of apology.

'Annabel?' Emma was looking at her curiously.

'Sorry. You made me think, that's all. About canonizing.'

'Your mother? I liked her; she was very sweet to me, that first holiday after Mummy's death. And she adored you. Looking back, she was very possessive, though; poor Uncle Douglas hardly got a look in. I once heard him say to Daddy, "She's very much Monique's baby." I think that's why Charlotte involved him so much with David and Holly.'

Annabel's mind reeled. Here was Emma, whom she'd thought most things passed by, proving herself both astute and observant. While her parents – but she needed time to assess her shifting attitude there.

They had rounded the final bend and were making their way down the steep path towards the beach and town, met by a strong smell of seaweed. Below them on their right was a line of beach huts, and several boats were drawn up on the pebbles, providing an irresistible play area for a group of small boys.

They skirted the car park and started up the slope towards Budleigh itself, pleased to discover that next to the newsagents was an ice-cream shop offering a wide range of

choices. After buying Edward's papers they treated themselves, savouring the exotic flavours as they leant against the
sun-warmed wall watching the crowds. It was Bank Holiday
weekend, and the little town was thronged with people.

The walk back, uphill, was more demanding and talk was
sporadic and, by unspoken agreement, on lighter matters.
But by the time they reached Dunes Villa, Annabel felt she
knew her cousin considerably better than she had before.

They found the rest of the party grouped in various stages
of undress round the pool. Flora, resplendent in a straw hat,
was seated under an umbrella, with Teddy's pram alongside.
The others, liberally coated in protective cream, lay out in
the sun.

Emma handed the newspapers to Edward, and Annabel,
eager for a swim, hurried back to the annexe to change. After
the long, hot walk home, the pool seemed very inviting.

The maids had drawn the curtains to keep the room
cool, and the sun pouring through them filled it with a
pale green light. She pulled open the drawer and frowned,
feeling a prickle of unease before realizing why. Then she
remembered: when she'd unpacked last night, she had
laid her paperback on top of her swimsuit, so she could
extract both together. Now it was lying half hidden and the
swimsuit itself, which she'd folded neatly, was crumpled in
a corner.

Annabel straightened, staring at her reflection in the
mirror. Simon must have been looking for something, she
told herself – though the drawers allocated to him were on
the other side of the dressing table. Almost fearfully, she
opened the next one down. It, too, was subtly different
from the way she had left it. Whoever had been here was
in a hurry, not taking time to replace things exactly as
they were.

Whoever had been here . . . The maids? Their bed was
made, the waste basket emptied, and fresh towels put
out. But Simon's watch and wallet lay on the dressing
table, where he must have left them when he changed

into his trunks, and such jewellery as she'd brought with her was undisturbed. And surely any cleaners would have more sense than to arouse suspicion on the first day of their contract? Their job depended on total honesty – why would they jeopardize it?

Had other rooms also been searched, she wondered. And if theft wasn't the object, what was?

She caught her breath as a possible answer came. Her mother's papers? Was that what the intruder had been after? But if so, why? Even if they included an account of the Welsh holiday, why assume that Monique knew any more than the rest of them?

Her eyes went quickly to the suitcases which, to make more floor space, Simon had put on top of the wardrobe. Pulling a chair over, she climbed up and took down first Simon's, then her own. With a huge sigh of relief, she saw that the envelope was undisturbed. The intruder had either not thought to look there, or had been interrupted. But he or she might come back.

Annabel replaced the cases, put the chair back in place, and quickly, with fingers that shook, undressed and slipped into the swimsuit. She mustn't be too long, or it might seem that her suspicions had been roused.

To remove any possible doubt, she'd ask Simon if he'd riffled through her things, though she thought it unlikely. She wouldn't, however, tell him of her conviction that the room had been searched, firstly because he wouldn't believe her, and secondly because she couldn't depend on his not repeating it, especially when he'd had something to drink. She must keep her suspicions to herself, at the same time being careful to act as though nothing were wrong.

Tomorrow she would make some excuse to go into Exeter, spend an hour or two in private reading through the papers, and then post them to herself at home. Obviously, they weren't safe here.

With her heart beating uncomfortably fast, she went to join the others by the pool.

Eight

As she'd expected, Simon confirmed, in answer to her casual query, that he'd not been through her things.

'Never fancied myself in your underwear,' he told her airily. 'Why, have you lost something?'

'No, it just wasn't where I thought I'd put it, that's all.' And she changed the subject, to show it was of no importance.

It was not a comfortable day. Lying back in the lounger, her eyes masked by her dark glasses, Annabel studied one member of her family after the other. Was it really conceivable that one of them had been in her room? Or had her memory played her false, and she herself had disturbed the articles in a search she'd forgotten about? If the Welsh holiday lay behind it, the suspects were narrowed to her father and Edward. On the other hand, the papers might not have been the reason for the search, in which case any one of them could be responsible, with the exception of Emma, who had been with her.

Tomorrow, alone in Exeter, she would abandon her chronological sorting and skip through the diary to see if the holiday *was* mentioned. Apart from anything else, in view of both her nightmare and the effect the room in Llandinas had had on her, she needed, now, to convince herself that her mother had known no more about the murder than the rest of them.

They were incredulous when, the next morning, she announced that she was going into Exeter.

'But Annabel, it's Bank Holiday Monday! Everywhere will be closed!'

'No, it won't, with the place full of holidaymakers. And I don't want to buy anything, just look round; I've never been there.'

'But why not wait till later in the week, when it's less busy? Then we could all go.'

'You'll never find a place to park!'

Smilingly she shook her head at all their objections, and at ten o'clock, with the envelope concealed in a carrier bag, she got into the suffocatingly hot car and set off.

The first part of the journey, through country lanes, was pleasant and she didn't meet much traffic, but as she came closer to Exeter this changed, and she joined a slowly moving line of cars which stopped and started, stopped and started, at a frustratingly slow pace all the way into the city centre. It was a further twenty minutes before she found a place to park, by which time she was ready to concede that her family had a point. She had also failed to take into account the fact that although some shops might be open on Bank Holiday, the post office would not.

She emerged from the car park, blinking in the sunshine, and turned towards the centre, relieved to find that the route took her past the post office. Though it was indeed closed, there was a machine outside and she bought a book of first class stamps. She had no means of weighing her package, but if she put several stamps on it, that should suffice.

There were signposts pointing to the cathedral, and these led her through a small square and past several cafés and shops until, down a cobbled alley, she emerged into the wide space of the cathedral close, and paused to look about her. The magnificent building with its towers and turrets was surrounded by a green, on which people were walking, sitting or lying in the sun. Several benches backed on to the low stone wall that enclosed it, and Annabel made her way purposefully towards one which was in the shade.

With a sigh of relief she sat down, reached for the file

and took out the jumble of papers, laying them in piles along the bench beside her. She turned first to the last in the pile in the hope these might be the most relevant, but a quick glance at a page or two showed them to be concerned with the build-up to the wedding. No short cut, then; she would have to sift through them and see what she could find.

On the grass a few yards from her, people were beginning to eat lunch, producing sandwiches and fruit from bags and picnic hampers, but Annabel, having had a cooked breakfast at the villa, was not hungry, though she might be glad of a drink before too long. To work, then.

The page now uppermost began, like most of them, in mid-sentence:

> 'traditions' which cannot be broken. Always we must spend Christmas at Hazelwood; we must go there each month for the Sunday lunch; we must have a week away over Madame's birthday. Sometimes it seems I have married the entire family! When I say to Douglas that perhaps we shall not go to lunch today, that I should like to drive into the country, he says, 'But it is the first Sunday of the month!' As though the commandment were written in stone!
>
> Once I spoke to Hilary about it, and she agreed. 'She smothers the boys,' she said, 'but she means well.' So it seems I shall get no support from her.

Poor Maman, Annabel thought ruefully. Her independent spirit hadn't taken kindly to domination by Flora, and who could blame her? Surely Daddy could have made a stand sometimes, when he saw how she felt? But Douglas, she knew, was one for the quiet life – or, as Monique had scornfully remarked, weak.

Annabel sighed and picked up a few pages that were still attached to each other. But they weren't about the holiday either, and she was about to discard them for another batch

when a sentence seemed to leap out of the page at her,
riveting her attention.

> Douglas is so boring these days no one could blame me
> for having a little fun, though I should not need to look
> elsewhere if only Edward would admit the feelings we
> have for each other. He watches me whenever we're
> together, but he never comes close except to kiss my
> cheek when we meet or leave, as Hilary does. That is
> not at all how I want him to kiss me.

Annabel looked up, and the grass, the grey stone building
and the sky beyond spun together in a dizzy whirl. Her
mother and *Edward*? And instantly, before she could stop
it, came the thought: could that be a motive for murder? Yet
Hilary's death hadn't brought them together.

She felt faintly sick, reluctant to read any more, yet
knowing she must. Now more than ever, she had to know.
After a minute she forced her eyes back to the page.

> Robert and I have met twice now, in the room behind
> his shop – he has a sofa there. It is quite exciting,
> making love between all the packing cases!

Robert? Annabel tried to anchor her darting thoughts.
When would this have been? Where was she when all
this was taking place? Monique had not been like Hilary,
dumping her child on friends while she followed her own
pursuits. She had given up work when Annabel was born,
and even after the separation, had limited herself to coaching
students at home in the evenings. Was it before she was
born, then? If so, Monique must have been married less
than two years.

Annabel closed her eyes, passionately wishing she could
turn the clock back. If Sally had never met Martin and told
him of the Carlyle connection, she would not have gone to
Wales and experienced her traumatic reaction to the house.

And if George had not handed over those three lethal cartons, she could have gone on remembering her mother as she always had, a warm, amusing, loving companion. Above all, she wanted to obliterate the in-depth analysis that Emma's remarks had prompted and the picture, emerging from these papers, of someone very different from the person she had loved.

'Annabel?' said a voice above her. 'It is, isn't it?'

She looked up through a prism of tears to see three figures standing on the grass in front of her. Dr and Mrs Cameron – and Neil! Thank goodness for her dark glasses!

'Hello!' she said haltingly. 'I didn't expect to see you here.'

'Nor we you,' Moira replied. 'But of course, it's Flora's birthday week, isn't it? I'd forgotten you were coming down this way. We're on a motoring tour of the south-west, and spending a couple of days with Neil.' She turned to her son, silent at her side. 'He's rented a house in Topsham for a couple of months, to do some painting.'

Annabel looked up at him. 'I thought you were in South America?'

He smiled. 'Not any longer. How are you, Annabel? Lord knows when I last saw you.'

She said awkwardly, 'Would you like to sit down?' and began to shuffle the piles of paper together. For the second time in three days they were causing her embarrassment.

'What's all this, then?' Rex asked jovially. 'Someone give you a holiday task?'

'No, I—' But she was too emotionally battered to think up any more lies. 'It's my mother's diary,' she said. 'George found some cartons of her papers when he moved house, and this was among them.'

'I never knew she kept one,' Moira commented, sitting down in the first cleared space. 'In French, I see. Very wise!'

Annabel's raw nerves quivered. Was that a harmless joke, or did Moira know something of her mother's affairs?

'It's lovely to see you, dear,' she was going on. 'You don't often come to Cheltenham these days. Look, we're just about to go in search of lunch. Will you join us?'

'Oh, I don't—'

'Of course she will,' Rex said firmly.

Which was how, fifteen minutes later, she found herself at a table in a tiny restaurant tucked into the corner of the close, and, having removed her sunglasses, was able to take her first proper look at Neil. He was as attractive as she remembered, tall, blond and broad-shouldered, with steady grey eyes and a tan left over from his South American trip. Catching his eye, she smiled and asked brightly, 'How's Marina?'

He made a grimace. 'History, I'm afraid.'

She was startled. They'd been together for years, though the relationship had been broken off more than once before. 'I'm sorry,' she said awkwardly.

'We just grew out of each other,' he replied with a shrug, and picked up the menu.

It must have been over a year since she'd seen Mrs Cameron, and her fair hair was noticeably greyer. Her face still looked youthful, though; it was a pleasant face without being pretty, a face that one instinctively warmed to, and Annabel knew she'd been a good friend to both Monique and Hilary. When she herself grew up, Moira had invited her to call them by their first names, but she thought of them as she always had, as Dr and Mrs Cameron.

The doctor was as charming as ever, his hair, darker than that of his wife and son, still thick, though it, too, was flecked with grey. And on closer inspection, Annabel noted with concern, his face also had a greyish tinge, and the hand that held his glass trembled slightly. She felt a rush of protective affection, remembering how he'd kept a packet of chocolate biscuits in his surgery for his younger patients.

She glanced back at Neil, found his eyes consideringly on her, and cast around for something to say.

131

'Your godson's growing apace.'

He smiled. 'I haven't seen him recently.'

'Why not come over to the villa, then? It's not far – between Budleigh and Exmouth, and we're there till the end of the week.'

'Oh, I wouldn't dare invade Flora's birthday gathering! Actually, though, I was about to make a counter-suggestion. As Mother said, I have this house in Topsham, which is a lovely spot a couple of miles away. How about you and Simon coming over for lunch? I see the others when I go home, but it's years since we got together. Mother and Dad will still be here tomorrow, but any day after that would be fine.'

'That would be lovely – thank you.'

'You'd better give me your mobile number, so we can arrange it.'

The meal passed in an exchange of news, and Annabel, who had thought herself not hungry, was surprised at the ease with which she dispatched her warm chicken breast and Caesar salad. They sat for some time over coffee, and it was after three when they finally parted.

'I'll be in touch,' Neil promised, and she watched them cross the road and begin to skirt round the green. Then she turned back to the table, using its surface to address the envelope and slip the papers inside. It wasn't heavy, but she put three first-class stamps on it and went in search of a pillar-box. She'd not found what she wanted in the diary, she reflected, but what she had discovered had been unsettling enough. Better to dwell on the more positive aspect of her visit to Exeter, her meeting with the Camerons. As she made her way back to the car, she was looking forward to seeing Neil again.

Before leaving that morning, Annabel had set two small traps in her room: she'd tucked an old label attached to Simon's suitcase between it and her own case, and, in her portion of the wardrobe, had draped the sleeve of

132

her dressing gown across the garment hanging next to it. If they'd been disturbed, it would be proof not only that an earlier search *had* taken place, but that the intruder was desperate enough to risk a second.

On her return from Exeter she went straight to her room and opened the wardrobe. The sleeve of her dressing gown hung limply down. She stood staring at it for several minutes, not sure whether to be glad or sorry that her suspicions had been confirmed. Then, heart fluttering in her throat, she climbed up to inspect the cases. The label also hung free, no longer lodged between them. Lucky indeed that her suitcase was empty and the diary safely on its way back to Bristol.

The others were interested to hear of her meeting with the Camerons, and Simon welcomed the suggestion of lunch with Neil.

'He's going from strength to strength with his painting,' Edward remarked. 'Rex told me there's an important exhibition coming up in a month or two.'

Annabel glanced across at him. Dear Uncle Edward, of whom she'd always been so fond. Had there really been anything between him and Monique, or had the fancy been only in her mother's head? And was it he who'd been in her room during her absence today?

Neil phoned shortly afterwards, and, since Wednesday was Flora's birthday, their visit was arranged for Thursday. Annabel took down the directions he gave her, and promised to be there by twelve thirty.

At dinner that evening she was sitting next to Charlotte, slimly elegant in a coffee-coloured silk blouse. Her fair hair hung smooth and straight in a bob and her skin bloomed with health, though laughter lines were etched round eyes and mouth.

'Douglas tells me you've invited us down one weekend,' she said in a low voice, under cover of the general conversation. 'That's sweet of you – he was very touched.' She paused, then added quietly, 'He missed you a great deal, you know, when your mother left. I know you often stayed at Hazelwood, but he felt you'd grown apart from him and he didn't know how to get close again.'

Annabel could think of nothing to say. After the separation, Douglas had let their house and moved back with his parents. Vaguely, she remembered some of those early visits; her father kneeling on the floor with her to play tiddlywinks or dominoes, and her own short attention span; going for walks in Pitville Park and playing Pooh sticks on the bridge. Yet even then, instinctively, she had kept her distance, subtly influenced, no doubt, by Monique. What had Emma said? *Poor Uncle Douglas hardly got a look in.*

Charlotte crumbled the bread roll on her plate. 'I probably shouldn't be saying this, but quite apart from losing you, it took him a long time to get over your mother. Until she married again, I think he still hoped she'd come back.'

The words she'd read that morning burned in Annabel's mind, but she managed to say – truthfully – 'I always thought it had been mutual.'

Charlotte shook her head, then, possibly guessing at Annabel's confusion, put a hand briefly over hers. 'Sorry if I'm talking out of turn,' she murmured. 'Let me just say, though, that any time you feel like coming to see us, you'd be most welcome. I'd like you to know my offspring better.' She smiled, adding confidentially, 'Between you and me, I'm afraid they consider this annual week rather a drag!'

Annabel laughed aloud, glad to have her mood lightened. 'It can't be much fun for them, with everyone so much older. But David's still at university, isn't he? He's not been with us for the last couple of years – how did he manage this time?'

'It's his year out, working for a company, so he's able to take normal holidays. Though I suspect that, having escaped twice, he thought he'd managed to wriggle free.'

'It's amazing, when you think of it, that we all manage to turn up year after year,' Annabel commented, thinking of her sacrificed half-term.

'Not when you know your grandmother, it isn't!' Charlotte replied.

On Flora's birthday it was the practice for her to be presented with her cards after breakfast, but no gifts were offered until they gathered for drinks before dinner, a ceremony Annabel found embarrassing, since everybody felt bound to exclaim appreciatively over everyone else's offerings.

It was also tradition that, weather permitting – and it had never dared do otherwise – they had a picnic lunch on the nearest beach. This year, since it was stony close by, it had been decided to drive to Exmouth, a few miles along the coast. Accordingly, armed with a cool-box packed by the caterers, they set off mid-morning in a hired minibus. The day was dull and warm, with high, greyish clouds moving sluggishly over the sky.

When Annabel and the twins were younger, games had been organized – rounders, pig-in-the-middle, and races on the sand. Now, everyone was much more sedentary, setting up their folding chairs and reading, knitting, or doing the crossword. Remembering Charlotte's words of the night before, Annabel turned to David. 'I'm not ready to sit down yet; do you feel like a walk along the beach?'

She saw his surprise, and felt ashamed. This young man was her half-brother, and she barely knew him.

'Fine!' he said, with gratifying eagerness. 'Can Holly come too?'

The three of them set off together, Annabel keenly aware of Douglas and Charlotte looking after them.

'This can't be much fun for you,' she said frankly.

Brother and sister exchanged a quick look. 'No, it isn't,' Holly agreed. 'I've got my mocks when we go back, and I'm having to spend a lot of time revising.' She smiled shyly. 'I'm afraid my French isn't so hot!'

'Would you like us to speak French now?'

'I wouldn't!' David said quickly.

Annabel laughed. 'If it's any help, I could give you a bit

of coaching after supper each evening. Though not tonight, of course, since it's the birthday dinner.'

'That would be great!' Holly said. She looked very like Charlotte, thought Annabel; the same clear skin and pale gold hair, though Holly wore hers long. She felt an unexpected surge of affection for this younger sister.

The sand here was soft, making walking an effort as they manoeuvred their way past little settlements where families had set up their deck chairs and spread their rugs. There was the usual plethora of sandcastles, of varying originality. The smell of the sea and the rock pools brought back vivid childhood memories – and, more recently, the walk with Stephie along the Welsh beach.

'It's always warm for Gran's birthday,' David commented. 'Sometimes, it's all the summer we get!'

'I hear you were in France recently?' Annabel said.

'Not us – just the parents.'

'So what are you doing for holidays?'

'I'm off to the States in July,' David said, picking up a pebble and sending it skimming over the surface of the water. 'There's a crowd of us going from university – ten or so. All done on a shoestring, of course, but it should be fun. We're flying to the west coast and taking it from there.'

They talked easily about America, and about Italy, where Holly was going, and the initial reserve between them soon evaporated. She should have made an effort long before this, Annabel thought; she was certainly getting to know her family this week, which, she supposed, was the object of the exercise.

Flora would have echoed that sentiment. She'd been considerably surprised, after her earlier reflections, to see Annabel not only deep in conversation with Charlotte but more relaxed with Douglas. Now she had rounded up her siblings and taken them off down the beach. What had brought about this sea change? On previous occasions she'd seemed so aloof, not really one of the party – unlike Simon, who wholeheartedly entered into the spirit of it. Such a nice young man he was, good-looking, charming, and at his ease with everyone. She found him much easier to talk to than her granddaughter.

Simon, lounging on a rug with Tom, was also surprised by Annabel's actions. As far as he remembered, she'd never gone out of her way before to talk to the kids, and she'd been chatting up Douglas and Charlotte, too. All very cosy. No doubt it was down to her current obsession with raking up the past. They mightn't be so pally if they realized that. He'd also been amazed that she'd brought those papers of her mother's with her – almost as though she couldn't bear to be parted from them. All very well giving him grief for identifying them, but she'd only herself to blame. God, old Flora had gone positively glacial!

They'd made love last night, for the first time in weeks, and it had been good. A pity they couldn't always be as relaxed as they were now, but he supposed it was the holiday atmosphere. Back home, no doubt the pressures would build up again. Things had been pretty bad these last few months; he'd been bored, restless and generally discontented, and, no doubt unfairly, had blamed Annabel.

Without volition Lucy came to mind, and as heat sluiced over him, he hastily turned on his stomach and buried his head in his arms. Since their night out, he'd caught only a few brief glimpses of her – Miss Efficiency in her business suit. He bet the rest of the staff didn't know what a hot number she was under that cool exterior. He remembered pulling her hair free, its heaviness on the back of his hand, the warmth and passion of her. Well, he could have her if he wanted, she'd made that clear – as long as it was on her own terms. Only pride – and panic – had made him back down.

'When is it you're seeing Neil?' asked Tom beside him. Simon wrenched his thoughts back. 'Tomorrow.'

'Give him my regards, won't you? I had a card from him

a couple of weeks ago. When this Topsham let ends he's coming up to Cheltenham for a while. It'll be good to see him again. I think he's still smarting a bit over the rift with Marina.'

'Don't think I ever met her,' Simon said, feeling it safe to turn round again. 'What was she like?'

'Oh, beautiful, of course, and sultry. Long black hair and flashing eyes. Terribly temperamental, though; she was always flying off the handle. I don't know how he stuck it so long. She's an artist, too, though personally I don't like that ultra-modern stuff. You know the kind of thing – an enormous canvas covered completely in dark blue, with a white triangle in the middle, entitled *Perplexity* or something equally pretentious. I could do that myself – in a month or two, even Teddy could!'

Simon laughed, following the direction of Tom's eyes to where the baby kicked happily on the rug beside his mother. What would a baby of his and Annabel's be like? It might be rather good to find out.

He looked up in time to see her and the others coming back, still talking animatedly, and as though their return were a signal Flora motioned to Edward to start unpacking the picnic. There was smoked salmon, asparagus rolls, bite-sized vol-au-vents, shrimp patties and cold chicken, with three different kinds of salad, fruit and white wine. Flora did not care for red in the middle of the day.

'Glyndebourne-on-Sea!' Edward teased, handing out linen napkins and uncorking the wine.

They ate hungrily, the salt air giving an edge to their appetite. The sun had still not appeared, but it was warm and pleasant enough. Emma wasn't joining in the conversation, Annabel noted, nor had she eaten much. Remembering her own sadness on her mother's anniversary, she sympathized. She tried unsuccessfully to catch her eye, and Edward, intercepting her glance, murmured something to Emma, who gave her a reluctant smile.

The remnants of the meal were packed away, Teddy was

given his bottle, and the rest of them dozed, read or chatted. By three thirty they were ready to return to the minibus and be driven back to the villa.

At seven o'clock they assembled in evening dress for the present-giving ceremony. Flora, wearing an elegant gown of steel-grey satin, sat by the window, and as they all came in, they laid their parcels on the table beside her. Edward was in charge of the champagne, and when everyone had a glass, he proposed the toast.

'To Flora Cicely Carlyle – mother, mother-in-law, grand-mother and great-grandmother! Many Happy Returns of the Day!'

'Happy Birthday!' came the reply as glasses were raised.

Flora nodded and smiled, raising her own glass in acknowledgment. 'Bless you all. As always, I'm delighted to have you with me to celebrate my birthday, especially, as Edward reminds us, my great-grandson. May he be the first of many!'

She leaned forward and picked up the nearest parcel. *'To dearest Gran, with all love – Emma,'* she read aloud. The gift was a silver photograph frame, which was duly exclaimed over.

Annabel leant back in her chair, watching as the pile of wrapped parcels decreased and an array of presents took their place. From herself and Simon she had bought a Caithness glass paperweight in a swirl of colours that would look well in the Hazelwood drawing room, and she was relieved when, on opening it, Flora's pleasure was evident.

Their glasses were topped up, and at last all the gifts were unwrapped. Flora made a general speech of thanks, but they knew that after they'd returned home, they would receive another, more personal thank-you note. Grandmother was nothing if not punctilious.

Dinner followed, more formal and elaborate than their previous meals. Annabel was seated between Tom and David and opposite Simon, who had Emma on his left.

Although Emma had become briefly animated when her present was admired, she had now withdrawn again and spoke only when directly addressed. The wine flowed freely, and Annabel noted, a trifle anxiously, that Simon was becoming flushed and his eyes over-bright.

Individual spinach soufflés were followed by lemon sorbet, strips of plaice in a cream sauce, and noisettes of lamb on croutons, with a selection of vegetables. A delectable cheese board was then produced, and finally, as the lights dimmed, the birthday cake, extravagantly iced and with a few token candles glowing brightly. They sang 'Happy Birthday', Flora blew out the tiny flames, and the staff cut the cake quickly and efficiently into portions. The level of conversation was by this time quite high, and Annabel had to lean forward to hear what people said. Then, suddenly, it dropped away, and she saw that Emma had risen to her feet and everyone was looking at her expectantly.

'I think we should have another toast,' she announced, her voice ringing nervously in the suddenly quiet room. She raised her brandy glass. 'To those no longer with us – Grandpa, my mother Hilary, and Aunt Monique!'

There was an embarrassed pause, then they all raised their glasses and drank.

Emma was still on her feet, her eyes a little wild. 'I know you all think I'm neurotic, but I'm telling you now that I'm going to find out who killed my mother. I'm not sure how, but I won't give up until I do.'

By now the silence was electric. Annabel found her hands were tightly clenched, and made a conscious effort to relax them. Edward, on Emma's left, touched her arm placatingly, but she shook him off.

'I went back to Llandinas,' she went on defiantly. 'I persuaded Tom to take me, and we went down on the beach, to the same place where we'd sat that day. And we went to look at the house.'

'So did—' Simon began, and broke off abruptly. Annabel went hot.

Emma turned to look down at him. 'So did who?' she demanded. 'You?'

Miserably aware of his slip he shook his head, avoiding her eyes.

'Annabel?' she persisted, and looked across the table. Annabel's cheeks flamed, but there was no way out of this.

'Yes,' she admitted quietly.

'When?'

'A couple of weeks ago.'

Douglas was staring at her in consternation. 'But why, after all this time? Because you'd found Monique's diary?'

'No.' She shook her head violently. 'It was before I knew about that.'

'Then for God's sake, why did you go?'

Flora hadn't spoken, but the quick glance Annabel flashed her showed she'd grown pale.

No hope, now, but to tell the truth. 'I met a journalist who'd been in Swansea at the time,' Annabel said in a low voice. 'It was his idea I should go back.'

'A journalist!' Flora spoke at last, a wealth of incredulity in her voice. 'You went back with *the press*?'

'No, I went with a friend, but it was because he'd roused my curiosity. It didn't do any harm, for Heaven's sake!' she added with a flash of spirit.

'Nor any good either, I imagine,' Flora returned drily.

Annabel was silent. She was damned if she'd tell them about Janet Evans or her inexplicable blackout, and she prayed Simon wouldn't, either. Fortunately, he was subdued after his faux pas. Emma was still on her feet, staring at Annabel.

'Why didn't you tell me?' she asked accusingly. 'When I was talking about that last day?'

'It – didn't seem the right time,' Annabel said lamely. She hoped Emma wasn't going to run from the room again, but after an interminable minute, she finally sat down.

'Has anyone else been back to Llandinas?' Flora asked

with an edge to her voice. 'If so, let's get it over, once and for all.'

No one spoke.

'Right,' said Flora firmly, 'then we shan't speak of it again.'

With which edict they were all glad enough to comply.

Nine

B efore breakfast, Annabel tapped on Emma's door.
'Now it's my turn to apologize,' she told her. 'I'm
sorry, Emma. I didn't mean to upset you last night.'

Emma turned away. 'You're just like the rest. I thought
I could talk to you – we *did* talk, and I thought we were
being frank with each other. But when I told you about that
last day, surely the natural thing would be to say you'd just
been there?'

'If you'd said you'd been back yourself, I would have
done,' Annabel defended herself, 'but we started talking
about our mothers, and the moment passed.'

'Tell me now, then,' Emma invited.

The request hung on the air a fraction too long, and
Annabel, who should have been expecting it, floundered.

Emma's eyes narrowed. 'Something happened, didn't
it?'

If she admitted her blackout, Annabel reasoned, Emma
would immediately connect it with her infant self, screaming
in terror on the night of the murder. And the assumption
would follow that Annabel – and by default Monique – must
have been there when it took place. She was incapable of
laying her mother open to such suspicions, even if she was
uncomfortable with them herself. Instead, as a substitute,
she threw in Janet Evans.

As she recounted the meeting and the story Janet had
to tell, Emma's face lit with excitement and she clasped
her hands together. 'There! I always knew there must be
someone who knew something!'

'Emma, it's not much use, really. She hardly saw the man, and his appearance will have altered. She wouldn't be able to identify him.'

'But if she's existed all these years without anyone tracing her, there could be other people, with even more important information.'

'I don't want to give you false hope,' Annabel said weakly. 'The police—'

'The police!' Emma exclaimed scornfully. 'They've had all this time, and what have they done, apart from grilling poor Daddy?'

'An enormous amount of questioning and statement-taking, I should think.'

Emma shook her head dismissively. 'Could I have Janet Evans's address?'

'Sorry, I haven't got it; she just gave us a number to ring, and Stephie – my friend – threw it away.'

'But I must speak to her!' Emma cried. 'Don't you see, Annabel? She might have remembered something else! Will you ask your friend if she still has it? Please?'

'Emma, I saw her throw it away.'

'Then I'll have to go there, and track her down.'

Annabel said with a smile, 'There are a lot of Evanses in a Welsh phone book!'

Emma sighed in frustration. 'There must be something I can do. Would the journalist be any help?'

'He'd want to splash it all over the papers – "Daughter still searching for mother's killer" and so on.'

Emma grimaced and thought for a minute. 'Your mother's diary,' she said diffidently, 'did she mention that holiday?'

'I don't know. I've been looking through it, but so far I've not found anything.'

'You will tell me, if you do?'

'If there's anything relevant, yes.'

'Thanks. Right, let's go to breakfast.'

*   *   *

144

The first part of the drive to Topsham was the way Annabel had come on Monday, but after a while they turned off, following a long road which, after a level crossing, eventually led to a winding village street dropping down to the River Exe.

'The Quay Car Park is at the bottom of Fore Street,' Annabel read from her scribbled directions. *'If it's full, there's a free one up the hill.'*

They were lucky enough to find a space, and, having parked, set off as instructed along the Strand. It was an attractive road, with gardens on one side and on the other tall, gabled houses built in the Dutch style and painted in pastel colours. It was one of these that Neil had rented for the past two months.

A brass ship's bell hung beside the door and Simon gave it a tug. They could hear it jangling inside, and a minute later Neil opened the door.

'Good to see you!' he said enthusiastically. 'Come in.'

He was wearing a vivid blue open-neck shirt, stone-coloured denims and sandals. Quite the artist, Annabel thought with amusement.

He led them into a large, light room at the back of the house which overlooked a paved garden, made colourful by tubs of multi-coloured geraniums. The room was pleasantly if impersonally furnished, and they seated themselves on a chintz sofa while Neil poured their drinks.

'Where are your parents making for now?' Annabel asked.

'Torquay – they set off yesterday. The intention is to follow the coast round as far as Plymouth, then start wending their way back home. I hope the weather holds for them.'

'How's the painting going?' Simon enquired. 'Edward was saying you've an exhibition coming up.'

'That's right; which is why I came down here, away from any distractions. I've done quite well, too, several new canvases. A large part of the display will be work I did in South America, but I needed some variety, so over the last few weeks I've been concentrating on river- and seascapes.'

'May we see them?'

Neil made a small, apologetic gesture. 'Would you mind if I said no? They still need quite a lot of work, and I prefer no one to see them till they're finished.' He smiled. 'Mother can never understand this; when I'm working from home she's forever wanting to "take a peep", as she calls it, at the end of each day.'

'Fair enough,' Simon said easily. 'I'm not surprised you've done well here, though, it's a picturesque spot. I'm almost inspired to paint myself!'

'It's great, isn't it, and I'm particularly lucky to be living on the Strand. These were originally merchants' houses, you know, built in the seventeenth and eighteenth century, at the time when Topsham was a bigger port than Exeter. After lunch we'll walk out along the Goat Walk, and you can see more of it. Incidentally, I've booked a table at a local eating place. It's excellent food, and I wouldn't want to submit you to my cuisine!'

Just before one o'clock they left the house and walked back past the car park and a short way up Fore Street to the restaurant.

'Looks impressive,' Simon commented, as they were handed menus.

Annabel chose potted shrimps followed by fresh crab salad. 'With the sea so near, I might as well be fishy!' she said.

Neil was sitting across the table from them, and once or twice she looked up to find him watching her. Eventually, perhaps feeling an explanation was called for, he put his knife and fork down and leaned back in his chair. 'It's time I owned up and admitted I had an ulterior motive in inviting you here today.'

They looked at him enquiringly.

'I have a proposition for you, but don't say anything until you've had a minute to consider it. All right?'

'All right,' they agreed, exchanging a puzzled glance.

'The point is, I would very much like to paint a couple of portraits of Annabel,' he said.

She put her glass down, gazing at him wide-eyed.

'Good God!' said Simon.

'You see,' Neil went on quickly, speaking now directly to her, 'my portrait collection's a bit sparse, and I need at least a couple more. I've been keeping my eyes open for someone who would fit the bill, and over lunch in Exeter, I knew I'd found her. If you agree, of course.'

'I – don't know what to say.'

'How about yes? But I don't expect a definite answer today. Go away and think about it, but what I propose is this: my let here ends next week, and the parents have talked me into going back home for a while. I would need quite a few sittings, which would each last about an hour. Either I could come to Bristol, or you to Cheltenham, whichever you prefer.'

'She hasn't much spare time,' Simon put in. 'She often brings work home in the evening, and the weekends are pretty frantic.'

'Obviously I'd fit in any way I could.'

Simon turned to Annabel. 'What do you think, darling?'

'I really don't know. I suppose it would be quite exciting.'

'On the contrary,' Neil assured her, 'boring is the word that springs to mind! Sitting still for an hour is incredibly difficult, and you'll get very stiff. But you have an expressive face, Annabel, and I'd very much like to paint it.' He paused, and when neither of them spoke, added, 'I'd be happy to present you with one of the portraits afterwards.'

'Oh, Neil, I couldn't take it! It would be worth a great deal of money!'

'Think of it as a thank-you, for agreeing.' He smiled. '*If* you agree!'

The waiter came to remove their plates, and a minute later wheeled over the dessert trolley. Annabel's mind was spinning. Did she want to be painted, or not? It was an honour to be asked, but did she really want thousands of people staring at her picture? Suppose she didn't like it?

They made their choices, and as the trolley was wheeled away, Neil said firmly, 'We won't talk about it any more. I'll phone you before you go home, and you can give your answer then, though if you've any questions in the meantime, call me any time.'

He handed her a card giving his mobile number. 'Right, now let's enjoy the rest of the meal.'

When they left the restaurant twenty minutes later, Neil having insisted on paying the bill despite Simon's protests, they walked to the end of the Strand and on to a narrow path running alongside the estuary. The river was quite wide here, and on the far side they could see a tiny train moving behind some trees. It was cooler by the water, with a stiff breeze blowing, but Annabel welcomed it on her hot cheeks.

'That's Exmouth right at the end,' Neil pointed out, 'and on the opposite bank is Dawlish.'

As they walked, Annabel joined in the conversation but her mind was circling round and round Neil's proposition. She might never again have the chance of having her portrait done, and he'd made an extremely generous offer, with the gift of a finished picture. She'd be a fool to refuse.

By the time they returned to the house it was nearly four o'clock and they declined Neil's offer of a cup of tea. 'I think we should be making a move, before the rush-hour traffic builds up,' Simon said. 'If you have such a thing down here?'

'Round Exeter, certainly, but you should be all right the way you're going. Give my regards to the family; obviously I'll look them up when I get back to Cheltenham. When are you leaving here?'

'Saturday morning,' Annabel said. 'We have to be out of the villa by noon.'

'Then I'll phone you tomorrow evening.' He held out

his hand, and she took it. 'I'll be keeping my fingers crossed!'

'Thanks for the lunch, Neil,' Simon said, shaking hands in his turn. 'And good luck with the seascapes.'

As they walked back to the car, Simon gave an expressive whistle. 'Well, what do you think about that?'

'I don't know. One minute I think yes, the next, definitely not.'

'He might want to paint you in the nuddy,' he remarked casually, with a sidelong glance.

'In that case, the answer would most certainly be no.'

'I've not seen any of his portraits, have you?'

She shook her head.

'No idea whether he goes in for photographic representation or the more airy-fairy stuff. Could be no one would recognize you anyway.'

It had clouded over by the time they reached Budleigh, and a few spots of rain were falling. At the villa, the family had retreated to the sitting room for tea, and extra cups were brought for Annabel and Simon.

'Where's Emma?' Annabel asked, looking round the room.

'She went for a walk,' Douglas replied. 'She should be back soon. How was Neil?'

'Full of bright ideas.' Simon sat down and accepted his cup of tea. 'He wants Annabel to sit for him.'

There was a general murmur of interest. 'For the exhibition?' 'What fun!' 'How interesting!'

'She hasn't agreed yet,' Simon said quickly. 'There are a lot of practicalities to consider, time being one of them.'

'What does Neil suggest?' Charlotte asked.

'He says either he can come to Bristol or she can go to Cheltenham. It would have to be at weekends, of course.'

'Annabel?' Flora prompted. 'You're keeping very quiet about this; how do you feel?'

'Well, it's an honour, of course, to be asked.'

'You could become famous,' Celia told her, 'like Picasso's model. Neil's in the top league now; I read a crit recently that said he's regarded as one of the most important modern artists.'

Annabel was startled; she hadn't appreciated that. 'Well, as Simon said, it's a question of fitting it in. If Neil came to Bristol—'

Flora cut her off with a sweep of her hand. 'Totally impractical. He would have to bring all his equipment and set it up somewhere in your home that has enough space and the right light, and all for an hour's sitting. Whereas if you spent a few weekends in Cheltenham, you could probably fit in two sittings each day, and everything would be to hand. And, of course, you would stay at Hazelwood.'

'Well, that's very kind of you—'

'Not at all. I like the idea of my granddaughter's portrait in a prestigious exhibition. Also, it will give us all a chance of seeing you, which we don't often have.'

She meant Douglas, Annabel knew, and was touched.

'Naturally,' Flora went on, 'Simon will be equally welcome, though since you'll be engaged all the time, it might not be very interesting for him. And I'm sure he wouldn't mind sparing you for a few weekends, for the sake of posterity.'

It seemed Annabel's mind had been made up for her. Looking at Simon's face, though, she knew he resented Flora's intervention, and, in fact, probably didn't want Neil to paint her anyway.

'That's settled, then,' Flora announced with satisfaction. 'You must let me know which weekends you'll be up.' She glanced out of the window, where the rain had increased to a steady drizzle. 'If Emma doesn't come home soon, she'll be drenched.'

'She's probably sheltering somewhere till the worst of it blows over.'

'What's everyone been doing today?' Annabel asked,

glad of the change of subject. 'Have we missed any-thing?'

'No,' Edward said, 'we tended to split up and do our own thing. Tom, Celia and I followed your example and went into Exeter. We were most impressed with the cathedral.'

'I never managed to go inside,' Annabel said ruefully. 'Meeting the Camerons upset my plans.'

'Well –' Flora rose to her feet – 'I think I'll go and have a rest before changing for dinner. I still have some postcards to write.'

The rest of them chatted for several more minutes before dispersing in their turn, Annabel and Simon making a dash to the annexe through the now heavy rain.

'You're going ahead, then,' Simon said flatly, when they reached their room.

'Why not? It's a chance I'm not likely to have again. You heard Grandmother – you're invited too. You could play golf with Tom, or—'

'No, thanks; the idea of hanging about waiting for you to come back doesn't appeal. If I have to do it, I'd rather do it at home.'

'You don't *mind* about the portrait, do you?' she challenged him.

'I can't say I'm all that keen.'

She smiled. 'Because it will interfere with your creature comforts? Never mind, it'll probably only be for a couple of weekends. I'll stock up the freezer, and as you know, your parents will be more than happy to see you. You could spend the night with them, if you wanted.'

'Thanks, but I can think of better things to do,' he said.

It wasn't until they gathered again for drinks that it was realized, with a sense of shock, that Emma had still not returned.

'But she's been gone over five hours!' Douglas exclaimed. 'Where on earth can she be?'

'Did she say where she was going?' Tom demanded.

151

'No, just for a walk. Said she needed some exercise.'

'She might have had an accident,' Flora said anxiously. 'Someone should go and look for her.'

'I will,' said Tom instantly.

'I'll help you,' offered Simon and David together.

Tom laid a hand quickly on Edward's arm. 'Don't worry, Dad, it'll be OK. We'll find her.'

'We'll have your meal kept hot for you,' Flora assured them, as they hurried in search of raincoats.

It was a depleted and subdued gathering who sat down, all at one table, that evening, and conversation was sporadic. Etched on Annabel's memory was a picture of Emma at this same table the night before, and her defiant declaration: *I'm going to find out who killed my mother.* But surely no one could have taken that as a threat; they were all *family* here. As they had been in Wales, said the small voice inside her. Had whoever searched her room taken more drastic action this time?

None of them had eaten much, and they were halfway through their dessert when they heard the front door burst open and almost immediately Tom appeared in the doorway, dripping with rain, his face red with exertion.

'We've found her,' he announced breathlessly, 'but it's not too good, I'm afraid. She's halfway down a cliff, on a ledge of some kind.'

Edward had started to his feet. 'She is – all right?' he demanded hoarsely.

'We're not sure, Dad. The ledge broke her fall, thank God, but it depends how she landed. We've alerted the police and ambulance, and the coast guards are there with ropes and pulleys. I just popped back to tell you.'

'I'm coming with you.'

'No, Dad, really. There are enough people milling about, and it's pretty treacherous up there, with all the rain. Honestly, there's nothing you can do.'

'I'm coming with you,' Edward repeated grimly, and, with a shrug, Tom gave in.

'You'll be bringing her back here?' Flora asked, her voice shaking.

'It depends if she's hurt, Gran. All being well, we will. Try not to worry; she's in good hands now.'

Edward reappeared in his raincoat, and the two of them left together.

'Be careful, Tom!' Celia called after him, but the front door had already slammed shut. Edward's pushed-back chair and abandoned gateau added to everyone's unease.

'I wish I'd thought to ask if she's conscious,' Flora said.

Douglas put his hand over hers. 'I think a spot of brandy in the coffee wouldn't go amiss,' he said. 'We're all in need of it.'

The next hour was one of the most uncomfortable Annabel had spent. To add to the tension, Teddy awoke crying, and, most unusually, refused to settle. Eventually Celia brought him down and sat rocking him in her arms, her face pale, while Annabel, pushing stories of telepathy from her mind, tried not to read any significance into his distress.

Someone turned on the television and they sat watching the news, every nerve stretched for the sound of the front door. Surely they must have pulled her up by now? Suppose she was seriously hurt – or worse? Would Tom and Edward have gone with her in the ambulance? But then Simon or David would come back to tell them.

There was a knot of anxiety in Annabel's stomach which no amount of reasoned logic would dispel. The wet evening had darkened prematurely, but no one made a move to draw the curtains, and the rain pattering against the windows could be heard over the low murmur of the television.

At last there was the sound of voices outside, and they all came instinctively to their feet, staring at the door as Simon and young David came in.

'Well?' Flora's voice was hoarse.

'She's all right, Gran,' David said quickly. 'At least, she's not seriously hurt; she's sprained her ankle, but it's shock and hypothermia they're worried about. She's been taken to hospital and will probably stay in overnight. Uncle and Tom have gone with her, but they'll be back later.'

Flora reached out behind her, and lowered herself into her chair. Only then did Annabel realize the depth of her grandmother's fear, and her heart went out to her. What was it Martin had said? *I hope history doesn't repeat itself.* It seemed she had not been the only one to fear that.

When Simon and David had changed out of their wet clothes, their dinner was brought through on trays. They ate ravenously, while more questions were fired at them, but it still seemed unclear exactly what had happened, nor how long Emma had lain on the ledge. When, eventually, they reached their room, Simon was more forthcoming.

'She was hysterical,' he said, 'going on about someone following her. We couldn't get any sense out of her.'

Annabel went cold. 'She's not saying she was *pushed*?'

'Not in so many words, and you know what she's like; ten to one it's all in her mind.'

'But she's not badly hurt?'

'No, she was damn lucky there. Concussion, bruises, a sprained ankle, that's all.' He paused. 'It's her mental state that worries me. She's never been the most balanced of people – I hope this doesn't tip her over the edge.' He smiled grimly. 'No pun intended.'

Annabel lay in bed listening to the rain still beating against the windows. Suppose the stalker had *not* been in Emma's imagination, and had been after her as a direct result of her comments over dinner? Of those present, only her father, Flora and Edward had been among the adults in Llandinas. Flora, Annabel immediately discounted. Edward would never harm his daughter, whatever the provocation – he was devoted to her. In any case, he, Tom and Celia had been in Exeter. Which left Douglas. What had her father been doing this afternoon, and on that other afternoon twenty-eight years ago, for which he had no alibi?

She turned over, pulling the duvet more closely about her and evoking a protesting grunt from Simon.

Then there was her dream, which, rightly or wrongly, she now attributed to the tragedy. If she had been in the house at the time, then so had her mother.

A woman's as capable as a man of hitting someone over the head. Did Martin's remark have any hidden meaning? Had rumours been circulating about her mother at the time? Perhaps that was why he was so anxious to keep in touch with her.

Desperately, she tried to reason away her fears. All right, Monique had a temper; it was not inconceivable that she might have lashed out at Hilary, with no intention of any lasting harm. But why? Surely not because of some passing attraction to Edward?

As, finally, she fell into a disturbed sleep, she realized with a feeling of total despair that, by her own reasoning, the two people most likely to have killed Hilary were her own parents.

The rain had cleared away by morning, leaving everything drenched. The sky was a clear blue with high white clouds, but the day's brightness was not enough to lift the spirits of those gathered round the breakfast table. Edward and Tom, who had arrived back late the previous night by taxi, had little more to report. Edward had phoned the hospital first thing, to be told that Emma had had a reasonable night and could return home after the doctors' rounds later in the morning.

'Did she say any more about what happened?' Charlotte asked.

'Not really. She thought there was someone behind her, but I don't think she actually saw anyone.'

'But even if there was, why should that alarm her?'

Douglas asked reasonably. 'There are always people on the coastal path, there's nothing sinister about it.'

Edward shrugged helplessly. 'I think she got herself thoroughly worked up. She does, sometimes.'

Annabel spoke in Emma's defence. 'When we walked into Budleigh on Sunday, she was very calm and self-possessed. It's a long time since I really talked to her, and I was impressed by her common sense.'

Tom said in a low voice, 'She has mood swings, Annie, that's the trouble. One minute she can discuss anything with you, the next, she withdraws inside herself. Sometimes, even I can't reach her.' He paused. 'Since Gran isn't here, I can say that these weeks away always put a strain on her.'

'Well,' said Charlotte comfortably, 'we're going home tomorrow.'

It was an oddly disjointed day; none of them seemed able to settle. Edward was filling in time before he could go and collect Emma from the hospital, Holly and David had gone off in search of a tennis court, and Celia seemed concerned about Teddy, who was still fretful.

'Probably getting a tooth through,' Charlotte suggested.

Despite the sunshine, there was a cool breeze and none of them fancied going in the pool. Douglas, Charlotte, Simon and Annabel had a game of croquet in the garden, which generated a lot of good-natured competitiveness, and when it ended, set off to walk into Budleigh for a pub lunch. The width of the path dictated that they walked two abreast, and Annabel found herself with her father. How, she wondered, could she tactfully ask where he was yesterday afternoon? Or, for that matter, on the afternoon of the murder?

'When you come up for your sittings,' he said, 'I do hope you'll come and visit us.'

'Thank you – yes.'

She'd seldom been to her father's house since Monique had left him. On her visits to Cheltenham, they usually met at Hazelwood – neutral ground, Annabel belatedly realized.

Perhaps that was Flora's doing, for her grandmother must have known that on the few occasions Annabel had revisited the house, it no longer felt like home. When Douglas and Charlotte married, they had virtually gutted it – put in a new kitchen, added en suite bathrooms, completely refurnished and redecorated. Perhaps, she thought now, they were trying to lay Monique's ghost. Certainly the original house had borne a strong imprint of her personality.

Douglas glanced sideways at her, and, perhaps guessing the direction of her thoughts, said quietly, 'She was happy, wasn't she, your mother? In her second marriage?'

'Oh, yes. George adored her.'

'Adoration isn't always enough,' Douglas said, and Annabel cursed her thoughtlessness.

'They were happy,' she assured him gently, 'like you and Charlotte. You were both given a second chance.'

'And how about you and that handsome young husband of yours? Are you happy, too?'

'Of course!'

'Then all is well,' he said quietly.

The pub lunch was mainly notable for the fact that, for the first time, the four of them were alone together, sitting round a table like a normal family. There were no awkward pauses, and conversation flowed lightly and pleasantly throughout the meal. A first, successfully negotiated.

Afterwards, they walked along the beach for some distance in the opposite direction, so that by the time they returned to the villa it was mid-afternoon. They found Edward alone in the sitting room. He looked tired, Annabel thought.

'How's Emma?' she asked quickly.

'Not too bad, but she has to keep her foot up to help the swelling. Fortunately she'll be able to rest it on the back seat going home.'

'Could I go and see her?'

Edward hesitated. 'She might be asleep. I think, despite hospital assurances, she had rather a disturbed night.'

'I'll go in quietly,' Annabel promised.

Over in the annexe, she gently turned the handle of Emma's door and put her head round. Emma was sitting up in bed and turned quickly at the sound, relaxing when she saw who it was.

'How are you?' Annabel asked, going over to the bed.

'Alive, thank God.' Her voice was jerky.

'I brought you a magazine. Flowers didn't seem a good idea, with going home tomorrow.'

'Thanks.' Emma glanced at it absentmindedly, then, catching hold of Annabel's arm, said in a taut voice, 'Someone was there, Annabel. I swear it.'

'I should think a lot of people were,' Annabel said gently, remembering Douglas's comment.

'*Following* me, I mean.'

'Or just going in the same direction? A pity you didn't stick to your original plan of staying in the garden.'

'I wanted some time to myself, but up there on the cliff I suddenly felt so *vulnerable*! I can't imagine what possessed me to go in that direction.'

'Can you remember what happened just before you fell?'

'I've been over and over it in my head. It was starting to rain, and I wanted to turn back, but then I'd have come face to face with – whoever it was. So I had to keep going. It was like one of those ghastly dreams, when you know you're going further and further from safety, but haven't any option. Then the rain came on more heavily and I knew I was a good half-hour from here. I thought, *This is ridiculous!* and turned quickly – and I'm *sure* I saw someone dart behind a bush. I panicked, I suppose, and decided to make a run for it, giving him as wide a berth as possible. But I went too near the edge, slipped on the wet grass, and the next thing I knew, I was going over the top.'

'So no one actually pushed you?'

Emma held her eyes and gave a long sigh. 'No.'

'And you didn't actually *see* anyone?'

'Only out of the corner of my eye.'

'But it was just an impression, wasn't it, Emma? Because you were frightened?'

There was a silence. Then Emma said listlessly, 'Perhaps.'

'Did you scream as you fell?'

'Too right I did! Long and hard.'

'And no one came? No one looked over the top to see what had happened?'

'I don't know; I banged my head against the rock and passed out for several minutes. When I came round, my head was aching agonizingly and my ankle throbbing, and I was alone with the cliff and the sea. I didn't dare move, the ledge was so narrow, and I couldn't have stood anyway, with my ankle. So I started to call.'

'And no one came?'

'No. Eventually I think I passed out again, because the next thing I knew was my name being called, and Tom peering down at me from the cliff-top. And by that time I was shaking so hard with cold and shock that I couldn't speak, and I was terrified of rolling off the ledge.'

'What a ghastly experience.'

'If the ledge hadn't be there, that would have been it.'

'Don't think about that – you're safe now. God, Emma, you gave us a fright.'

'I gave myself one.' She smiled a little. 'Tom's always complaining that I'm over-imaginative. He blames it on all the books I read.'

'I'd rather have too much imagination than too little.'

'So would I, most of the time.'

They smiled at each other. Annabel said, 'At least one good thing has come out of this holiday; I feel I know you all better. And when I come up to Cheltenham—'

Emma looked surprised. 'You're coming up?'

'Of course, you won't have heard: Neil wants to do a couple of portraits of me, for the exhibition. I haven't confirmed it yet, but as he's going to be with his parents for a while, the sensible thing seems to be for me to come up at weekends, for the sittings.'

'That's great, Annabel, congratulations! If Neil's as good as everyone says he is, people might be looking at your picture hundred of years from now!'

'What a terrifying thought!' Annabel stood up. 'Well, I must let you get some rest and make a start on the packing. Are you coming over for dinner?'

'I think I should make the effort, since it's the last night. Tom has offered to carry me across. Thanks for looking in, and for the magazine.'

'See you later, then.'

Outside the door, Annabel drew a deep breath of relief. It seemed, after all, that any specific threat had been solely in Emma's head, for which she was inordinately thankful.

Neil phoned half an hour later, and was delighted to hear her decision. He would be driving to Cheltenham the following Wednesday, and it was decided she should go up for the first sitting the next weekend.

'Since I'll be doing two portraits,' he said, 'I'd like you in contrasting outfits. For the first, an evening or cocktail dress with a fairly low neckline and bare shoulders. Have you anything suitable?'

'There are a couple that might do.'

'Bring them both, and we'll see which would be best. For the second we'll need something less formal – a shirt and trousers, say, but that can wait for the moment. How soon could you get there? Will you be going up on Friday evening?'

She hesitated, aware of Simon pretending not to listen. 'No, I don't want to be away more than one night. But I can leave early and be with you by nine.'

'Fine. The first session will be less structured, anyway. I often spend most of it talking to the subject, getting to know the person behind the face, deciding on clothes, the

160

best position, and so on. So – nine o'clock on Saturday, at number seven.'

'I'll be there,' she said.

'Not wasting any time, is he?' Simon commented sourly, when she relayed the arrangements. 'Probably afraid you'll change your mind.'

'I shan't be in the nude, anyway, you'll be relieved to know!'

He grinned reluctantly, and she reached up to kiss his cheek. 'One of these days we might have a masterpiece hanging on our wall, so make the best of it, there's a love. Now, hurry up and have your shower, it's time to get ready for dinner.'

Ten

Annabel was relieved, on reaching home, to find the bulky package she had posted in Exeter awaiting her.

'What's that?' Simon asked curiously, as she picked it up off the mat together with a pile of smaller envelopes.

'Nothing much.'

'But it's in your handwriting!'

'If you must know, it's Maman's diary. You were right, I shouldn't have taken it to Devon, so I posted it back here.'

He stared at her. 'Why the hell bother, once it was there?'

She shrugged and he gave a deep sigh of incomprehension, which she ignored. The diary, she reflected ruefully, seemed to be causing trouble on all fronts.

She had just put the first load in the washing machine when George phoned.

'Hello, my darling, welcome home! How did the ordeal go?'

'Suffice it to say I survived!'

'Not as bad as you feared, then?'

'It had its moments, but this year I really felt I got to know them all better.' She paused. 'Especially Daddy. In fact, I invited him and Charlotte to come down one weekend.'

'That's great!' George said heartily.

'You don't mind?'

'Why on earth should I mind you seeing your father?'

'I – felt a bit disloyal. To you, I mean.'

'My darling girl, what nonsense! I'm delighted you're

coming together after all this time. From what I saw of Douglas, he seemed a decent enough chap. So – what were the bad moments you spoke of?'

She bit her lip, annoyed with herself for mentioning them. 'I brought them on myself,' she admitted. 'I stupidly took Maman's diary with me, thinking I might have more time to go through it down there. And they found out.'

'So? It's not a hanging offence, surely?'

'No, but Grandmother went frosty, the way she always does when Maman's name comes up.' She paused, and he was sure she was holding something back.

'And *did* you get a chance to look through it?' he prompted.

'Only very briefly.'

He couldn't stop himself asking, 'Anything come up about the holiday?'

'No.'

'But something else did,' George pursued intuitively, 'something that's worrying you.'

'It's just—' She broke off, and started again, glad that he couldn't see her face. 'I found out that their marriage wasn't right almost from the start. I hadn't realized that.'

'She mentioned other men?' George asked quietly.

Annabel caught her breath. 'You knew?'

'She admitted there'd been one or two – indiscretions.'

Had she told him about Edward, Annabel wondered, almost sure she had not.

'Annie, listen. I loved your mother dearly, but I knew she wasn't a saint. Don't judge her, darling. She was just a normal, passionate woman, and she had her faults like the rest of us.'

'Yes,' Annabel said after a moment. 'I probably put her on a pedestal.'

'No one can stay up there for long,' George commented wryly.

'No.' Anxious, now, to change the subject, she hurried on. 'By the way, I have some news for you: Neil

Cameron's going to paint my portrait! What do you think of that?'

Talk of the portrait took up the remainder of their conversation, and by the time he replaced his receiver, George was more or less convinced that all was well. Ever since Nigel saw Simon with that woman, he'd been worrying about his stepdaughter. And he was also anxious about that infernal diary; if only he'd kept those papers to himself, and simply destroyed them. He'd had no idea how frank Monique had been in her writing, but if she'd mentioned the affairs which had upset Annabel, it was quite likely there'd be a full account of what happened in Wales. As far as she knew it, of course, George told himself hastily. And what would happen when Annabel found that?

Annabel's second phone call that evening was much less welcome.

'Ah, the wanderer returns!' said Martin's voice in her ear. 'All in one piece, then?'

She said stiffly, 'Hello, Martin; do you want to speak to Simon?'

'No, I want to speak to you. How did the jaunt go? Anyone else murdered?'

'I told you I didn't want to hear from you again. You promised—'

'Ah, but you forfeited that by going to Wales behind my back. Furthermore, you compounded the felony by keeping quiet about that witness you found. Underhand dealing all round. You need to be taught a lesson, my girl.'

'What do you want, Martin?' she asked coldly.

'Suppose I said I'd found out something?'

'I shouldn't believe you.'

'Your loss, then, if you prefer to read about it in the papers.'

He was bluffing, Annabel told herself. Of course he was.

'Look, my lovely,' he went on, when she didn't speak, 'I

was prepared to play it by the book, but you bent the rules. Your privilege. But the gloves are off now, so don't expect any favours. If I find what I'm looking for, and it blows your cosy little family apart, you'll have the satisfaction of knowing you brought it on yourself.'

'Goodbye, Martin,' she said, and put down the phone.

Simon poked his head round the kitchen door. 'Who was that?'

'Your friend Martin, uttering threats.'

'What about, for God's sake?'

'The family scandal, what else?'

'You're not still on about that? Honestly—'

'Speak to him rather than me, Simon,' she said crisply, and ran past him up the stairs, leaving him staring after her.

At breakfast the next morning, Simon announced his intention of spending the day in the garden. 'The grass will take ages to cut, it's grown amazingly this last week. I just hope it keeps dry long enough for me to finish it. Did you hear the forecast?'

'Cool, with showers,' she replied.

'Flaming June!' he said. 'What are you going to do? You won't have any schoolwork today.'

'No,' she answered steadily. 'When I've finished the ironing, I'm going to have a real go at Maman's diary.'

She braced herself for a sarcastic comment, but none came and he merely nodded, his mind obviously on the garden. Accordingly, after a swifter than usual session with the ironing board, Annabel collected the envelope and took it into the sitting room, where she curled up in a corner of the sofa. This time, she resolved, she wouldn't stop until she found what she was looking for.

When she tipped out the papers, the topmost page was the one she'd been reading when interrupted by the Camerons in Exeter. *It is quite exciting, making love between all the packing cases!* She bit her lip, flicked through the next dozen or so pages, and, out of sequence, came across some earlier comments on Robert the shopkeeper.

10th November.
This evening, I went to the home of Sarah Lloyd for her first coaching session. It is an interesting house, full of antiques, paintings and old books in leather bindings. It seems her father is an antiquarian bookseller who has a shop just off the High Street. He told me he has several French volumes, if I'd care to go along one day. Sarah is much better behaved in her own home, and really concentrated on her work. Afterwards, Mr Lloyd insisted on walking home with me, and raised his hat when we parted at the gate. He is quite old – well in his forties, I would guess – and his waistline has expanded. But he has a nice face and warm brown eyes which are *très sympathique*.

17th November.
Again to Sarah Lloyd, and again Monsieur walked me home. He spoke of his book shop, and invited me to go and see his treasures. I think he is quite interested, which I find amusing.

20th.
Today I was shopping in the High Street and decided to look at Mr Lloyd's shop. I don't think he does much business; no one came in all the time I was there. He was very glad to see me, and showed me some early editions of Maupassant and Victor Hugo, though if he hoped I would buy them, he was disappointed. While we were looking at them, I deliberately brushed against him, and he became flustered. So I was not mistaken! This could be interesting!

So that was how it had started – very much, it seemed, at her mother's instigation. Annabel had no wish to read of the wooing of Robert Lloyd, and riffled quickly through the next few pages. She was working on a system of checking the first sentence on a page against the last on the preceding one, but this wasn't infallible. Once or twice they seemed to follow on perfectly, and it was only after several paragraphs that she realized they didn't belong together.

In the end, it was almost too easy. She came across a jumble of pages written in a slightly different coloured ink which she hadn't registered before. They were all mixed up, some facing inwards, some upside down, but as she sorted them out as she'd done so many others, the word 'Llandinas' jumped out at her.

She stopped dead, heart pounding, scarcely able to believe she'd found it, nor the lucky chance that Monique should have used a different pen while away on holiday. Once she'd assembled this wad into order, she would have the account she'd been looking for. And quite suddenly, she wasn't sure if she wanted it. What would she know, minutes from now, that perhaps it would be better for her not to know?

She stood up abruptly and walked to the window. Simon, his back to her, was setting off down the lawn behind the mower. This, she told herself, was here and now. Whatever she might read in the next few minutes wouldn't alter the fact that she and Simon were here, safely in their own house, in the present. What had happened twenty-eight years ago was powerless to alter that.

Slightly comforted, she returned to the sofa and the waiting pile of papers.

Saturday 27th May 1972.

The same date as they'd travelled down this year, Annabel thought, with a superstitious shiver.

Today, we came to Llandinas. Annabel woke early, so Douglas played with her while I finished the packing. So much to take for one small child! The journey

167

was uneventful, and now that more of the motorway is open, a lot quicker than when we last visited Wales. Monsieur et Madame came down yesterday, so everything was ready for us.

The house is on the sea front, the last of three, with trees to one side. It is quite narrow, especially the hallway; it will be necessary to keep the pushchair in the porch. There is only one reception room, which runs from the front to the back of the house. The front portion is the sitting room, with the dining area at the rear. As there are only four bedrooms, Annabel's cot is in with us. The twins are next door; I hope they do not make too much noise.

So – for the next week, Edward and I will be under the same roof. I am sick with excitement, but frightened, also, that I might give myself away. It has been so long now, with never a word between us that others could not hear, yet we do not have to speak, and I think we both accept that sooner or later we will come together.

Annabel settled with no trouble – the journey must have tired her – and we went downstairs for drinks. Edward turned as I entered the room and our eyes met for a long moment. God, I want him so badly!

Fortunately, Monsieur Henri came forward to kiss me and I had time to collect myself. He is a dear man – I am so fond of him. When Annabel was born, knowing I'd never known how to address them, he told me I could now call them Grand-mère et Grand-père. While I did not suggest 'Mémé' for Madame – it is far too informal – I said I should prefer to call him Pépé, explaining it was the more familiar name for Grand-père, and he laughed and agreed. I do not think Madame approves; she does not like the French. Hilary calls them Ma and Pa, like Edward, but I could not do that. And even though I now address Madame as Grand-mère, I still think of her as Madame.

Annabel looked up suddenly as a scene she had long forgotten came clearly into her head. She saw herself in the drawing room at Hazelwood, aged, probably, six or seven – it was, at any rate, after Pépé's death. Flora was handing her a bar of chocolate, and she took it, murmuring, 'Thank you, Grand-mère.'

Whereupon Flora said, quite sharply, 'What is the English word for "Grand-mère", Annabel?'

She had not understood, and remained shyly silent. Flora repeated the question, adding for clarity, 'What does "Grand-mère" mean?'

'Grandmother,' she had whispered.

'Exactly. Well, you're a little English girl, aren't you, so don't you think it would be better if you called me that?'

So it was not of her own volition that she used that stiff form of address, Annabel thought. She had been told, very early on, how to address Flora, though she'd forgotten until the passage she'd just read provided what Martin would call a 'trigger'. She returned to the text.

> Hilary seemed a trifle *distraite* this evening. I asked what was wrong, and she said there was a problem at work, but she did not intend to think about it on holiday. The meal was enjoyable, cooked and served by outside staff. I had a headache, and the strain of trying not to look all the time at Edward made it worse. I excused myself soon after dinner and came upstairs. Annabel is sleeping soundly, the little love. I hope that tomorrow, there will be a way to be with Edward.

Annabel, by now frantic to read about the murder, flicked quickly through the next few pages until, in a hand very different from normal, she came to the date Tuesday 30th May. Taking a deep breath, she began to read.

> Oh God, God, God, God, GOD! I must write down

everything that happened today, or I shall go out of my mind. Over and over I ask myself, was there anything we did that would have made a difference? I cannot see it, but this guilt is beyond bearing. And Edward – I do not know if we shall ever speak again. Madame was right to dislike me; though she does not know it, I have destroyed her family.

I hear the voice of Tante Aimée in my head – 'Calme toi, cherie, calme toi!' as she used to say so often. I shall try. I write this in an hotel bedroom, but I do not think any of us will sleep tonight. Annabel has been screaming and crying for hours, and only now is she quiet, from sheer exhaustion. If I have in any way harmed my baby, caused her lasting damage by my actions today, I shall never forgive myself, never!

But I must set it all down in order, to try to make sense of it. If only at some point in this terrible day I could stop the clock, make everything right again! I DO NOT BELIEVE IT HAS HAPPENED!

So – breakfast was as always. Madame took hers in her room, the rest of us discussed what we should do today. The twins want, always, to go on the beach, but the day was a little overcast. Pépé suggested we drive somewhere this morning, and they could go down this afternoon. They argued, of course – they always argue – but when Pépé told them there was an old castle they could explore, they agreed quite readily.

We went in two cars, Douglas and I, with *la petite*, in that of Monsieur et Madame, and drove across the peninsula to Weobley Castle. It is a curious name, and is pronounced 'Webley', though the twins thought it amusing to call it 'Wobbly'. It is in ruins, and they amused themselves running and hiding and climbing, while the adults walked about reading the guide book, which was very interesting.

There seemed to be a coolness between Hilary and Edward; she continually walked ahead of him, talking pointedly to Douglas or *les vieux*. On the way home, as is the custom, we stopped to buy ham and cheese and fresh bread for lunch, which is not provided by the staff.

As Pépé had thought, the sun had by this time come through, and we had a picnic in the garden. It was, I think, the last happy time of our lives. The picture is clear in my mind, of the twins on the grass, of Madame in her straw hat, of Edward and Douglas talking together, and Hilary – Hilary supervising everything, as she always does. Did. So little time ago, but now another world.

When we had finished eating, the twins at once asked Edward to take them to the beach, but he said he must first buy a battery for his shaver. Hilary asked why he had not bought it while we were out that morning, and he replied there was nowhere suitable, which was true. So she said she would take them, and Madame offered to go with her. Annabel is too young for the beach and tries to put the sand in her mouth, so I decided to take her for a walk instead. Earlier, Douglas had asked me if I'd mind if he went to the cinema that afternoon; there was a film he wanted to see, which did not interest me. I did not, of course, care what he did; all I could think of was Edward. Pépé, who is a fit man for his age and takes a lot of exercise, then announced he was going to climb Cefyn Bryn, a nearby hill which has some prehistoric remains. (I have gone into detail here, because it is important.)

Since we often split up during the day, each couple has a key to the house. Douglas gave me ours, because he would be later back than I should, and Edward gave theirs to Hilary. We have an arrangement that the first one back leaves the door unlocked for the others. Oh God, if only we had stayed all together! But with no thought of disaster, we went our separate ways. Annabel has a sleep after lunch, so I was the last to leave the house. I sat in the garden reading for a while, but I could not concentrate. Inside me there was such a hunger for Edward, I did not know how I could bear it.

At about three o'clock, long after the others had left, Annabel woke. I put her in her pushchair and set off in the opposite direction from the village, past the trees and on to the cliff path that runs all the way along the coast. The afternoon was warm and there were several people walking up there. A lady spoke to Annabel, who was looking very pretty in her pink sunbonnet. She was fascinated by the seagulls swooping overhead, and when a little boy threw some bread for them, they landed quite near to us. She pointed at them and struggled to get out of her pushchair, but we were too near the cliff edge and I dared not let her out.

Stupidly, I had forgotten to take her drink of orange juice, and soon she started asking for it. I distracted her as long as I could, but finally she became upset, so I turned and started to walk back to the house. It was quite a long way, and by the time we reached it she had fallen asleep again. I did not want to wake her by lifting her out of the pushchair, but nor could I leave her alone in the garden, so I pushed her inside, closing the door on the latch.

Annabel looked up with a frown. If the door had been on the latch, why had Hilary needed a key to let herself in, as Janet Evans had described? Perhaps that would be explained later.

I'd intended to leave her in the hall, but it was so narrow that anyone coming in would be unable to pass her, so I wheeled her into the sitting room and pulled the door to. Then I went up to my room. I was hot after my walk, and since before dinner there was always a queue for the bathroom, I decided to have my shower then.

And now I come to the part that is so hard to write, with my emotions in such turmoil. *Calme toi.* I had just pulled my shirt over my head when I heard a sound behind me. I spun round and there, standing in the doorway, was Edward. He said, 'Monique.' That was all. And then I was in his arms and he was kissing me and everything exploded inside me as we tore off each other's clothes and fell together on to the bed. And it was wonderful and unbelievable and heart-stopping and all the other words which fall so far short of describing it. And the strange thing was that neither of us said a word except each other's names, over and over.

And then I heard it – a sudden, terrified cry which I knew was Annabel's – and my heart seemed to freeze. I rolled off the bed, grabbed my dressing gown and fled downstairs, wondering if she had somehow fallen out of the pushchair and hurt herself. The front door was standing open and as I turned into the sitting room, the first thing I saw – to my total disbelief – was Hilary lying face down on the floor, her head covered in blood. Beyond her, Annabel was sitting up in her pushchair, her face scarlet, screaming and sobbing and beating her little hands on the cover. I stood immobile, frozen with shock, until Edward, seconds behind me, pushed me aside and knelt by Hilary, feeling for a pulse. Then he looked up at me, totally without expression, and slowly shook his head.

Stumbling past them both, I ran to the baby, scrabbled to free her from the pushchair and clasped her to me, trying to soothe her. Edward said, 'Get dressed as quickly as you can and take her away.'

'Where?' I stammered, not understanding.

'Anywhere! Where you were this afternoon. Don't come back for at least an hour. And Monique – listen to me!' This because I had started to sob and shake. 'Whatever happens – *whatever happens* – you are to say *nothing* about all this. Do you understand? You have not been back to the house, you have not seen either me or Hilary, and everything I say you will accept. *Do you understand?*'

And as I nodded, he steered me out of the room and gave me a shove towards the stairs. I fled up them carrying the screaming baby, and pulled on my clothes. By the time I reached the hall again, he had moved the pushchair into the porch. Annabel struggled violently as I tried to strap her in, and my shaking hands made it even more difficult.

'Wait!' Edward said, again in that hard, cold voice, and he went outside and looked up and down the road. There was no one in sight. There never is, in mid-afternoon.

'Go,' he said, 'and remember – not a word!'

The next hour is a blur. My mind had gone into overdrive after experiencing such powerful emotions in so short a space of time. The joy of our lovemaking had, in the space of a moment, been obliterated by the sight of Hilary lying in her own blood. How? Who? Why? None of the questions had an answer. I prayed endlessly, uselessly. Please God let it be a mistake, don't let her be dead – let her just be injured. Please do not let this happen. But underlying it all I knew that this was our punishment, for what we have done.

So I arrived back at the house an hour later, with the baby still fretful and crying, to find police cars lining the road and the rest of the family gathered in the front garden. Douglas came running to meet me, his face white.

'Darling, the most appalling thing has happened!' he said, holding on to my arms. 'It's Hilary – someone has killed her! Edward found her when he got back, about an hour ago.'

I stared at him blindly, and past him, to Edward who was kneeling on the grass hugging the twins. And then the tears came, and I could not stop crying. And Douglas held me, soothing me, as I had Annabel.

We were allowed only briefly into the house to collect overnight things. The sitting room had been sealed off with tapes and there were men in white coats moving around inside. Then we were brought to this hotel, and the police interviewed us each in turn. I did as Edward told me, and did not mention my earlier return to the house, or what had happened then. We are all in shock, and do not know what to say to each other. Hilary was so alive, so busy always, so much in control. It seems impossible that this could happen.

Simon's voice called, and it was a moment before she registered it.

'Hey! How about some coffee for a thirsty worker?'

Annabel put the diary down and stood up, totally disorientated. 'OK,' she called back. 'Coming!'

She went through to the kitchen, her mind still reeling, but with a feeling of overwhelming thankfulness. Her mother had not after all been involved in Hilary's death, and the reason for her lifelong reticence and guilt was now explained. And unless Edward had killed Hilary before going upstairs – which was surely inconceivable – he, too, was in the clear. Which left Pépé and her father.

She ran water into the kettle, her mind still in the past. *Had* Douglas gone to the cinema that afternoon? Had her grandfather gone hill-climbing? Neither had been able to prove it.

The back door opened again and Simon came in, running a hand through his hair. 'That looks a bit better, doesn't it?' he said.

She turned a blank face towards him. 'What does?'

'The grass,' he explained with heavy patience. 'What do

you think I've been doing for the last couple of hours? I need to go over it again, but I've got the worst off. It'll make a difference when I've done the edges.'

'It's fine,' she said numbly.

'What have you been doing?'

He'd obviously forgotten what she told him, but she couldn't, possibly, go into it. Not just now. 'Reading,' she said, and he laughed.

'All right for some! How about a spot of weeding, then?'

'After lunch,' she promised, glancing at the clock. It was eleven thirty.

He nodded, apparently satisfied, and took his mug outside with him. Annabel watched him go.

Her dream. All her life, she as well as her mother had been haunted by that scene. And all the years that Monique had come to her when she woke, frantic and crying, from the nightmare – how must she have felt? *If I have in any way harmed my baby, caused her lasting damage by my actions today, I shall never forgive myself.* Her punishment had certainly been long-lasting.

Slowly Annabel returned to the sitting room and the discarded heap of manuscript. There was one final brief entry, dated a month later.

28th June

These last weeks have been a continuing nightmare. Edward was arrested and spent two days in custody before being released without charge. I know the police still suspect him. I managed a word with him, on one occasion only, and begged him to allow me to give him an alibi. He refused. 'For the sake of Douglas and the family,' he said. I knew then that he was bitterly ashamed of what had happened, that he blamed me, and hated me for his own weakness. He will never forgive either himself or me for what we were doing at the moment that his wife was murdered.

Though there were dozens of pages still to be sorted, Annabel knew instinctively that they'd been written earlier, and that this was the last entry her mother ever made in her journal. For herself, she didn't want, or need, to know any more. What had started pleasurably with the account of Monique's first visit to Hazelwood had become a task less and less to her liking. She wished she hadn't learned of her mother's early disenchantment with her marriage, or her liaison with Robert Lloyd. There might be more names if she dug deeper, and she did not want to know. As it was, her image of her mother had altered irrevocably, though as George had pointed out, Maman's past had made her into the woman she was, and Annabel did not love her any the less.

She gathered all the papers together, slipped them into the envelope, and returned it to the cardboard carton under the stairs. At least her nightmare had been explained, and could surely now be consigned to oblivion.

Except— She paused, her hands still on the lid of the box. The dream had started to progress; it was only very recently that Monique's face had materialized, bending over her. Suppose – just suppose, in its next visitation, she saw that of the murderer? And recognized him?

She straightened suddenly, catching her head on the low ceiling of the cupboard. The killer himself was unlikely to know about her dream, but he *could* be concerned that by some quirk of memory she might remember seeing him, as he must have seen her, in her pushchair.

Oh, God, she thought, let him after all have been the passing tramp that Martin had so contemptuously dismissed. There *were* cases of random killings, quite a lot of them, and the question of motive still remained unsolved. It seemed unthinkable that either her father or grandfather could have committed the deed, yet who else was there?

Annabel frowned, then, kneeling in the cramped space, took out the envelope again and flicked back to the beginning of the murder account. Monique had written: *Hilary*

177

seemed a trifle distraite *this evening. I asked what was wrong, and she said there was a problem at work.*

What kind of problem? What kind of work? Could that conceivably be of importance, or was she clutching at straws? When she was in Cheltenham, she would find a way of asking Edward what Hilary had been engaged on prior to her death, and whether she'd discussed any problems arising from it.

She dropped the envelope back into the box, closed it determinedly, and stood up. It seemed her detection work was not, as she'd hoped, quite finished after all.

Eleven

At break the next day, Stephie was eager to hear about the holiday.

'How was Devon?'

'All right, thanks.'

'Did your cousin provide the flashpoint you'd feared?'

'A couple, actually, but nothing too drastic.' Annabel steered her gently off the subject. 'The big news, though, is that I'm going to have my portrait painted.'

Stephie, bless her, was easily diverted. 'My goodness! Who by?'

'Neil Cameron, a friend of the family, who's an artist.'

'The dishy one you always fancied?'

Annabel flushed. 'When I was eight or nine,' she said repressively.

Stephie laughed. 'Come off it, your eyes lit up when you mentioned him in Wales! Anyway, tell me more. When and where is this great event to take place?'

'I have to go up to Cheltenham for the next few weekends, for sittings. I'll be staying with Grandmother.'

'Into the lion's den, eh? Or the lioness's, I should say. And what's the object of the exercise? Does he want a memento of those days of innocence?'

'No,' Annabel answered steadily, 'it's for an exhibition he's giving in London.'

'Wow! Imagine all those toffee-nosed people with catalogues, gazing at our little Annie!'

Annabel smiled. 'It's a daunting thought, isn't it?'

'What does Simon think about it?'

'He's not too impressed, actually, but only because I shan't be there to cook his dinner.'

'So how did all this come about?'

'I bumped into Neil and his parents in Exeter, and we had lunch together. Then he invited Simon and me to the house he's renting in Topsham, and put the idea to us.'

'*Very* exciting,' Stephie said. 'I shall make a point of going up to London to look at it.'

'You might not need to; Neil's going to make us a present of it afterwards.'

'Well! I've never heard of that before! You *have* got him hooked, haven't you?' She paused. 'As a matter of fact, I've some news, too – of a sort. I had a phone call from Martin.'

So her diversionary tactics had been in vain. 'Whatever did he want?' she asked irritably.

'He enquired solicitously after my health, then asked if we'd found out anything more about the murder.'

Annabel looked quickly round the staff room, but no one seemed to have heard. 'What did you say?'

Stephie grinned wickedly. 'I said, "Not for publication"! I thought that would get him going! He rose to the bait beautifully.'

'At least he was more civilized than he was with me. I had a call, too, last night. He told me I'd blotted my copybook, and that given the chance he'd tear the family apart.'

'Charming! He's bluffing, though; he was anxious enough for more info when I spoke to him. I can't think why he's so hung up on this case; there must be dozens of others he's worked on.'

'Spite,' said Annabel. 'Basically, he's punishing me for going to Wales with you, having turned him down. Oh, and he heard from one of his contacts that Janet Evans had been to the police; so that was another black mark, for not telling him about her.'

'But he'd gone home!' Stephie objected.

'Exactly; that's what I said, but it wasn't a good enough excuse.'

Stephie, fiddling with her coffee cup, shot her a glance from under her fringe. 'He thinks it was probably your mother,' she said diffidently.

'Does he really? And how did he reach that conclusion?'

'Search me. Probably spite again!'

'Well, I'm as certain as I can be that it wasn't.'

Stephie nodded, thinking it a predictable reaction. It was frustrating, but Annabel couldn't admit to having proof and she was glad, now, that she'd not confided in Stephie about the diary; she might have had difficulty fending off her questions, and she'd no intention of betraying her mother's secrets, even to vindicate her.

'Have you had the dream again?'

'No, thank goodness.' Of course, Annabel reflected, it would have been the dream that aroused Stephie's suspicions of Monique; it had been she who'd picked up the 'toddler height' factor.

The bell rang for the end of break, and to Annabel's relief the conversation necessarily came to an end.

Simon sat at his desk, staring through the glass partition to where Lucy stood talking to a colleague. She was wearing a linen skirt that came just above her knees, and his eyes lingered on her legs. If Annabel was going swanning off with Neil, he didn't see why he shouldn't have a bit of fun too, he thought rebelliously. It was a bit much, leaving him alone for an unspecified number of weekends. Come to that, if she hadn't gone to Wales without him, the thing with Lucy would never have started.

She'd been odd again last night, too, withdrawn, not listening to what he was saying. He'd hoped that after the holiday things might have been better between them, but there wasn't much sign of it. Well, two could play at that game. He'd give Lucy a ring later in the week and, if she was free, arrange to see her on Saturday. They could be discreet – he was as concerned as she was about that. He'd no intention of scuppering his marriage, just of pepping it up a bit with some outside interest.

Decision reached and conscience assuaged, Simon opened the file on his desk and settled down to work.

Annabel was feeling guilty about Simon as she drove home. After much consideration she had decided not, after all, to tell him of her findings. It wasn't, she argued to herself, as though he'd shown any interest in the diary, but the main reason was to protect her mother and Edward. He was sure to make some ribald remark, and would henceforth regard her uncle in a different light, which she didn't want. Edward had already paid highly for his infidelity, and Simon wasn't known for his tact. He could easily blurt out some reference which would be picked up by Flora or Douglas, with unknown but probably disastrous consequences.

And since she couldn't mention the diary, nor could she confide her fears about the possible interest of a murderer. But here, she told herself firmly, drawing up outside her home, she was letting her imagination run away with her.

The phone was ringing as she opened the front door, and she hurried in, catching it up with a breathless, 'Hello?'

There was silence. She said again, 'Hello?' and heard, very distinctly, a receiver being replaced.

Wrong number, she thought. They could at least have apologized. On impulse, she dialled 1471, only to be told that the caller had withheld their number.

Dismissing it from her mind, she went into the kitchen and began the preparations for supper.

'Edward, what is it? You haven't seemed yourself ever since you came back from Devon.'

'I'm sorry, love. I've a lot on my mind, that's all.'

'But what? Wouldn't it help to talk about it?'

'In this instance, no.'

Suzanne studied him worriedly. She knew he hadn't been

looking forward to this enforced holiday, and had been increasingly unsettled as it approached. But now that it was over, she'd expected him to revert to his normal, gently humorous self.

She had cooked a special meal to welcome him back, and had looked forward, after more than a week's absence, to being with him again, but so far he had been quiet and withdrawn, obviously having to force himself to respond to her increasingly desperate attempts at conversation.

She sat beside him on the sofa and took his hand. 'Please tell me,' she said quietly.

He sighed. 'It's just that, either rightly or wrongly, I've always thought I was a reasonably civilized individual.'

She smiled. 'I doubt if anyone would argue with that.'

'Well, they should, because I've proved to be quite the opposite.'

'In what way?'

'I've behaved appallingly badly, totally in my own interests, and in the process no doubt caused considerable anxiety, to say the least.'

She frowned. 'When did this, whatever it is, happen? In Devon?'

'I don't want to talk about it,' he said.

And that was all she could get out of him. It was obvious he was in no mood for lovemaking, and she could see he was about to make some excuse and leave early. But she wanted to comfort him in the only way she could, not to mention satisfying her own need, which was stronger than she cared to admit. So they made love, tenderly rather than passionately, after which, unusually, he fell asleep.

Suzanne lay looking at him, at the pronounced eyebrows, the stubby lashes lying on his cheek, the greying brown hair. He looked younger in sleep, more vulnerable, but the creases either side of his nose and between his eyes were still apparent. For the first time, with a twist of pain, it struck her that his was not a happy face, and she wished passionately that she could put right what was worrying him.

Her eyes moved to the clock on the bedside table. He would never forgive her if she allowed him to sleep beyond his set time for leaving. Gently, she put a finger on his mouth.

'Edward,' she whispered, 'time to wake up.'

He stirred, moved his head restlessly, and, as she bent forward to kiss him, said, quite distinctly, 'Monique.'

The second phone call came on the Tuesday, again as she returned from school. Again there was silence on the line; again, after a long minute, it went dead.

Annabel stood immobile, the phone slippery in her suddenly sweaty hand. Then she dropped it back on its cradle and rubbed her hand down her skirt. Could this after all be deliberate? If so, did the caller know she had just come in, that she was alone? Was he standing across the road watching her? Or was it all just chance, a coincidence? Without hope, she dialled 1471, and again learned that the number had been withheld.

Well, she told herself, it hadn't been an obscene call, nor even a heavy-breathing one. All the same she was relieved that the next time the phone rang, an hour later, Simon was there to answer it.

'For you!' he called. 'Cassie.'

She dried her hands and picked up the kitchen extension. 'Hello, Cassie! How are you?'

'Fine, thanks. Annie, we were going to invite you both over at the weekend, but Pop says you'll be away.'

'That's right, in Cheltenham.'

'Well, it's short notice, but could you manage an evening during the week instead? It's a long time since we've seen you. Especially Simon,' she added, her voice changing slightly.

Annabel noted the change, and wondered at it. 'I have a girls' night tomorrow,' she said, 'but otherwise I think we're free. Simon tends to arrange things at the last minute. Just hold on, and I'll ask him.'

He appeared in the doorway, and she put her hand over the phone. 'We've nothing on this week, have we? Cassie and Nigel would like us to go for a meal.'

He made a brief grimace, which annoyed her. The times she had to suffer his parents! 'Nothing definite, no,' he said. 'Which evening?'

Annabel relayed the question.

'Would Thursday be all right? If Saturday's an early start, you won't want a late night on Friday.'

'Thursday would be fine,' Annabel said, lifting an enquiring eyebrow at Simon, who nodded confirmation.

'As soon after seven thirty as you can make it, then. Look forward to seeing you.'

'Did you say you were out tomorrow?' Simon asked, topping up his glass.

'A girls' night – I told you. We're trying out that new restaurant down by the river.'

'You're never in these days,' he said in an aggrieved tone.

'Come on, Simon! This is a once-a-term thing! Go to the pub; you haven't seen them for a while.'

'Oh, don't worry, I'll find something to amuse myself. It's a bit of a drag, though, having to trail over to Marlborough midweek. I hope you'll drive home!'

'Don't I always?' she said.

The following evening when Annabel returned home, she was almost expecting the call, and was not disappointed. She stood just inside the door, watching the bleeping instrument and making no attempt to lift it. After several rings the answerphone cut in, and she listened to Simon's message. There was a pause, then the call was terminated.

'Gotcha!' she exclaimed inelegantly. If she pursued that course of action, he'd get tired eventually. All the same, it was an uncomfortable feeling; whoever it was seemed to know within minutes when she arrived home each day.

With time in hand, she had a leisurely bath and washed

her hair. Then, a towel wrapped round her head, she opened her wardrobe, surveyed the clothes hanging there, and took out the two dresses which might be suitable for the portrait. One was an apricot chiffon, off-the-shoulder with a draped bodice and tight-fitting skirt. She wasn't sure how comfortable it would be to sit in for any length of time. The second was more formal, a brocade evening gown in turquoise and gold which she'd worn to Simon's office ball.

Take them both, Neil had said. She shrugged, put them back, and, towelling her hair dry, went out on the veranda and leant on the rail. The sun, brilliant in a stormy sky, was hot on her damp head. It had been a day of sunshine and heavy showers, and the evening seemed set to continue the pattern.

The last time she'd stood here had been the night she had her dream. A lot had happened in the intervening weeks, she reflected: Wales, the discovery of the diary, Devon. Behind her, she heard the sudden ringing of the phone, and her mouth went dry. Robbed of catching her the first time, was he trying again?

She fled on bare feet down the stairs and stood, heart pounding, as the answer machine again clicked into action.

'Hello, Annabel,' came Neil's voice, and with a gasp of relief she snatched up the instrument.

'Neil – hello, I'm here!'

'Hi. Just phoning to say I've arrived back and am looking forward to seeing you on Saturday. You're still OK for that?'

'Yes – yes, of course.'

'And you'll bring both outfits with you, so we can make a choice?'

'I've just been looking at them.'

'Fine. About nine, you said? See you then.' And he rang off.

She put down the phone, resenting her moments of panic and determined not to let the unknown caller reduce her to that state again. Simon's key sounded in the lock, making

186

her jump, and he came into the house, pausing as he caught sight of her.

'What on earth are you doing, standing there in your dressing gown?'

'I've been on the phone. But as a matter of fact, there've been one or two odd calls lately. No one there when I pick it up.'

'Wrong number,' Simon said dismissively, dropping his briefcase on the floor and flicking through the mail on the hall table.

'Three days running, and always at the same time?'

He frowned. 'Have you tried 1471?'

'Of course. Number withheld.'

'So who do you think it is?'

'I've no idea.'

'Could be some sales promotion – computer-operated. Programmed to keep phoning till they get a reply.'

'But they did get a reply, twice.'

'Faulty machine, then. It happens.'

'Does it?'

He put a careless arm round her. 'Often. Don't worry, it's not likely to be Jack the Ripper after you.'

'That's a relief,' she said.

They had an enjoyable evening, the six of them, at the Riverside. It was good to meet outside the confines of the staff room and exchange sometimes scurrilous gossip about other members of staff. Good, too – though they kept it to a minimum – to compare the progress of difficult pupils, which methods had achieved the best results. For the most part, though, their conversation was strictly non-shop – clothes, films, books, plays, relationships.

When they emerged from the restaurant, the pavements were glistening and wet but the rain was over. Calling goodnight to each other, they separated and went in search of their cars. Annabel, still smiling at a joke Josie had told, turned into the multi-storey and started up the steps towards the third level. Behind her, out of sight round a bend, she heard the sound of other footsteps. Nothing unusual in that, she told herself, aware nonetheless of her lack of foresight; a more open parking place would have been more sensible. She began to hurry, imagining that whoever was below had also quickened his pace. She'd have been happier to hear voices, but it seemed he was alone. If, of course, it was a he.

To her relief, however, the footsteps stopped at the second level. Those phone calls must have worried her more than she'd realized. To convince herself that all was well, she went down a couple of steps and peered through the entrance to the second floor. Only a few cars were still there, and she was in time to see a man get into one of them. A minute later its door slammed.

There! she told herself. Satisfied?

She hurried up to the next level, let herself into her own car, and drove carefully down the winding exit way. At the second level, a car moved into place behind her. The man from the stairwell? Surely he'd have been on his way before now?

Her heart was pounding again as she drove down to the exit, fumbled for her ticket, and, with an anxious glance in the rear-view mirror, pushed it into the machine. The car was directly behind her, ignoring the vacant machine alongside. In an agony of impatience she waited for the barrier to rise and drove quickly through, seeing the other vehicle emerge a minute later. Trying to ignore it, she turned right and then left, and the car behind did the same. As she drove round the busy Centre, she was praying he wouldn't follow her up Park Street, but his headlights were still remorselessly behind her as she turned up the hill.

By now, her hands were sticky with sweat. Hundreds – thousands – of people came this way home, she told herself, and only a couple of days ago she'd warned herself against an overactive imagination. But suppose he really *was* following her? Wasn't she supposed to drive to a police station and ask for help? Where *was* the nearest police station? The last thing she must do was lead him to her home – though if this were the anonymous caller, he already knew where she lived. Oh God, Simon, I wish you were here! What price the faulty computer now?

When, after negotiating the Triangle, he was still behind her, she forced herself to think clearly. If he lived round here, he would merely be going home and she'd been panicking unnecessarily. If, on the other hand, her fears were justified, she could only hope that her local knowledge was better than his and she'd be able to shake him off.

Translating the thought to the deed, she turned sharply down a side street and, without indicating, immediately turned again. Deciding on each move only seconds before putting it into operation, she darted in and out of the residential streets, dodging parked cars and the occasional cat, twisting, turning, doubling back, cutting through.

She was not sure at what point she lost him, but it was a full ten minutes after her last sighting before she felt safe, and, with dry mouth and thundering heart, at last dared to drive home. Fortunately there was a space quite near her gate. She stumbled out of the car and looked behind her. No one was in sight. Hastily she locked the car, ran up the path and, with another quick glance over her shoulder, scrabbled the key into the lock. Come *on*! she instructed it. Open, damn you! Then she was inside, in the blessed sanctuary of home, with the door slammed shut behind her.

Simon did not appear to be in. Annabel went into the dark sitting room and felt her way over to the window. Positioning herself to one side and screened by the curtain, she kept watch for five long minutes. No one drove past. She'd either shaken him off or, confident he knew where she was going, he'd given up the chase. On the other hand – she drew a deep breath – wasn't the most likely explanation that he hadn't been following her at all?

She considered the implications more calmly. Firstly, to be rational about it, the car which had emerged from the second floor was in all probability not the one she'd seen the man get into. Secondly, if it *had* been a personal stalking, he must first have followed her from home to the car park, then to the restaurant, then back to the car park. And for what? It seemed more and more unlikely. The truth, surely, was that her nerves were on edge as a result of the phone calls and her room being searched in Devon. Consequently, she had worked herself into a panic over a harmless citizen innocently driving home. It wasn't his fault he happened to live in the same direction as she did.

Nevertheless, she drew the curtains before putting the light on, and poured herself a restorative brandy. Just as well Simon hadn't been here when she'd stumbled into the house; he must already be starting to think she was paranoid. If she didn't take herself in hand she'd end up like poor Emma, who'd also believed someone was after her.

On which sobering thought, she went upstairs to bed.

'You're looking a bit pale,' Simon said critically at breakfast. 'Not got a hangover, have you?'

'No, I just didn't sleep too well.'

'Did you have a good evening, all blue-stockings together?'

'Very, thank you. Did you?'

'Yep; I rang Phil and we went for a curry.' He paused, eying her shrewdly. 'Not still worried about those phone calls, are you?'

'A little,' she admitted. A lot!

'If it would make you feel better, we could report them as nuisance calls. BT would put a tracer on the line.'

'Let's just wait a while and see if they continue. There've only been three so far.'

He shrugged. 'Up to you. What time do you want to leave this evening?'

'Cassie said be there about seven thirty.'

'I'll try to leave the office a bit early.' He kissed the top of her head, and went to collect his briefcase.

By the sheerest chance, he arrived at the office building at the same time as Lucy.

'Hello, stranger,' she said coolly.

'Hi. I was going to phone you, actually. Are you by any chance free on Saturday?'

She turned to look at him, and he held her glance, though to his annoyance he felt himself flush.

'Why?'

'I thought we could have a spot of supper.'

She raised an eyebrow. 'And what about your wife?'

'She'll be away.' He felt his flush deepen.

'Again? Well, you know my terms, Simon.'

'They're OK by me.'

'I thought you'd taken fright,' she said, amusement in her voice.

'Not at all. Just biding my time.'

She smiled. 'Tactical withdrawal, more like.'

'Well?' he demanded urgently. They had reached the steps, and the conditions she'd referred to demanded no contact within the office.

'Luigi's at seven?' she suggested over her shoulder, and went ahead of him through the swing doors without waiting for his reply.

Simon arrived in his office in a state of triumph tinged with resentment. Why did she have to be so damned offhand? Well, young lady, he thought grimly as he took off his jacket and hung it on the hook, like it or not, I'll be the one calling the tune on Saturday.

The daily phone call came as she was changing to go out – slightly later than usual – but Annabel didn't even go downstairs. There would be no message, and she was more occupied by what exactly she was going to say to George that evening. Of course she'd tell him Monique was in the clear, but she was reluctant to mention Edward. Play it by ear, she told herself – always supposing the chance offered of a private word with him.

As it happened, it came at once. George emerged from his own door as they turned into the drive, and walked to Annabel's side of the car. He nodded pleasantly enough to Simon, and, opening her door for her, kissed her as she got out.

'I was hoping to catch you, darling. I'd like you to have a look at something, if you can spare me a minute.' He turned to Simon. 'You go on in, old chap. We shan't be long.'

Simon nodded and strolled over to Cassie's front door while George shepherded Annabel through his.

'I'm still sorting through boxes and cases after the move, and came across some more of your mother's things.' He gestured to a few items spread out on the sofa. 'I thought we'd disposed of everything, but these must have been overlooked. I wondered if you'd like them.'

Annabel looked, with a catch in her throat, at the familiar scarves which Monique had made so distinctively her own. She could see her mother now, standing in the garden with the wind in her hair and a scarf, casually but expertly tied, fluttering at her throat. She picked up the gauzy things and ran them through her fingers and a lingering memory of Monique's scent drifted from them. Annabel felt her eyes sting, and turned quickly to examine some belts, a couple of handbags and a handful of costume jewellery.

'Yes,' she said huskily, 'I'd love to have them. Thank you.'

'Fine, I thought you might.' He collected them together and slipped them into a carrier bag.

She put a hand on his arm. 'George – Maman had nothing to do with the actual murder.'

He stared at her, relief flooding his face. 'You're certain? You found the passage?'

She nodded, and he asked, as she'd known he would, 'Then why would she never talk about it?'

'Remember I told you about my dream?'

'Of course. Don't tell me it was memory after all?'

'It must have been, because I was there, in my pushchair.'

He looked bewildered. 'Then where was Monique?'

Annabel moistened her lips. 'Upstairs. She heard me scream, came running down, and – and found Hilary lying there. She was horrified – you can imagine – and didn't know what to do. I suppose she panicked – grabbed me, dashed out of the house, and didn't come back till Hilary'd been found.'

George frowned. 'Then why didn't she say so, later?'

Annabel improvised wildly. 'She would have done, once the murderer'd been caught. But he never was, and she was afraid she'd be suspected herself if they knew she'd been in the house. And the longer she kept quiet, the harder it became.'

'She could have told *me*,' George said. 'No –' he shook his head – 'there must have been more to it than that.' He studied her averted face and went on slowly, 'Or are you trying to spare my feelings, my darling? Was she with someone?' His voice sharpened. '*With Edward?* Now that really would make sense, and he hadn't an alibi.'

Annabel let out her breath in a sigh. 'I never could keep anything from you,' she said.

He hardly seemed to have heard her. 'No wonder she could never forgive herself. Poor darling, what infernal luck.'

Annabel flung her arms round his neck. 'Oh, I do love you!' she said.

They found Cassie, Nigel and Simon waiting for them on the terrace. The sun was off the back of the house but spreading itself prodigally over the garden, bathing it in a mellow light, sharpening the colours of the flowers and defining every leaf and twig against the cloudless sky.

'Ah, gathering complete!' Nigel said, rising and coming to kiss Annabel. 'I'll see to the drinks.'

'Simon has been telling us about the holiday,' Cassie commented. 'Did you enjoy it?'

'I'm not sure enjoyed is the right word, but it was OK. I did get on better with them than usual.'

'That has to be a good thing! And I hear you're about to achieve immortality, *grâce à* Neil Cameron?'

'Something like that!'

'Should be fun. What will you wear?'

'I have to take two eveningy dresses with me, and we'll decide then.'

Annabel looked up as Nigel returned bearing an ice bucket and a bottle of champagne. 'My goodness, you're pushing the boat out, aren't you?'

'A family celebration – why not?'

He opened the bottle expertly and poured the fizzing liquid into the flutes. Then he moved round to where Cassie was sitting and put a hand on her shoulder.

'Now, my love, are you going to tell them the real reason for the champagne?'

She smiled, and Annabel was struck by her sudden radiance. 'We've some rather exciting news,' she said. 'We're going to have a baby!'

'Oh, *Cassie!*' Annabel jumped up to kiss first her, then Nigel. 'How absolutely wonderful! I never thought—' She broke off in confusion, and they both laughed.

'Nor did we!' Cassie said. 'We've been trying for ages. Would you believe I'm regarded as an "elderly primigravida" – *elderly*! I've been longing to tell you for weeks, but wanted to be quite certain all was well.'

As Simon bent over her with his congratulations, she proffered her cheek but didn't look up at him, and again Annabel wondered if he'd offended her in some way.

'So when is it due?' she asked eagerly, pushing the thought aside.

'Christmas, would you believe? It'll be quite a celebration this year!'

Annabel turned to George. 'You knew, of course?'

'I was sworn to secrecy. It's wonderful news, isn't it?'

Simon, who'd returned to his seat after shaking Nigel's hand, watched his wife's animated face and remembered his fleeting thought about babies on the Devon beach. They hadn't discussed a family since the early days of their marriage, when they'd agreed to wait a few years. But 'a few years' had now passed, and he wondered if this news of Cassie's would spur her into bringing up the subject again. Though in Devon he'd been quite taken with the prospect, now, his impending date with Lucy very much on his mind, he was not so sure. A baby was an added commitment; was he ready for it?

He looked up to find Nigel's eyes thoughtfully on his face, and took a hasty sip of his drink. For an uncomfortable moment it was almost as though the man had been reading his thoughts. Come to think of it, there'd been a slight cool-ness in both Nigel and Cassie's manner towards him, and even George seemed to have to work at being friendly.

Well, stuff the lot of them. He met Nigel's eyes challengingly and raised his glass. 'We've not had a toast yet,' he said, breaking into the women's chatter. 'So here's to the expected new arrival! Long life and happiness!'

'I'll drink to that!' said George heartily, and they all repeated, 'Long life and happiness!'

Sitting at the dinner table later, Annabel watched Cassie and Nigel with a pang of envy. Love and happiness shone in their faces, in the way Nigel laid a hand on her shoulder as he passed, the way she smiled up at him. Seeing them together like this made her realize just how far apart she and Simon had drifted, and she felt a touch of panic. What was going to happen to them?

In the car going home, she said suddenly, 'You haven't had words with Cassie, have you?'

So she'd noticed it, too. 'Nope. Haven't even seen her for yonks.' He paused. Let her spell it out. 'Why?' he added.

'I just thought she seemed a bit – distant with you.'

'Well,' he said lightly, 'I can't be all things to all women.'

Seeing he was not prepared to discuss the matter, she let it drop and switched on the radio, absolving them from the need for conversation for the rest of the journey.

Twelve

A lthough only just after eight o'clock, the motorway was busy this Saturday morning, though most of the traffic seemed to be going south. She should do the journey comfortably in under an hour.

Forty-five minutes later, as she approached Cheltenham, Annabel felt the usual mixture of anticipation and apprehension she'd known as a child, when being brought here to stay with her grandmother. Still, she wasn't going straight to Hazelwood this time, but to the Camerons' home, off Christchurch Road. The gates were open, but she decided to park in the road, in case the doctor was on call. Originally, so her mother had told her, he had run his surgery from home, but ever since Annabel could remember he'd worked at the prestigious group surgery with the much respected Dr Harrow, who retired a few years ago, making Cameron the senior partner.

Leaving her overnight bag in the boot, Annabel extracted the two dresses, swathed in dry-cleaning covers, and carried them up the drive as the front door opened and Neil came out to meet her.

'You made good time,' he said, kissing her cheek. 'How long did it take you?'

'Just over fifty minutes – most of the traffic was going the other way.'

'Mother insists you'll be in immediate need of sustenance, and has the coffee on.'

She smiled. 'It will be very welcome.'

The Camerons' house was familiar to her from childhood,

when she and the twins came regularly to play with Neil. This large square hall had served as a pirate ship, a space-craft and a desert island, among many other guises. She had a momentary vision of Tom, in a paper tricorn, leaning over the banisters and shouting orders to his crew below.

Moira appeared from the kitchen, and embraced her fondly. 'How was the rest of the holiday?'

'Fine, thanks. We had the usual good weather. "Gran's Weather", Tom calls it.'

'And the birthday itself passed off well?'

'Yes, all according to form: picnic, present-giving, special dinner.' Annabel spoke lightly, holding down the memory of Emma's toast and the embarrassing disclosures that had followed it.

Moira laughed. 'Flora's traditions are set in stone. Neil, take Annabel into the sitting room and I'll bring in the coffee.'

Rex rose to his feet as they went in, and Annabel, noting again his pallor and the hollows under his eyes, was reminded of that unfocussed glimpse of George at the cemetery. Returning his kiss, it pained her to realize that the doctor, too, was growing old.

Rex in his turn was studying her, and – ironically, in view of her own thoughts – remarked, 'You're looking a little peaky, young lady.'

'Hey!' Neil protested. 'Don't go insulting my model!'

'It's not an insult – pale and interesting, that's what she is. But you are all right, my dear?'

'Yes, fine,' she said quickly, embarrassed to find herself the subject of their scrutiny. 'I haven't slept too well the last couple of nights, that's all.'

'Don't worry,' Neil said, as Moira came in with the tray, 'a touch of carmine will work wonders!'

They chatted easily while they had their coffee, and Annabel relaxed. She had known the Camerons all her life, and felt much more comfortable with them than with her in-laws – a thought she hastily buried.

As she put down her cup, Moira said, 'Well, I've strict instructions not to delay you too long, so off you go – and happy sitting! We'll have a snack lunch at about one, if that's all right. What time will you finish this afternoon, Neil?'

'It depends how long Annabel can put up with me.' He added for her benefit, 'Sittings are usually an hour, but can stretch on a bit if things are going well.'

They all looked at her.

'Since I can only come át weekends, no doubt you'd like to get as much done as possible. Provided I have a few breaks, I don't mind carrying on.'

Moira glanced from one of them to the other. 'Half-past three? Four? I promised to phone Flora and let her know what time you'd be over.'

'Make it five,' Neil suggested. 'Then Annabel can relax here for a while.'

In the hall, he took the two dresses out of their sheaths and studied them critically. After a minute, he said, 'I'd like to see you in both of them, if that's OK. You can change in the parents' room.'

She ran up the stairs, not needing to be told where to go; she'd hidden too many times under the Camerons' bed. Quickly she took off her shirt and jeans and slipped the apricot chiffon over her head. Then, self-consciously, she walked down the stairs while he watched her from below.

'I didn't ask you – will it be head and shoulders, or full length?'

'One of each, I think.' He was studying her carefully, not, she knew, as herself, but as the subject of his painting. 'You know, Dad's right; you are a bit pale, and that shade drains your colour even more. Let's have a look at the other.'

Back upstairs, she slithered into the turquoise and gold brocade and, leaning over the dressing table, pinched her cheeks before going down again.

'Ah!' Neil said at once. 'That's the one – it complements your skin tones. Right, up we go, then.'

One of the attics had, many years before, been converted

into a studio for him – a large, bright room with the necessary north light. An easel had pride of place, and, beside it, a table covered with paints, brushes and charcoal. There was an assortment of chairs and chaises longues draped with different coloured cloths, and one or two upright chairs with gold-lacquered legs. To one side stood long trestle tables piled with canvases, and more lined the walls, all facing inwards.

Neil pulled one of the chairs forward, turned it slightly sideways to the easel, and gestured to her to sit down. 'I shan't be using oils today,' he told her. 'I need to get the feel of the picture, how I want to depict you, and so on, so we'll just chat while I make some preliminary sketches. Don't be embarrassed if I stare; I'm afraid it goes with the territory!'

She smiled and settled in the chair, draping her rich skirt about her, and he dragged a tall stool over to the easel and lounged half on and half off it, a piece of charcoal in his hand. *Getting to know the person behind the face*, he'd called it. She wasn't at all sure that she wanted him to.

'So – tell me what you've been doing since I last saw you. Not in Devon, I mean before that.'

Under his prompting, she told him about St Helena's and her routine there.

'You speak fluent French?'

She looked surprised. 'Of course. Maman and I always spoke it at home – when we were alone, that is. Neither Daddy nor George could.'

'And you always wanted to teach?'

'It seemed the natural thing. It was what Maman did, and I wanted to be like her.'

'Things must have been difficult for you, after your parents split up. I never really thought about it at the time.' He smiled. 'I remember you gamely tagging along after Tom and me and doing everything we did. You always had scraped knees and bruised elbows, but you were a brave little thing. You left poor Emma standing, even though she was older.'

'My parents might have split up,' Annabel said quietly, 'but at least they were still both alive. I don't think Emma's ever got over losing her mother.'

He sobered at once. 'No. Again, I didn't make allowances at the time. I just thought she was a typical girl, whining and crying, while you were an honorary boy!'

'Thanks!'

'Hard to believe now, mind!' He hesitated. 'Do you mind all these probing questions?'

'I'll let you know! What's the next one?'

'I was wondering how long your mother was alone after the break-up, and how she coped. You went straight to Bristol, didn't you?'

'Yes. She was determined not to go out to work till I started school, so as she had to earn money coaching privately at home, she thought there'd be more chance of pupils in a big town. Cassie, George's daughter, was one of them.'

Annabel broke off as it struck her for the first time that history had, in a way, repeated itself, though she refused to consider George in the same category as poor Robert Lloyd. In any case, their circumstances were quite different; he was a widower, and Monique by this time a free agent.

For the first time in years she thought of the cramped little flat in one of the most popular districts of town. (Though it stretched their budget, Monique knew that parents wouldn't take their children to less respectable – though more affordable – areas.) And she recalled how, little by little, George had started to stay longer when he came to collect Cassie – for a drink, for supper – and how both she and Cassie had resented it. She'd been five at the time, and Cassie fifteen, jealous of anyone competing for her father's attention.

A picture, long forgotten, flashed into her mind from that time, of them all sitting round the kitchen table with its checked oilskin cloth. 'French seems a strange language to me,' George was saying teasingly. 'My name is George, but Madame here writes it with an "s" on the end, as though there were two of me!' She had reluctantly smiled back at him, even as Cassie exclaimed scornfully, 'Oh, Daddy, *really*!' Annabel smiled at the memory.

Then had come the day when, to her utter bewilderment, Maman told her they were going to leave the flat and go and live with Mr Woodbridge and Cassie.

Neil broke into her musings. 'And then they were married?'

'Not immediately. She said one marriage was enough for anyone, but George finally talked her round.'

'Good for him! And they were happy?'

'Very,' she said firmly.

'So it all turned out well. Excellent. How long have you been married yourself?'

'Nearly four years.'

'I've forgotten what Simon does?'

'He works for an insurance company.' She paused. 'Am I allowed to ask you questions, or is it all one-way?'

Neil laughed. 'Feel free! What can I tell you?'

'What *you've* been doing over the years. Apart from painting, that is.'

'Apart from painting, very little. A bit of a rolling stone, I'm afraid, off on a whim to wherever I thought there might be something worth capturing on canvas. Which was all very well in my salad days, but as my mother keeps telling me, it's time I settled down.'

'But not with Marina?' she asked boldly.

'Not with Marina,' he agreed after a pause, probably surprised by her directness. 'It was a good relationship at first, but it ran its course. We were two opposites, and we tore each other to shreds.'

'You were together a long time, though.'

'Twelve years, on and off. We met at art school.'

Twelve years. Annabel thought back to the first time she'd met the glamorous Marina, and of how jealous she'd been. She had spent most of her life half in love with Neil, and none of her boyfriends measured up to him. Until Simon. Mentally she compared them, dark, charming, moody Simon and blond Neil with his steady grey eyes and enigmatic smile. Which made him sound like the Mona Lisa, thought Annabel, and smiled involuntarily.

'A penny for them?'

'Nothing,' she said hastily, 'just a passing thought.'

'It must have been a good one. You know,' he went on, after sketching for a few minutes, 'it's amazing that I never realized how lovely you are.' Seeing her flush, he added quickly, 'Sorry – I didn't mean to embarrass you; I was speaking as an artist. It must be because I've known you so long; you were just little Annabel, Tom's cousin. But seriously, your bone structure's perfect. Do you ever wear your hair up?'

'I used to sometimes, but I'm not sure it's long enough now.'

He came round the easel and gently swept her hair on top of her head. Then, holding it in position with one hand, he stepped back and surveyed her critically.

'Yes, that's good; it shows off your neck. I think we should be able to secure it with combs and pins. We'll have it like that for one of the portraits, but perhaps the more casual one.'

He let it fall. 'Sorry, now I've messed it up. Do you want to comb it?'

'Not unless you're going to draw it.'

He shook his head. 'I'm not ready for details yet.'

He went back to the easel and made a few more sweeps of the charcoal before coming over to reposition her chair. 'Now, I want you to keep your body in that position but turn your head slightly towards me. No, that's too far. Yes – fine. Hold it there. And relax those shoulders.'

He returned to his stool, but made no further additions to his drawing. 'Have you any long earrings?'

She put an instinctive hand to her ear. 'Sorry – I forgot. I have some drop turquoise and pearl which I wear with this dress; I meant to bring them.'

'Perfect. Next weekend?'

She nodded, watching his intent expression as at last he began to work in earnest. From time to time he spoke, and a brief conversation ensued, but for long stretches of time there was silence. He had put some classical music on the CD player, and she was content to sit and listen to it. It was soothing, after the turmoil of the last few weeks, to empty her mind to the music. Just as she was becoming conscious of stiffening up, Neil said, 'OK, we'll stop for a minute and you can have a stretch.'

Thankfully she stood, arching her aching back, and watched as he switched on a kettle and put out a couple of mugs. 'More coffee! It's what keeps me and my sitters going!'

Remembering his refusal to let them see the painting in Topsham, she made no attempt to go over to the easel. 'Did you finish your seascapes?' she asked.

'Yes, I did half a dozen in all, and several of the estuary. I'm quite pleased with them.'

'So work for the exhibition is going well?'

'I think so; I've been preparing for it for the last eighteen months.'

She took the cup of steaming coffee he handed her.

'You will, of course, be invited to the private view.'

She had barely time to finish her coffee before he moved back to the easel and, taking her cue, she again took up her position. It interested her to see the way he worked, totally absorbed in what he was doing, the quick, decisive strokes and the long periods of inaction while he contemplated first her and then his canvas. At the beginning of the session, those long, searching looks had embarrassed her and she'd wanted to fidget and look away;

but he had warned her it 'went with the territory' and she knew it was not herself as a person he was studying. She schooled herself to relax, and eventually was able to ignore them, concentrating instead on the swelling music.

She was jolted from her reverie by the strident ringing of a bell at the foot of the stairs, and Moira's voice calling, 'Lunch is ready!'

'Damn!' said Neil softly. Then he looked up and smiled. 'Sorry, you must be more than ready for it, after an early breakfast. Let's go down.'

Holding up her long skirt she went carefully down the two flights to the ground floor, Neil following behind. Moira was coming out of the kitchen bearing a tray. 'My, don't you look gorgeous!' she exclaimed.

'Thank you, ma'am!'

However, it was her face, not her finery, that caught Rex's notice, and as they went into the dining room he commented, 'If I were your GP, young lady, I should recommend a tonic.'

'Oh, really, Rex!' Moira exclaimed. 'Leave the poor girl alone!'

'Any reason why you're not sleeping well?'

'Once a doctor, always a doctor!' Neil commented. 'Ignore him, Annabel!'

Hoping to deflect him, she glanced down at the quiche lorraine in front of her. 'That smells gorgeous,' she said, taking the salad bowl from Neil. But she could feel Rex's eyes still on her, waiting for an answer, and reluctantly she looked up to meet them. 'Things have been a bit fraught lately,' she admitted.

'Would it help to talk about it?'

It just might, Annabel thought. It was useless discussing things with Simon – though to be fair he had offered to have the calls traced – and if she confided in George, he would only worry.

'I'm probably getting a persecution complex!' she said

with a forced laugh. 'Weird phone calls, cars following me, that kind of thing.'

'My dear child!' Moira exclaimed. 'Have you been to the police?'

And Rex said sharply, 'What kind of phone calls?'

'Silent ones. Every afternoon, as I walk into the house after school. It's as though someone knows the exact time I arrive home. Nobody speaks, and after a minute the line is cut. Now I just leave the answerphone to deal with them.'

'But somebody's making them,' Neil said with a frown. 'And what was that about a car?'

Comforted by their concern, she told them about her experience returning from the restaurant. 'With hindsight, though, I'm sure it was nothing – just my imagination working overtime.'

'Can you think of any reason why someone could be subjecting you to all this?'

Annabel bit her lip, then shook her head.

'You're sure?' Rex probed.

'Drop it, darling,' Moira told him. 'If she doesn't want to say, that's her business. Now, no more diagnoses, thank you. How did the sitting go?'

Across the table Neil's worried eyes were still on her, but he answered lightly, 'Not bad, for the first one. Annabel's very patient, and she can sit still for inordinate lengths of time. I wish all my sitters did.'

For the rest of the meal conversation was determinedly light, but back upstairs, Neil immediately said, 'Are you sure you feel up to this? Would you like to call it a day?'

'Neil, I'm not ill!' she protested with a little laugh. 'Of course I'm up to it!'

'Well, relax on the chaise longue for a while. I'm not working on your pose for the moment, just your expressions, so you might as well be comfortable.'

'I'm not an invalid, you know. I'm tougher than I look.'

'You always were!' he said. 'I don't like to think of you being harassed, though. Can't Simon do anything about it?'

'He did offer to get on to BT.'

'Then let him. What about the car?'

'I didn't mention it.'

He frowned. 'Why not?'

'Because, as I said, by the next morning I'd convinced myself there was nothing to tell. It's just that with the stresses of the week away, and then the phone calls, it all got on top of me. I was susceptible because I was under par, but I'll soon get my bounce back.'

'Why was the week away stressful? I thought it was supposed to be a holiday?'

She hedged, not wanting to go into details. 'I just meant that it's difficult being with Daddy and his new family; added to which Grandmother never approved of Maman, and it rubs off on me.'

'But that's ridiculous! How could she not approve of you?'

Annabel shrugged. 'Let's just say I've never been close to her.'

'But all those times you came to stay as a child—'

'They weren't easy. Which is why,' she added with a smile, 'I was so glad to come round here to play. Oh, look,' she went on, seeing his expression, 'I'm not after a sympathy vote! I had a secure and happy childhood with Maman and George.'

'And now,' he said, 'you have Simon.'

'Yes,' she acknowledged after a minute.

'You know, Annabel, I'm beginning to think I never knew you at all. What an insensitive clod I was.'

'You were a *boy*! And I was very proud that you and Tom let me join in your games.'

'And now, because of the portraits, you're having to spend more time at Hazelwood. If I'd known, I'd have suggested you stayed here. The parents would have been delighted.'

'And Grandmother mortally offended! Please, Neil, forget it. It's nothing I can't handle. You won't say anything to Tom, will you?'

'Of course not.'

'She's never been unkind, you know. Just not – affectionate.'

He didn't reply, simply turned back to the easel and took up the charcoal again. He worked steadily for about an hour, with sporadic bouts of conversation, and then pushed himself away from the easel.

'I know it's only three, but I think that will do for today. I don't want to tire you.'

'I told you—'

'I know. But I've done as much as I can for the moment. If you'd like to change out of your finery, we can go and join Mother in the garden.'

'As long as you're sure,' she said doubtfully.

'Leave your dress in the bedroom; it's pointless to carry it backwards and forwards.'

She nodded and went down to the Camerons' room, where she changed back into shirt and jeans. She hadn't meant to go into all her troubles, and regretted being coerced into doing so. At least she hadn't mentioned the diary, and fortunately they seemed to have forgotten it. They wouldn't have thought it important, anyway.

So the next two hours were spent in the shade of the cedar, with Moira knitting and Rex pottering among his vegetables. And at five o'clock, she left to drive the half-mile to Hazelwood.

'Tomorrow at nine?' Neil confirmed, opening her car door for her.

'I'll be here.'

'Sleep well.'

She smiled. 'I'll try to have a little more colour for you!'

As she turned the corner on to Christchurch Road, he was still standing at the gate, looking after her.

Hazelwood looked as it always did, a tall, handsome, solid

house set in its established gardens, and with a red gravel driveway leading to the door. Annabel retrieved her bag from the boot and went up the steps to the front door. She rang the bell, and it was a minute or two before Sarah, who'd been Grandmother's maid for many years, came to open it.

'Miss Annabel! Nice to see you, miss. Madam said I was to show you to your room, and perhaps you'd like to relax and have a bath before dinner.'

'That would be lovely, Sarah.'

At Hazelwood you never felt free to wander; you stayed in your room until your presence was required. Was this how it was with Tom and Emma, or David and Holly? But they, living in or near Cheltenham, would never need to spend a night here.

She let Sarah precede her up the red-carpeted staircase, glancing as she passed at the oil paintings which, as a child, had seemed to frown disapprovingly down on her. Perhaps, she thought fancifully, her own portrait might hang on a staircase some day. She hoped she wouldn't look as forbidding as these long-dead Carlyles.

The room she was shown into was the one she had as a child, but since it had been redecorated, the wallpaper she used to lie looking at, and imagining pictures in, was no longer there. Also, a door had been inserted leading to the bathroom next door, and making it en suite. As Sarah left her, with the information that drinks would be served in the drawing room at seven, Annabel reflected that perhaps she was being unjust to her grandmother. At the moment, she was not ready to face company, and the prospect of relaxing in a hot bath was undeniably attractive.

She took out the dress she had brought for dinner and put it in the cavernous wardrobe, where it hung forlornly amid the smell of mothballs. Then she carried her spongebag through to the bathroom, with its huge cast-iron bath on legs. No change here, then.

She bent over and turned on the taps, thinking of Neil

Cameron. She'd been touched by his obvious concern for her – more, admittedly, than Simon had shown. There was an old-fashioned jar of bath crystals – goodness knew how long they'd been there – and she tipped them lavishly into the steaming water, breathing in the scent of freesia or whatever it was. Cramming her hair into her shower cap, she remembered the feel of Neil's hands gathering it up on top of her head. Careful! she thought; I'm no longer an impressionable sixteen-year-old, but a respectable married woman. It would be as well to keep thoughts of Neil Cameron firmly on a business footing.

Voices were coming from the drawing room when she reached the hall, and as she went in, the first person she saw was Edward. Caught off-guard, she paused for a minute, and their eyes met and held. Then she forced a smile as he came over to kiss her. Silly not to have realized he'd be here.

'Good to see you again so soon,' he said. 'Ma will be down in a minute.'

She turned to her father and Charlotte who, with Holly, were waiting to greet her. 'I didn't expect such a gathering!' she said.

'It's the monthly reunion,' Douglas explained. 'The first weekend in June we were travelling back from Devon, so it was rescheduled for the second. And since you won't be able to join us for Sunday lunch, Mother shifted it to this evening. I hope you appreciate the honour!'

'I do indeed.' She turned to Holly. 'Sorry we didn't manage any French coaching,' she added. 'Events seemed to overtake us. Good luck with the mocks.'

'David's sorry to miss you,' Charlotte told her. 'He's spending the weekend with a university friend.'

'And Tom and Celia couldn't manage it, either,' Edward put in. 'Their babysitter let them down at the last minute, and Saturday nights are always tricky. But Emma's here.' He moved aside and Annabel caught sight of her cousin, sitting on the sofa with her leg up.

She went over and bent to kiss her. 'How's the ankle?' she asked.

'Taking longer to recover than I'd hoped.'

They all turned as Flora came into the room, and was kissed in turn by her family. Over the sherry that followed, Annabel was asked about the progress of the sitting, and Charlotte produced some photographs of the holiday. It was odd to be standing here in Hazelwood, looking at themselves on the beach and at the birthday dinner. To Annabel's eyes, several of the captured smiles looked strained.

Dinner was lamb cutlets, with the sauté potatoes that were a speciality of Sarah's, and garden peas from the vegetable patch. Strawberries and cream followed, and then the traditional cheese board, with a slab of the Lancashire that was Flora's favourite. In fact, Annabel noted, all the cheeses on offer were English: Leicester, Sage Derby, Stilton. Nothing French at Hazelwood.

It was just after nine when they returned to the drawing room, and Douglas, knowing his mother's fondness for the game, suggested a round of whist. 'We can manage two tables, with a dummy,' he said. But Holly wanted to watch a programme on television, and Annabel said quickly that she would be quite happy to sit and watch.

'I don't know about anyone else,' Edward remarked, 'but after all that food, I need to stretch my legs. I think I'll have a stroll round the garden. Will you join me, Annabel?'

Startled, she began to make excuses, but Flora was saying, 'An excellent idea. I'm sure she could do with some fresh air, after the drive and being cooped up in that studio all day.' The two-hour break in the Camerons' garden hadn't been mentioned.

Annabel glanced at Edward, who raised his eyebrows interrogatively, and she had no option but to smile and say, 'Yes, of course.'

They went out of the front door and round the side of the house, pushing aside the climbing roses which hung exuberantly over the path. Across the cobbled back yard, with its ancient outhouses where she'd played hide and seek as a child, past the kitchen window where Sarah could be seen washing pans, and under the stone arch into the back garden.

Neither of them had spoken since leaving the house, and Annabel's heart was beating high in her chest. Still in silence, they started down the right-hand path, where the philadelphus scented the air with its heavy perfume. And Edward said quietly, 'You know, don't you?'

She nodded.

'I knew you'd find out, as soon as you mentioned the diary, and as Tom would say, I totally lost my cool.'

'So you searched my room.'

'Twice. I can scarcely credit it. God knows what got into me.' He smiled bleakly. 'But you were one step ahead of me, weren't you? I realized, later, that must be why you went into Exeter. If it's any consolation, I'm bitterly ashamed of myself.'

They followed the path round a bend, out of sight of the house, past the raspberry canes which would soon be glistening with fruit. Another childhood memory – being given bowls and sent down the garden to pick some for tea. Purple stains on mouth and fingers and sometimes on shorts and shirts too. Mosquitoes hung in the still air, and somewhere a dog barked. If Edward was waiting for her to speak, she was unable to help him. He was walking beside her, hands behind his back, eyes on the ground, seeing who knew what pictures from the past.

'Your mother and I,' he began at last, 'it was a kind of madness, Annabel, for both of us. Not really love, more a desperate need of each other.' His mouth twisted. 'You could call it lust, I suppose, but it was much more than that. I'd never experienced anything like it, and don't want to ever again. It was like having a painful rash, or toothache, a throbbing pain that gave you no peace. Believe me, not a pleasant sensation. And it went on for *over three years*; three years of meeting regularly at dinner parties and family

gatherings, and trying to behave naturally. I knew that if we
so much as touched each other, we'd be lost.'

Annabel swallowed past the dryness in her throat. 'Where
were you that afternoon?'

Edward shot her a swift glance. 'What did she put in
the diary?'

'That you'd gone off in the car to buy a battery.'

'God, yes. And if I *had* bought one, I'd have had at
least a partial alibi. But halfway to Killay I remembered
putting a spare in my case before leaving home – it had
gone completely out of my head. You can imagine how
convincing *that* sounded to the police.' He stopped, staring
into the shrubbery. 'I could have turned straight round, gone
back and joined them on the beach. I wish to God I had; it
might even have saved Hilary's life. But we'd had a bit of
a tiff that morning and I was still annoyed with her, added
to which I was in complete turmoil about my feelings for
Monique. It was sheer torture being with her every day and
having to keep my distance. So I spent an hour or so cruising
round the Gower blowing off steam, which is why, of course,
nobody saw me.'

There was a long silence. They'd started walking again,
and wound their way round to the summer house. By mutual
consent they went inside and sat side by side on the warm
bench. The garden stretched in front of them – croquet lawn,
herbaceous borders, graceful old trees. Dusk was beginning
to fall, and an owl hooted nearby.

He started speaking again. 'It must have been about four
fifteen when I got back to the villa; too late to go down to the
beach, but as Hilary had our key, I didn't think I could get
into the house. On the off-chance, I went and tried the door,
and to my relief it opened. So I went in, looked round the
living-room door, and saw you asleep in your pushchair.'

He leaned forward, his hands gripped between his knees.
'Which meant that Monique must also be in the house –
and Douglas had gone to the cinema. I knew instantly and
irrevocably what was going to happen. I even put the snip

down on the door, so no one could take us by surprise.' He was silent for a minute, then added flatly, 'I imagine you know the rest.'

'She thought you hated her,' Annabel said in a low voice.

He rubbed a hand across his eyes. 'I wish I'd known; I could have told her differently.'

'You refused to let her give you an alibi.'

'It would have destroyed the family – you must see that. And although I loathed being under suspicion and unable to defend myself, I knew that eventually they'd have to let me go, for the simple reason that I hadn't done it.'

'Poor Uncle Edward,' Annabel said softly. He reached for her hand and for several minutes they sat unmoving, their thoughts in the past. Then he sighed and released her.

'I suppose we'd better go back.'

It was almost dark now, the house a blurred shape in the twilight, all the lights at the front. They stood up and walked slowly across the lawn.

'Even if I had bought the blasted battery,' Edward said suddenly, 'I'd probably have thrown the receipt away. Douglas couldn't produce a ticket from either the cinema or the car park. Typical, isn't it, just when he needed them most? And for that matter, Pa couldn't prove he was up Cefn Bryn, either. What a hopeless lot we were!'

'Innocent people don't think about alibis.'

'You have a point there.'

Back round the side of the house and in at the front door, blinking in the brightness of the hall. The whist game was still in progress. Annabel put her head round the door.

'Could I just interrupt to say goodnight?' She looked at Douglas and Charlotte. 'I might see you next weekend, but if not, I'll be in touch about your coming down.'

There was a chorus of goodnights. In the hall, Edward

was waiting. She put her arms round him and he held her close.

'Thank you for understanding,' he said, and, as she started up the stairs, went into the drawing room to rejoin his family.

Thirteen

The date was going much better than the last one. Since it was a Saturday, Lucy wasn't in the formal clothes which had been such a turn-off but in a floaty, low-necked summer dress that showed off her tan. Her hair was loose round her shoulders and she was bare-legged. If any of this was intended to send out signals, they were the right ones.

'Is your wife in Wales again?' she asked idly, twirling the stem of her glass.

'No, she's in Cheltenham; having her portrait painted.'

'Does she make a habit of leaving you alone at week-ends?'

'She will be doing, for the next few weeks.'

'How very convenient!'

Damn it, she was far more composed than he was. Perhaps she made a habit of this kind of thing. He could feel the sweat breaking out under his arms and it was taking him all his time to swallow the food. He'd never cheated on Annabel before, not really. The odd kiss and cuddle at the office party, yes, but everything within bounds. Tonight, he accepted that those bounds would be broken, that Lucy was expecting it. Well, it was no big deal, he assured himself, emptying his glass. He knew for a fact that Phil regularly had a bit on the side, and no harm done. What the eye doesn't see—

'Are you going to eat that pudding, or just push it round your plate?'

He moved it away. 'I've had enough.'

'Shall we go, then?'

He nodded, called the waiter, and paid the bill by cash so

it wouldn't appear on his credit card statement. Lucy took his arm as they walked to the car.

'Where are we going?' she asked.

'My place.'

She turned to look at him. 'Isn't that a bit risky? Suppose someone sees you?'

'No one will – it's dark, isn't it?'

She shrugged. 'As long as you know what you're doing.'

So they drove back to Clifton, and incredibly there was a parking space right at his gate. A good omen, he told himself. He opened the front door, his heart momentarily quailing at the sight of the familiar hall and Annabel's raincoat on the hook.

'You go on up,' he said. 'I'll get the drinks.'

'Where do I go?'

'The door opposite the top of the stairs.'

She started up, then turned to look back at him. 'That's not your room, by any chance?'

He met her gaze defiantly. 'Yes, why?'

'Insensitive devil, aren't you? Well, I tell you this: I'm not going to cavort with you in your wife's bed. I have some limits, even if you haven't.'

'The next one along, then,' he muttered sulkily. 'I think the bed's made up.'

She held his eye for a minute and he wasn't sure what he read there. Acceptance? Contempt? Desire? Then she turned and went on up the stairs and, wiping the sweat from his face, he went in search of the drinks.

Annabel arrived at the Camerons' house just before nine the next morning. Her talk with Edward had resulted in yet another disturbed night. He'd not asked if she'd any memories of that day, she reflected; it couldn't have occurred to him. It was as well he knew nothing of the nightmare that haunted her even now.

Neil came down the path to meet her. 'All right?' he asked, his eyes raking her face.

'Fine.'

'Coffee's waiting.'

The day followed much the same pattern as the previous one. Neil sketched, talked, kept silent. They listened to the music, had coffee, broke for lunch.

'What time do you want to leave?' Moira asked. 'Sunday evening traffic can be a nightmare.'

'No later than four, if that's all right.'

'It's good of Simon to spare you!'

But the afternoon session proved less satisfactory, and finally, just before three, Neil stood up. 'Sorry; I've hit the equivalent of writer's block!'

'Oh dear! Is it serious?'

'No, it's just that I'm not concentrating. There's no point in wasting any more of your time, if you'd like to be on your way.'

She stretched. 'Well, if you're sure, I might as well. You are quite pleased, though, with the way it's going?'

'Oh, yes. I'll work on it during the week, then next weekend should show real progress.'

She nodded, satisfied, and went down to change. All three of them came to the gate to see her off.

'Remember what I said about a tonic,' Rex reminded her. 'And if there are any more phone calls, get them checked out.'

Simon sat moodily at the rosewood table in his parents' dining room, staring into his glass. Although the sex had been good last night, it had left him feeling dispirited, and Lucy's phrase 'cavorting in your wife's bed' echoed unpleasantly in his ears. She'd made it sound so sordid – which, he supposed, it was. In retrospect, he was appalled that he could even have contemplated using their own bed, and resentful that it was Lucy who'd prevented him.

'More meat, darling?' his mother asked brightly.

'No, thanks.' For two pins he'd have wriggled out of coming here today, but he couldn't swing it a second time.

'You've not eaten much, old man,' Giles said genially. 'Not sickening for anything, are you?' And he laughed, to show it was a joke.

Simon smiled weakly.

'Perhaps he had a night out with the boys, and is feeling the after-effects!' Sally hazarded. She looked at her son's bent head for a minute, then asked casually, 'What time is Annabel due back?'

'God knows. When the sitting ends, presumably.'

'But in time for the evening meal? Would you like me to come back with you, and cook something ready for her?'

'No, of course not,' Simon said irritably, adding ungraciously, 'thanks.'

'You could have stayed here, you know, if you're lonely. We'd be—'

'For God's sake, Mum!' he burst out. 'Give it a rest, will you? I'm not going into a decline just because my wife's away for a couple of days, and I'm not entirely helpless. Stop fussing!'

He glared across at her, saw her hurt expression, and hated himself. God, if this was what having an affair did to you, he'd rather not know.

'Sorry!' he said gruffly, and held out his hand. After a minute she took it.

'Just trying to help,' she said.

On the way home he stopped to fill up the car, and, on impulse, extracted a bunch of flowers from the bucket near the pumps. He couldn't, to his shame, remember when he'd last bought any.

Oh, Lord, he thought, driving off with them on the seat beside him, what was he going to do? Lucy knew Annabel would be away for the next few weekends; she'd expect their meetings to continue, and he wasn't entirely sure he wanted them to. How had he ever got into this mess?

*   *   *

Annabel arrived home an hour after him. 'You're earlier than I expected,' he said, going to kiss her.

'The muse dried up.'

He produced the flowers from behind his back. 'For my lovely wife!'

'My goodness, what brought this on? A guilty conscience?'

He stared at her, dumbfounded, but she had turned away with a laugh and was looking for a vase. He cleared his throat. 'How did it go, then?'

'I don't really know; Neil warned me we wouldn't get much done the first sitting. Most of the time, I just sat listening to the music.'

'And what does it look like?'

'I didn't dare peep, after what he said in Topsham. Anyway, it was only preliminary sketches.' She paused. 'Have there been any more phone calls?'

'Not while I've been here, but I'll check.' He went out into the hall, returning a minute later. 'According to the machine there were three; two yesterday, one at 10 a.m. and one at 10.15, and another at 12 p.m. today. No messages, and numbers withheld. It could have been anyone, though.' He glanced at her tense face. 'For a start, the two yesterday would hardly both have been the same person, and none of them were at the usual time.'

She said aridly, 'They wouldn't need to be, at the weekend.'

'Well, if you never answer it, how will you know if they are the same? It could be someone different each time, who just didn't bother to leave a message. We can't contact BT unless we've got the facts straight.'

'All right,' she said, 'next time, I'll answer it.'

The following day was wet, and as she balanced her umbrella under her chin and fumbled for her key, she heard the phone start to ring. Pushing the door open, she dropped the wet umbrella into its stand and picked it up.

'Yes?' she said curtly.

Silence. But before he could cut the connection, she rushed into her prepared speech. 'Listen, this is your last chance. If you ring again, BT will trace the call.' And she slammed down the phone, fiercely triumphant that this time it had been she who ended it.

She had just taken off her raincoat when the doorbell rang, and she froze. Suppose he'd been standing across the way, as she suspected, and, deprived of his cut-off, had come to confront her? She stared at the door, straining for sounds from the other side, and jumped as the bell rang again.

'Who is it?' she called, heart pounding, and, with an enervating wave of relief, heard her mother-in-law's voice.

'It's Sally, darling. Could you open up, I'm getting drenched!'

Annabel hastily flung the door open, to see her standing on the step under a cherry-red umbrella. 'Sorry, do come in. I'm only just back myself.'

Sally came into the hall, dripping water, placed her umbrella next to Annabel's and shrugged out of her raincoat. 'What a pig of a day!'

'I'll put the kettle on,' Annabel said, and Sally followed her through to the kitchen.

'What time does Simon get home?'

'Oh, not till about six.'

'That's what I thought. It gives us time for a nice little heart-to-heart.'

Annabel, puzzled, tried not to think of the various tasks she'd hoped to get through before dinner. 'What about?' she asked warily, pouring water into the teapot.

'Well, darling, as you know, Simon came to us for lunch yesterday, and we both thought – that is, it struck us that he didn't seem too . . . happy.'

'I'm not too happy myself,' Annabel said, surprising them both.

Sally looked concerned. 'I'm sorry to hear that, dear. Anything we can help with?'

Ashamed of her retort, Annabel shook her head. She put out cups and saucers – no mugs for Sally – and a plate of biscuits, hoping they'd not gone stale.

'We were wondering,' Sally continued diffidently, 'whether it's really necessary for you to be away so much? I understood that this painter had offered to come to Bristol?'

She makes him sound like a decorator, Annabel thought irritably. 'It just isn't practical. It would totally disrupt the house; we'd have to move furniture around, Neil would have to bring all his equipment, and we haven't a room with the right light anyway.'

'I see.'

'But I'm quite sure my absence wasn't the reason for Simon's unhappiness – *if* he's unhappy, which I doubt. His life is a mad whirl of parties, pubs and general socializing. I'd say he's having a ball.'

Sally, picking up the implied criticism, changed tack to come to her son's defence. 'Men!' she said, with a light laugh. 'I suppose we must make allowances.'

'Why?' Annabel asked baldly.

Again, Sally was taken aback. 'I mean if they get a bit boisterous now and then,' she stammered. 'After all, they're just little boys at heart!'

'And who wants to be married to a little boy?'

Sally stared at her. 'I think you're deliberately misunderstanding me, Annabel,' she said stiffly.

'Not at all, I understand you perfectly. You've come round to tell me to be nicer to your little boy.'

As Sally continued to stare at her, speechless, she clutched her head in both hands, feeling tears rush into her eyes. 'Sally, I'm sorry, I'm sorry! I didn't mean that, really. It's just that I haven't been sleeping well, I've a lot on my mind, and I just – snapped.'

'You certainly did,' Sally agreed. She studied Annabel carefully, noted the tears and the fact that her daughter-in-law looked decidedly under the weather, and relented as her mothering instincts came to the fore.

'Sit down now, and drink your tea, and we'll say no more about it.'

Shakily Annabel bent to kiss her cheek, and did as she was told. The hot tea was a reviver and her rocky control gradually steadied.

Sally said abruptly, 'You're quite right; I'd no business coming round here interfering. I apologize.'

'Oh, please—'

'Really, I mean it.' She gave a slight smile. 'All in all, I got what I deserved.'

Annabel looked at the tanned, carefully made-up face, the expertly tinted hair, the casual elegance of the silk dress, and felt more warmth towards her mother-in-law than she had for some time. Perhaps, in the years ahead, she also would try to fight her children's battles. If so, she hoped she'd remember this moment.

'I was very rude,' she said contritely. 'I'm sorry.'

'What is it you have on your mind?' Sally probed gently, topping up her cup.

'It's all rather complicated. I won't bore you with it.'

'Nothing to do with that journalist, I hope?'

'Partly,' Annabel admitted.

'Oh, dear, I feel dreadful about that, raking it all up for you. It's not even as though anything new could come of it, at this late stage.'

'No,' said Annabel numbly. If only that were true.

It was still raining the next morning, and as she was again doing her balancing act with her umbrella, this time to unlock the car, the postman, gleaming like a seal in his wet cape, stopped beside her and held out some envelopes.

'Delivered by hand!' he said with a grin.

It would have been more convenient if he'd put them through the letterbox, but she couldn't blame him for saving himself a walk in this weather. She held out her open handbag and he dropped them inside.

Once in the car, she forgot about them, her mind on the

lessons ahead, and it wasn't until break, when she searched in her bag for a handkerchief, that she came across them.

Two were for Simon, one was a bill from John Lewis, and one addressed to her in block capitals. She looked at it for a minute, frowning, before slitting it open and drawing out the single sheet. The message, also in block capitals, was brief and to the point:

ASK YOUR HUSBAND WHO HE BROUGHT HOME
ON SATURDAY NIGHT.

Annabel stared at it, feeling slightly sick. Was this a practical joke? If so, she was not amused.

Stephie, absorbed, as usual, in the *Telegraph* crossword, raised her voice. 'Wake up, Annie! I said, "Tailless town in Massachusetts heralds flight, question-mark". Seven letters. What's a tailless town, for Heaven's sake?' She looked up, noting Annabel's stillness and the letter she held. 'Bad news?' she asked quickly.

Annabel slipped the paper back in the envelope. 'I hope not,' she said.

The note with its nasty little message lodged in her mind and would not be shifted. Its very existence made her feel disloyal, that it should cause her to doubt Simon even for a minute. Whatever their differences, other women had never featured in them, and that was surely the inference. She longed for the school day to end, so they could laugh over it together.

A surreptitious re-examination in the ladies' revealed that the Bristol postmark was stamped with yesterday's date, the midday collection. Bad news travels fast – or rather, she corrected herself, innuendo does. Belatedly, she realized she'd not asked Simon how he'd spent Saturday, and regretted the omission. He'd enquired about her weekend; she should have returned the compliment, but instead her mind had gone to the answerphone.

And suddenly it struck her that the writer of this note and

the mysterious caller might be one and the same. Surely there couldn't be two people out to harass her?

From the day she met Martin, she thought helplessly as she made her way back to the classroom, her world had begun to fall apart. Or had it started even sooner, with Simon's moods and his frenetic need for company? One thing was certain, which Sally's visit yesterday had underlined: it was high time they had a serious talk, and the sooner it took place, the better.

There was no phone call when she let herself into the house that afternoon, and she hesitated uncertainly, waiting for it to ring. Perhaps her warning last night had had an effect – or perhaps the caller had switched to anonymous notes.

As she prepared their supper, she turned over in her mind how to broach the subject. Casually? Jokingly? With concern? She pictured Simon's various reactions, indignation predominating. 'A chance would be a fine thing!' he'd say.

Then, as she was making the sauce for the pasta, the phone finally rang. Quarter to six. With a dry mouth, she hurried into the hall as the answerphone came on, relaying Simon's standard message. Then her stepfather's voice: 'Annie, love, if you're there, pick up the phone. It's George.'

She lifted it, her heartbeat slowly returning to normal. 'Hello, George.'

'Hi there, sweetie. Just ringing to say that after all the excitement the other evening, you forgot to take your mother's things.'

'Oh.' They'd gone right out of her head.

'I have to come into Bristol tomorrow, so I could drop them off, if you like.'

'Fine. Thanks.'

'Annie, are you all right? You sound a bit strained.'

The usual lies came into her head: Of course – I'm fine – just a busy day at school, that's all. To her horror, she heard herself say: 'No, actually, I'm not. I've had an anonymous letter.'

Immediately, she was appalled. How *could* she tell George before discussing it with Simon? Or at all, come to that? So embroiled was she in her guilt that it took her a minute to realize he had not replied.

'George?' she said sharply.

'Yes, my darling, I heard.'

'Aren't you going to ask what it said?'

'If you want me to know, you'll tell me.'

Too late, now, to turn back. 'It said, "Ask your husband who he brought home on Saturday night." That was when I was in Cheltenham,' she added stupidly.

'My poor love.'

'You don't sound very surprised,' she accused him. Then, her voice rising, 'Is there something you're not telling me?'

'It's probably nothing – there was no point in mentioning it.'

'Well, there is now! What is it?'

'Annabel, I really shouldn't—'

'Tell me!'

He said quietly, 'Nigel saw Simon having dinner with a young lady.'

Her throat seemed to close. She said huskily, 'On Saturday?'

'No, no, a week or two ago. Before you went away.'

'But – I don't understand. Where was I?'

'I don't know, my love.'

'Where was this?'

'Somewhere in Almondsbury, I believe. One of the school governors stood him dinner. Look, darling, it was probably only a business colleague. Nigel stressed that they didn't seem at all – close.'

'Assuming it's this same – business colleague – he brought here on Saturday, they're getting closer, wouldn't you say?'

He didn't answer.

She said rapidly, 'George, I'm going to ring off. Simon will be back soon, and I need to work out what I'm going to do.'

'Give him the chance to explain, sweetheart. It might have blown up out of all proportion.'

'Don't worry about Maman's things; I'll collect them next time I see you. Goodbye.'

She almost dropped the phone as a fit of trembling took her. Nigel had seen Simon. *That* was why they'd been offhand with him. A wave of fury superseded the shock. Oh yes, she thought grimly, I'll give him a chance to explain.

By the time Simon came home, she was outwardly calm. She'd thought back over the weeks, and could remember only one evening recently when he'd not been in to dinner – the night she found her mother's diaries, when he'd informed her he was going to a 'business thing'. Weasel words.

'That smells good!'

She hadn't heard the door, and stiffened as he came into the kitchen. Seemingly unaware of her lack of response, he talked lightly about his day at the office; about a new client who, after a lot of hedging, had signed on the dotted line, about a colleague's holiday in Greece.

She served the food, making minimal replies, somehow managing to eat a reasonable amount, while Simon finished his plateful with evident enjoyment. Finally, when he sat back in his chair, she said quietly, 'I had an anonymous letter today.'

He stared at her, obviously unsure whether she was serious. 'Good Lord!' he said after a minute. 'Well, I suppose it makes a change from anonymous phone calls.'

'It was more specific, at least. It said I should ask who you brought home on Saturday night.'

There was total silence except for the ticking clock and the intermittent hum of the fridge.

She forced herself to look at him. He was staring at her, his face scarlet.

'So,' she went on, when he did not speak, 'I'm asking you.'

He swallowed. 'You're surely not taking it seriously?'

'If I wasn't before, I am now. You have guilt written all over you.'

'You took me by surprise, that's all. My God, you don't really think—?'

'Who was it, Simon?'

'No one! Look, this is all a mistake!'

'Like the dinner you had in Almondsbury, the "business thing"?'

She watched curiously as his colour faded, leaving him abnormally pale. He licked his lips with a quick, nervous movement. 'Oh, that,' he said. 'Yes, that was business. I told you.'

'But you didn't tell me about Saturday.' Her voice changed, became sharper and he flinched. 'How long has this been going on?'

'Annabel, for God's sake—'

'How long?'

'*Nothing's* going on! I only—'

'Where did you take her, Simon? To our room?'

'No!' Thanks to Lucy. Too late, he realized that by that one word, he had betrayed himself.

'The guest room, then? Did you change the bed linen? Or were you planning to use it again next weekend?'

She pushed her chair back and ran from the room.

'Annabel – darling – please!'

He followed her up the stairs and into the guest room, where she tore the cover from the bed and began feverishly stripping off sheets and pillow slips. Then, bundling them in her arms, she hurried out again, pushing past him in the doorway. Back in the kitchen, she stuffed them unceremoniously in the washing machine, added soap powder and switched it on. He watched her from the doorway.

'Darling, I can explain.'

'Really? That should be interesting.'

'It was nothing, a one-off—'

'A two-off, at very least.'

He stood stricken, gazing at her.

She said carefully, 'There are clean sheets in the airing cupboard. I suggest you go up and remake the bed, because that's where you'll be sleeping for the moment.'

'For the moment?' he echoed weakly.

'Until I decide what to do.'

'Annabel, I love you!'

'You have a strange way of showing it. Now go and make the bed. I want to be alone.'

'But I have to try to—'

'Go away.'

He turned and went.

She leaned against the sink, taking deep breaths. At the moment, she felt she never wanted to see him again. That might pass. Whether or not, in time, she'd be able to forgive him depended on a lot of things, but at the moment she was too distraught even to consider them. Very slowly, she started to clear away the supper things.

Upstairs, Simon stood like a zombie in the middle of the guest room, while unwelcome memories of Lucy superimposed themselves on the bed. Who the hell had seen them together, not once, but twice? He remembered her warning about the risk in coming here, and his own, typically arrogant, dismissal of it. Well, she'd been right. But of all the sneaky, underhand things to do, he thought indignantly, sending a note to Annabel! Why not tackle him openly, if it was any of their damn business, which he couldn't for the life of him see that it was.

Miserably, he brought fresh sheets and began to make up the bed.

'Did you have that chat with Annabel?' Giles Kendal asked, looking up from the evening paper.

'Yes; yes, I did. Yesterday.'

229

'You never mentioned it. How did it go?'

'I don't think there's anything to worry about.' The reason Sally hadn't reported the discussion was because she still wasn't sure what to make of it, and her anxiety had shifted from her son to her daughter-in-law. That outburst had been so unlike her, but the girl had looked strained, and her unguarded admission that she wasn't happy lingered in Sally's mind. If only she hadn't blurted out about the Carlyle connection to that wretched journalist!

'Did you suggest the artist chappie came down here?'

'Yes, but apparently it isn't feasible. Too much of an upheaval. She didn't seem to think that was the problem, anyway. She says Simon has a busy social life, with something always on.'

She did not add that Annabel hadn't sounded too happy about it.

Giles grunted. 'Well, he wasn't so all-fired sociable on Sunday.'

'Probably a hangover,' Sally said, and was thankful when, after a minute, he nodded agreement and returned to his paper.

It was a relief to have straightened things out with Annabel, Edward reflected; in particular, that she had accepted his apology for searching her room. The memory of that still made him hot with shame. God knows what she thought of him, with that lapse swiftly followed by her discovery of his relationship with Monique. He thought back to their discussion in the darkening garden, accepting that it had gone better than he'd dared hope. She was a thoughtful, sensitive girl – he'd always been fond of her, and not only because she was his niece and Monique's daughter.

Monique. He still mourned her tragically early death. No doubt if she'd lived, she would at some stage have destroyed the incriminating diaries – if, indeed, she still remembered their existence. What was certain was that she wouldn't have intended them to fall into her daughter's hands. He wondered how she'd thought of him towards the end of her life. Not at all, perhaps, since she was under the impression that he hated her. He regretted that.

The storm of applause brought his attention back to the orchestra, now standing and bowing their acknowledgements in response to the conductor's all-embracing gesture. They filed off the stage and he and Suzanne went in search of their interval drinks. As he handed her a glass of wine, she said suddenly, 'Edward, who's Monique?'

He started, wondering for a wild moment if he'd been speaking his thoughts aloud. 'Now, where did you come up with that name?' he asked, toasting her with his own glass.

'You said it in your sleep the other night.'

'Did I really? How ungallant of me!'

'But who is she?' Suzanne persisted curiously.

'No one for you to worry about,' he assured her, 'just part of my chequered past!'

Fourteen

Annabel lay wide-eyed, staring at the ceiling, the empty space beside her emphasizing her aloneness. Was Simon serious about this woman? He'd tried desperately to disassociate himself, but that was self-preservation. Was she even the one Nigel had seen him with, or were there others? Anything seemed possible in her suddenly topsy-turvy world. He had brought her back *here*! she thought, with a renewed sense of outrage. How could he? The whole house felt contaminated.

With an effort she anchored her whirling thoughts, determining to take one day at a time. Weekdays posed no problem, since they'd both be out at work, and at the weekend, thank God, she was going back to Cheltenham. She considered going up after school on Friday, but since even from home she could be at the sitting by nine, they'd wonder why. So there were three evenings to fill; perhaps she could persuade Stephie or one of the others to go to the cinema, and if Simon had any decency he'd make himself scarce. Shoot off to his girlfriend, perhaps.

She hurled herself on to her side, buried her face in the pillow, and willed sleep to come.

Somehow, the next day passed. Annabel was grateful to have a full timetable, and when a member of staff was taken ill, she volunteered to stay on for a couple of hours after school, to supervise prep. There'd be less of the evening to fill in, she reasoned, and she wouldn't be subjected to the silent phone call. Simon would wonder where she was, but that was his problem. At the moment, she felt she owed him no consideration, and was, in fact, dreading their inevitable meeting; breakfast had been a silent and hasty meal, both of them anxious to be out of the house as soon as possible. By his pallor and the circles under his eyes, she deduced he'd slept no better than she had.

It was therefore after six before she emerged from the school gates, and, though it meant prolonging her return home still further, she turned in the direction of the supermarket. Its car park was, as usual, full, but after circling for a few minutes she found a space and eased the car in. Wrapped in her misery, she started towards the entrance, and was considerably startled when, within yards of it, someone caught her by the arm and spun her round as a voice said silkily, 'Well might you try to avoid me, my girl!' Uncomprehendingly, she found herself face to face with Mandy Prior. The bored manner was gone, and blatant hostility had taken its place.

'Oh, Mandy – hello,' she stammered. 'I'm sorry, I didn't see you.'

'You're clever, I'll grant you that,' Mandy said in a low voice, her fingers still digging into Annabel's arm. 'I never guessed what you were up to, but I'm telling you now it's over, so you can just forget it.'

Annabel looked at her blankly. 'I'm sorry?'

'Oh, don't give me that, Miss Innocent! You know what I'm talking about all right, so just you listen to me: Martin and I have been an item for two years now, and I'm not going to stand by and let the likes of you muscle in. Got it?'

'Mandy, I've no idea what you're talking about, but let me assure you I have no designs whatever on Martin, nor he on me.'

'Then what price all those phone calls? Oh yes, I know about them! He was working at home last week, and twice when I went into the study he was on his mobile instead of the desk phone. He wouldn't say why, but it must have been so they wouldn't show on our joint bill. I was curious, so I waited my chance and scrolled back, and guess what? Several calls were to the same number. I dialled it, and what did I get but Simon's message on your answerphone. So talk your way out of that.'

'Just a minute.' Annabel put out a hand. 'You're saying Martin's been phoning me?'

'That's exactly what I'm saying. You're not trying to deny it?'

'No,' Annabel said slowly, 'I don't think I am. Tell me, did you ever *hear* him making these calls?'

Mandy gave a dismissive gesture. 'Not actually speaking, no; he was always too quick for me.'

'Or he might not have said anything.'

She frowned. 'What do you mean?'

'What time of day were they?'

'As if you didn't know! Late afternoon; when you'd be back from that school of yours, but before Simon came home.'

Annabel drew a deep breath, feeling at least a partial weight slide off her. 'If you know so much, why didn't you confront him?'

Mandy hesitated, and Annabel caught a glimpse of insecurity behind the sophisticated exterior. 'I decided it was better to tackle it from your end,' she said, 'and as luck would have it, I just happened to catch sight of you. Providence, wouldn't you say?'

'Well, let me put your mind at rest. There is nothing – less than nothing – between Martin and me, except that he's angry because I wouldn't help in his detective work. So he decided to play a nasty little trick on me, and for the last week he's been making nuisance calls.'

Mandy stared at her. 'Nuisance calls?'

'Not saying anything, and then hanging up. Charming, isn't it? I'm not surprised he didn't own up to it.'

'Is this true?'

'Absolutely.'

She looked bewildered. 'But what about Saturday – you must have seen him then?'

Annabel frowned. 'Why should you think that?'

'Well, we'd been out for the evening, but when we got home he said he had to deliver some late copy – there was an envelope on the dashboard. He dropped me at the gate and drove straight off. After the phone business I was suspicious, so I ran to my car and followed him, and was in time to see him turn into your road.'

He'd probably intended to drop some unpleasant note through the letterbox, Annabel surmised; even, perhaps – thinking they'd be in bed – to ring the bell before driving off. Simon's arrival with his lady-friend had been an unlooked-for bonus. At least it proved she was right; the caller and the letter-writer were one and the same.

Still, Mandy had been given quite enough explanations. She said merely, 'I was in Cheltenham last weekend. Believe me, Mandy, Martin is all yours – and you're welcome to him.'

And, leaving her totally confused, she escaped into the safe anonymity of the supermarket.

Simon met her at the door. 'Where have you been? I was worried about you.'

'Did you think I'd left you?'

The flicker in his eyes was confirmation. He said, 'I didn't know what you planned for supper, but I've made some salad.'

She walked past him, put the carrier bags on the kitchen table and started to unpack them.

'It was Martin who made the phone calls and wrote the note,' she said expressionlessly.

'*Martin?* Are you sure?'

'Positive. I met Mandy at Waitrose and we had an interesting chat. She'll deal with him.'

'But – but why?'

'Sheer spite. I told you I never liked him. There's some ham here, which will go with the salad.'

'Right. By the way, this carrier bag was on the step when I got home.'

She glanced at it, recognizing the bag into which George had put Monique's scarves and belts. A folded piece of paper was sticking out of it. She bent to pick it up. It was an old bill, with a note in George's writing scrawled on the back.

Dearest girl, she read, *I'd been hoping to take you out for a meal this evening, but there's no sign of you. Perhaps tomorrow? I'll be in touch. In the meantime, take care. Thinking of you. All love, George.*

Simon was watching her, and she knew he'd also read it.

'I assume he knows?' he said.

She nodded.

'Annabel, I feel all kinds of an idiot—'

'I don't want to talk about it.'

'But—'

'*No*, Simon. Since we're living in the same house, we have to exchange the odd comment, but that doesn't mean I'm in the mood for a string of excuses.'

He subsided, the sulky look on his face. 'When *are* we going to talk about it, then?' he muttered.

'When I've decided what to do.' She paused. 'I trust you won't be bringing that woman here this weekend?'

He flushed. 'Of course not. Anyway, it's over. It was, really, even before you found out.'

Annabel fought with her curiosity and lost. 'Who is she, Simon?'

He avoided her eyes. 'Someone from the office. You've never met her.'

'She was the one you had dinner with last month?'

He nodded. 'Those are the only times I've seen her. Except . . .'

She waited, and after a minute he went on in a low voice, 'Except when you were in Wales; she came to

236

the Schooner that Saturday and joined us on the trip to Tetbury.'

'Ah!' So that was why he'd cancelled lunch at his parents'.

'Annie, I'm so sorry. It was – unforgivable.'

'Being found out?' she asked caustically.

'It's never happened before. I hope you believe that.'

'I'd like to,' she said. 'The point is, will it happen again?'

He shook his head, and she saw, to her surprise, that he was close to tears. Weren't they her prerogative? So far, she'd remained remarkably dry-eyed. The ringing of the wall-phone came as a relief to them both, and Annabel, freed from the worry of nuisance calls, picked it up.

'Annie – you're back.'

'Hello, George. Sorry to have missed you.'

'Can you talk?'

'Not really.'

'Well, how about tomorrow? A nice meal out some-where?'

'That would be lovely.'

'I'll call for you at five thirty and we'll go for a drink first.' He wanted to avoid seeing Simon, she thought.

'I'll be ready,' she said.

Annabel moved through the rest of that week at one remove from reality. Outwardly, she behaved no differently from normal, but she felt about a foot off the ground, that nothing was quite as it seemed. The evening with George was pleasant, though his worried face added to rather than lessened her misery, and she side-stepped his questions on her future plans. They ended up talking about Cassie and the baby.

On the Friday evening she went with Stephie to the cinema, being careful to park in a well-lighted area. She should have asked Mandy where Martin was the night she went to the Riverside.

Then at last it was Saturday morning, and she was driving back to Cheltenham, grateful for the two-day respite from Simon's white face and pleading eyes. Dr Cameron would not be pleased with her, she thought with a flicker of amusement; more bad nights and no visit to the GP. But medication couldn't cure her problems.

'How are you, Annabel?' Neil greeted her anxiously. 'We've been worried about those phone calls. I nearly rang you a couple of times, but I didn't want Simon to think I was interfering.'

'There haven't been any more,' she said. Admitting to having found the perpetrator would involve all kinds of explanations that she'd rather not give.

'Well, that's a relief.'

Moira was alone in the sitting room, Rex having been called out to a patient. Her eyes raked Annabel's face, but Neil gave an almost imperceptible shake of the head and she made no comment except to say brightly, 'Lovely to see you, dear. I'll get the coffee.'

Upstairs in the familiar bedroom, Annabel again changed into the brocade dress and fastened on the turquoise and pearl earrings which, despite the traumas of the last week, she had remembered to bring. Then she brushed her hair and applied more colour to her cheeks, resolving to put all her problems aside and simply enjoy relaxing with the music.

But when she joined Neil in the studio, he said quietly, 'Phone calls or no phone calls, you still seem on edge. Is anything else worrying you?'

She bit her lip and looked away, and after a minute he said, 'Sorry, none of my business. Right, then: I've done a fair bit of work during the week, so I'm hoping we can forge ahead today. Same position as last week, please.'

The sitting began, music filled the room, and she felt herself relax. If only she could stay here all week, away from the problems that awaited her in Bristol. After about an hour, they had a break to allow her to move about, and Neil made some coffee.

'Simon survived the weekend without you, then?' he asked jovially, passing her a mug.

Her hand jerked involuntarily, and the hot liquid spilt on her dress. He gave an exclamation, took the cup from her shaking fingers, and knelt to mop at the stain. 'I don't think it'll leave a mark,' he said. 'It's not had time to soak in, and fortunately it's on a patch of dark colour.'

When she made no comment he looked up, to see tears streaming down her face. He rose quickly to his feet.

'Annabel! For God's sake, what's wrong?'

But she was beyond speech, beyond control. The strain of the last month had finally, overwhelmingly, caught up with her, and as his arms came round her, all she could do was lean against him, crying helplessly. Eventually, as her sobs lessened, he passed her a handkerchief and she moved away from him, mopping her eyes and blowing her nose.

'Sorry,' she said unsteadily. 'I bet that was more than you bargained for!'

'And it was because I mentioned Simon.'

'I've discovered he's been seeing someone else,' she said. The need for loyalty had gone.

'I'm so sorry,' he said gently. 'You never suspected?'

She shook her head. 'I knew things hadn't been right between us for months.'

'So what will you do?'

She gave a faint smile. 'Everyone keeps asking me that.'

'If there's any way I can help, you have only to say.'

'Thanks, but it's something I'll have to sort out for myself.' She opened her bag, took out a mirror, and made a little face at her reflection. 'Not a pretty sight!'

'Ready to try the coffee again?'

She nodded. 'I'll be more careful this time.'

While she drank it, he talked lightly about his thoughts

on the portrait, and by the time she'd finished, her control was firmly back in place.

'I'm really sorry, Neil; I don't know when I last cried like that. I feel better for it, but I'm sorry to have inflicted it on you.'

'Not at all, the proverbial shoulder is always at your disposal. Now, shall we get back to work?'

She nodded, taking up her position again, and, deep in their own thoughts, neither of them spoke again until Moira's bell summoned them down to lunch, by which time, to Annabel's relief, all signs of her recent tears had vanished.

Rex had returned, and greeted her with a kiss. 'Did you follow my advice?'

'No!' she admitted with a smile.

'A difficult patient! Well, I did my best.'

'I'll be fine,' she said quietly, taking her place at the table.

'How's Mrs Harris?' Moira asked him, laying bowls of fragrant-smelling soup in front of them.

'The mother of a seven-pound boy – two weeks earlier than expected. I attended myself because of her age, but all was well, thank God.'

'My stepsister's expecting her first baby,' Annabel said a little anxiously. 'She's forty; are there likely to be problems?'

'Very unlikely, I'd say. These days so many career woman are putting off starting a family, primigravidas in their forties are more and more common.'

The Latin word struck a chord in Annabel's memory. 'She was most indignant at being referred to as "elderly"!'

Rex Cameron laughed. 'We don't often use that term now – for obvious reasons.'

Home-made pâté and French bread followed the soup, after which Moira produced a bowl of fresh fruit.

'I thought this was supposed to be a snack,' Annabel

protested. 'At this rate, I shan't be able to eat my dinner tonight, and then I'll be in trouble!'

'You have to build up your strength to sit like a statue all day.'

Rex helped himself to a pear and began to peel it meticulously. 'What happened about those phone calls? Have you had any more?'

Neil's warning hadn't been passed on, Annabel thought, but she felt more able to deal with it now. 'No, and I found out who was behind them. It was a friend – so-called. An acquaintance, anyway.'

They exclaimed with surprise. 'Why on earth should he do that? It *was* a man, I presume?'

'It's rather involved, but basically it was because I wouldn't – play ball.'

'Play ball in what way?' Neil asked with a frown.

She hesitated, but these were old friends, who knew all about the family tragedy. 'Actually, he's a journalist, who happened to be working in Swansea when Aunt Hilary was killed.'

They all stared at her, startled by the serious turn of the conversation.

'But why bother you?' Rex demanded. 'You were only an infant at the time.'

'He thought that if I went back to the house something might jog my memory.'

'You didn't go with him?' Moira exclaimed, aghast.

'No, but he'd roused my curiosity, so I went with a friend.'

'To the house?' Rex said incredulously.

'Yes. Anyway, Martin was annoyed that I'd gone without him, and hadn't passed on something else that came up, so he started this ridiculous vendetta.'

But they'd lost interest in the phone calls. There was a short silence, then Moira said tentatively, 'Wasn't it rather risky, going back like that?'

'Decidedly.' Rex answered her. 'Heaven knows, it was

trauma enough to witness violence at so young an age; re-experiencing it as an adult could have had serious consequences.'

A wave of heat washed over Annabel and receded, leaving her cold. '*Witness* it?' she repeated, barely audibly.

'Yes, you were there, weren't you?' He broke off, staring at her across the table with dawning awareness.

She'd never told him about the dream, Annabel thought in confusion, above the ringing in her ears. She said in a whisper, 'How do you know I was?'

Rex's face was suddenly white. 'It was in all the papers.'

'No,' she said, shaking her head vigorously, as though to clear it. 'No one knew; Maman ran off with me and didn't come back till Hilary'd been found. I didn't know for certain myself, till I read her diary.'

Moira said on a high note, 'What is all this? I don't understand.'

Annabel and Rex sat motionless, their eyes locked on each other. 'No!' Annabel said on an indrawn breath. 'Oh, please no!'

'Father—' Neil leant forward urgently. 'There has to be an explanation. Did Monique tell you later? Say Annabel had been there? But surely she couldn't have been? No one would have done such a thing in front of a *baby*!'

Rex Cameron seemed to shrivel before their eyes. 'God help me, I didn't know she was there,' he said in a strangled voice. 'Hilary was screening her. I only saw the pushchair when she fell.'

Moira gasped and swayed in her chair.

Neil said sharply, 'Father, you're not well. You don't know what you're saying. Let me get you a brandy.'

No one answered him. He pushed back his chair, strode to the cabinet in the corner, poured out a glass and, after a moment's hesitation, three more, and brought them to the table. No one had moved.

Rex reached out a hand for his glass, and emptied it in one mouthful. Then he gave a deep sigh. 'I've been dreading this moment for twenty-eight years,' he said more calmly. 'It's almost a relief that it's come.'

Neil said rapidly, 'Don't say any more, for God's sake. Somehow or other we have to get round this.'

Rex ignored him, still staring at Annabel. 'At first, it was Monique I was worried about. She had to have been in the house if you were, and she could have caught sight of me as I fled. I knew she'd have come running when you started screaming, and she behaved very strangely after Hilary's death. Eventually, though, I realized she knew nothing, though I had a nasty moment in Exeter, when we came across you reading her diaries. That lunch we had together was a nightmare; I kept expecting you to come out with some kind of accusation.' He wiped a hand across his face. 'But you didn't, thank God, and eventually I was able to convince myself that if Monique had known anything, it would have come out at the time.

'Which left you. I'd no way of knowing how much you'd understand or remember from such an early age, and I was obsessed by the fear that the diary might have triggered a buried memory, especially when you were so pale last weekend. But you were perfectly relaxed with me, bless you, and I began to think I was safe. I should have known Nemesis is always just around the corner.'

Moira had started to weep quietly. Neil got up and went to stand behind her, his hand on her shoulder. His face was chalk-white and there was a muscle jumping in his cheek. It seemed that neither the doctor's wife nor son was capable of questioning him, so it fell to Annabel. Having come this far, she had to know the full story.

'Why?' she asked simply.

He shrugged, gave the travesty of a smile.

'What were you doing in Wales?' she persisted. 'You weren't part of the holiday group.'

Moira added her own question, turning her ravaged face to her husband. 'Yes, Rex, why? I don't understand – Hilary was our friend!'

The doctor held up his glass to his son, and without a word Neil took it and refilled it.

'My darling,' Rex said, 'if I could have spared you this, I would, but the time has at last come to own up.' Again he emptied his glass, took a deep breath, and leaned back in his chair. Neil, realizing a confession of some sort was imminent, resumed his own seat.

'In the spring of '72,' Rex began, 'two things happened which, to any sane person, should have been mutually exclusive. First, I was approached by James Harrow, who invited me to join his new group practice. As you know, he was extremely highly thought of, and I was ecstatic; it was the kind of opportunity I'd been dreaming of, and would be an enormous boost to my career. And second, unbelievably, I became involved with one of my patients – a young married woman.'

He glanced tentatively at Moira but she seemed in a daze, incapable of absorbing any further shocks, and after a minute he went on.

'It was, of course, sheer madness; I knew what risks I was running, but they simply added to the excitement.' He paused, thinking back. 'We met on my free afternoons and drove out into the country, always in a different direction, and though we were almost obsessively careful, one day the inevitable happened. I'd parked in a remote country lane – off-road, in a gateway. And as luck would have it, Hilary drove past with the twins.

'She recognized the car, of course, and *said* she was concerned that I'd been taken ill or had an accident. So she stopped, got out and looked first in the car and then, when I wasn't there, over the hedge. And, of course, saw us, and recognized my – companion. We weren't aware of it at the time; the first I knew was when she booked an appointment at the surgery the next evening.'

Rex glanced at his son. 'I don't know how much you and Annabel know about Hilary. Your mother says she was a friend and that's true; though only by virtue of being Edward's wife. The downside is that she could be both bossy and self-righteous, especially when involved in community or charity projects. And, crucially, she was on the local Health Authority Board. So you can imagine how dumbstruck I was when she came straight out with the statement that she knew I was having an affair with a patient, and it was her duty to report me. She added that she hadn't yet mentioned it to Edward, since she'd had to check that the girl was indeed on my list, which she had now done.

'Well, I threw pride to the winds and begged, cajoled and pleaded with her, calling on our friendship and God knows what else, in an effort to persuade her to forget it. To no avail. I even told her about my forthcoming partnership with Dr Harrow, which at that time was under wraps, but she was still adamant that, in her position, she had no choice.

'I was convinced I could talk her round, given time. But there was a complication; it was the week before Flora's birthday, and they were leaving for Wales the next day. Finally, after the most wearing half-hour of my life, I wrung from her the promise to say nothing, even to Edward, until her return from holiday.'

He picked up his glass, saw it was empty, and put it down again.

'I didn't sleep at all that night. My whole future hung in the balance, and there was no way I could wait ten days before speaking to her again; her resolve would have hardened in the interval, and I'd never shift it. So in desperation I phoned first thing the next morning, but she wouldn't speak to me, much less see me. She was finishing off the packing and they were leaving within the hour.

'I put the phone down feeling suicidal – then a possible solution occurred to me. At dinner the week before, Edward had mentioned they'd rented a villa on the front at a small village called Llandinas, on the Gower coast. I devised a lunatic plan to drive down, with a cock-and-bull story that a crisis had arisen in one of the charities Hilary and I supported. It was full of holes but the best I could come up with, and should at least give me a chance to speak to her alone.

'So on the Tuesday, which was the earliest I could get away, I drove to the Gower. On the front at Llandinas there was a row of parked cars facing out to sea, and I drew in alongside. Stupidly, it hadn't occurred to me there'd be more than one villa there, but of course there was. My nerve failed me at the thought of ringing all three bells, but I walked past scrutinizing them. There was no sign of life, and as it was mid-afternoon, it seemed obvious that everyone was out. So I went back and sat in the car, getting more and more strung up. Eventually, I must have fallen asleep, because the next thing I knew it was nearly twenty to five, and, thinking they'd be returning any minute for tea, I hurried back along the road. And just as I was drawing near, Hilary herself came up the path from the beach. I couldn't believe my luck.

'She was startled and annoyed to see me, complaining that I'd no right to follow her, and that I could have saved myself the trip, because she'd no intention of dropping the matter. She started to walk up the garden path and I went after her, still arguing frantically that the affair was over, that nothing like it would ever happen again, and she couldn't let it blight a promising career.

'She had the door open by this time, and before she could shut it in my face, I slipped in after her. The hall was very narrow, I remember. I was still jabbering on, and suddenly she lost her temper. She turned to face me and declared in that hoity-toity voice of hers, "If you want the truth, Rex, I've never liked you. You've altogether too high an opinion of yourself, and it's time someone took you down a peg. It's Moira I feel sorry for, but now at least she'll see you for what you are."

'And having annihilated my future in a couple of sentences, she calmly turned away and pushed open a door on the left. Incandescent with rage, I snatched up an ornament from a table just inside the door and lashed out at her. She dropped like a stone, and as she fell I saw the pushchair behind her, and the baby staring at me with huge, frightened eyes.'

He stopped speaking, and the only sound in the room was his harsh breathing. After a minute he wiped a hand across his eyes and continued, his voice shaking. 'I couldn't take in what had happened – it had all been so quick. I started forward to help Hilary up, but the instant I moved, Annabel's little face puckered and she began to scream with terror. I realized to my horror that she thought I was coming for her. I turned and fled, still clutching the ornament, as I discovered when I got back to the car. Thank God there was no one about, because my headlong flight would certainly have attracted attention.'

It was no wonder, Annabel thought numbly, that the nightmare had had such a powerful effect on her all these years.

Rex went on: 'How I ever got back to Cheltenham I'll never know, but I swear I didn't realize Hilary was dead. I expected the police to come knocking at any minute to arrest me for grievous bodily harm, trespass, you name it. The next day, when I read that she'd been murdered, I was stunned. Then, to my shame, it dawned on me that however accidental her death it had in fact been my salvation. My reputation, my job and my marriage had, in a stroke, been saved from total destruction – and no one knew I'd even been to Wales.'

He poured himself a glass of water from the crystal jug on the table. 'I also realized, belatedly, that the lethal weapon was still under the front seat of my car. I smashed it into smithereens and threw the shards in the dustbin.'

He looked round at the three blank faces. 'Of course it was a shock when Edward was arrested,' he said, 'but I didn't see how they could charge him, when he hadn't done it. If by any chance they *had* – or anyone else, for that matter – then of course I would have come forward. I hope you believe that.'

No one spoke. Again that rictus of a smile. 'Well, if no

one has anything to say, perhaps, Neil, you would phone the police. I'm afraid I'm not up to going down there and turning myself in.'

Neil made a protesting movement with his hand, but the doctor shook his head. 'I'm more sorry than I can say for you and your mother, but now all I want to do is get this over.'

Moira still sat unmoving, the tear-tracks drying on her face. As Neil left the room, Rex pushed back his chair and stood up. Very gently, he took his wife's hand, helped her to her feet, and led her across the hall to the sitting room, closing the door behind them.

Annabel remained where she was, staring at the remains of their lunch, eaten in such happy comradeship. It was over, she thought, but the words had no meaning. Neil, glancing at the closed door across the hall, came back into the room.

'My God,' he said tonelessly.

Annabel stood up. 'Neil, I can't tell you how sorry I am. I would rather it had been almost anyone else. I can't bear what this is doing to you and your mother.'

'I keep thinking I'm going to wake up,' he said in a dazed voice. 'My God, Dad, of all people! What I don't understand is how could he have lived with it all this time, without our knowing.'

Annabel touched his hand and he pulled her gently against him. 'My father killed the mother of my closest friend. How can I come to terms with that? How can I ever face Tom again?'

She said brokenly, 'Why did I start talking about Martin? This is all my fault.'

'Darling Annabel, you mustn't think that. As Dad said, it was just that Nemesis finally came round that corner.'

She sighed, glancing down at the brocade dress she was still wearing. 'It seems wrong even to think of it, with all this happening, but what will happen about the portrait?'

'God knows. All that's clear at the moment is that Mother's going to need my support for the next few weeks and months. Eventually, though, life will have to go on – and presumably the exhibition with it. If they still want me, when all this breaks.'

'Of course they will!' she said quickly.

His mouth twisted. 'Publicity value, you mean? One thing's certain, though: having found you again, I've no intention of letting you disappear. After all, you're the best sitter I've had in years!'

She smiled as he'd meant her to, but she wondered if his words held a deeper meaning. And what of Simon? He had hurt her badly, but there was still something between them. No doubt time would provide the solution.

The doorbell rang, and she jumped. 'The police already?'

'I doubt it; it's more likely in response to my other phone call.' He patted her arm and went to open the front door. Annabel heard a familiar voice say, 'I've come to collect my granddaughter.'

She ran into the hall, to see Flora on the step, a reassuring figure in her shifting, uncertain world. 'Oh, Grandmother!' she cried with a catch in her voice.

Flora held out her arms, and she went running into them. Behind her, she heard the front door close.